PENGUIN BOOKS

AN EXPERIMENT IN LOVE

'The time is 1970, and it is wonderfully well evoked ... The skill with which Mantel manages her time-shifts, the precision of her writing, the acuteness of her observation, the seriousness of her themes, and the way in which she weaves them into a coherent whole, make this an unusually satisfying novel' – Allan Massie in the *Scotsman*

'A clear-eyed examination of female alliances may well be needed in these misleading times. *An Experiment in Love* may well be such an examination, cool, unsentimental, and unassumingly authoritative' – Anita Brookner in the *Spectator*

'Hilary Mantel's intelligent, funny, and disturbing new novel follows a trinity of girls as they grow up into young women in the Britain of the 1960s and 70s. About experiment, social, sexual, and emotional, this fiction also probes and dissects, brilliantly and experimentally, the human heart and a divided society' – Carol Anderson in the *Herald*

'*An Experiment in Love* has much to say about its turbulent era, and is replete with the atmosphere of the cusp, with the prospect of irreversible change ... It is also a profoundly sad novel, to which Mantel's liberal sense of comedy and dazzling acuity for metaphor add an almost excruciating flavour' – Rachel Cusk in *The Times*

HILARY MANTEL

An Experiment in Love

PENGUIN BOOKS

PENGUIN BOOKS

Published by the Penguin Group
Penguin Books Ltd, 27 Wrights Lane, London W8 5TZ, England
Penguin Books USA Inc., 375 Hudson Street, New York, New York 10014, USA
Penguin Books Australia Ltd, Ringwood, Victoria, Australia
Penguin Books Canada Ltd, 10 Alcorn Avenue, Toronto, Ontario, Canada M4V 3B2
Penguin Books (NZ) Ltd, 182–190 Wairau Road, Auckland 10, New Zealand

Penguin Books Ltd, Registered Offices: Harmondsworth, Middlesex, England

First published by Viking 1995
Published in Penguin Books 1996
3 5 7 9 10 8 6 4

The lines on p. 39 from T. S. Eliot's 'Whispters of Immortality' are reprinted from *Collected Poems
1909–1962*, 1974, by kind permission of Faber and Faber Ltd

Printed in England by Clays Ltd, St Ives plc

FOR GERALD

One

This morning in the newspaper I saw a picture of Julia. She was standing on the threshold of her house in Highgate, where she receives her patients: a tall woman, wrapped in some kind of Indian shawl. There was a blur where her face should be, and yet I noted the confident set of her arms, and I could imagine her expression: professionally watchful, maternal, with that broad cold smile which I have known since I was eleven years old. In the foreground, a skeletal teenaged child tottered towards her, from a limousine parked at the kerb: Miss Linzi Simon, well-loved family entertainer and junior megastar, victim of the Slimmer's Disease.

Julia's therapies, the publicity they have received, have made us aware that people at any age may decide to starve. Ladies of eighty-five see out their lives on tea; infants a few hours old turn their head from the bottle and push away the breast. Just as the people of Africa cannot be kept alive by the bags of grain we send them, so our own practitioners of starvation cannot be sustained by bottles and tubes. They must decide on nourishment, they must choose. Unable to cure famine – uninterested, perhaps, for not everyone has large concerns – Julia treats the children of the rich, whose malaise is tractable. No doubt her patients go to her to avoid the grim behaviourists in the private hospitals, where they take away the children's toothbrushes and hairbrushes and clothes, and give them back in return for so many calories ingested. In this way, having broken their spirits, they salvage their flesh.

I found myself, this morning, staring so hard at the page that the print seemed to blur; as if somewhere in the fabric of the paper, somewhere in its weave, I might find a thread which would lead me through my life, from where I was then to where I am today. 'Psychotherapist Julia Lipcott', said the caption. Ah, still Lipcott, I said to myself. Although, of course, she might have married. As a girl she wouldn't change her underwear for a man, so I doubt if she'd change her name.

The story beneath the picture said that Miss Simon had been ill for two years. Gossip, really; it's surprising what the *Telegraph* will print. The megastar's gaze was open, dazed, fish-like; as if she were being grappled suddenly towards dry land.

It was the year after Chappaquiddick, the year Julia and I first went away from home. All spring I had dreamt about the disaster, and remembered the dreams when I woke: the lung tissue and water, the floating hair and the sucking cold. In London that summer the temperatures shot into the mid-eighties, but at home the weather was as usual: rain most days, misty dawns over our dirty canal and cool damp evenings on the lawns of country pubs where we went with our boyfriends: sex later in the clammy, dewy dark. In June there was an election, and the Tories got in. It wasn't my fault; I wasn't old enough to vote.

In July there was a dock strike, and temporary shortages of fresh food. The Minister of Agriculture appeared on the news and said, 'What housewives should do this week is shop around, buy those things which are cheaper.'

When my mother heard this, she took off her slipper and threw it at the television set. It sailed over the top and landed at the back among the tangled flexes and cables. 'What does he think folk generally do?' she asked. 'Go down to the market and say, "What's dear today, give me two pounds, will you, and a slice of your best caviare on top? Oh, no, that's not dear enough! Please keep the change."'

My father creaked out of his chair and went to pick her slipper up. He handed it back: 'Prince Charming,' he said, identifying himself.

My mother snorted, and forced her veiny foot back into the felt.

As soon as my exam results came through I started packing. I didn't have many clothes, and those I did lacked the fashionable fringes and mosaic patterns. The papers said that purple would be the dominant shade of the autumn. I was old enough to remember when it had been fashionable last time: how jaundiced it made women look, and how embarrassing it was for them when the craze fizzled out and they had its relics crowding their wardrobes. The colour's just a rag-trade manipulation, because apart from prelates nobody would naturally choose it. Women have been caught too often; that's why we don't have purple now. Except, of course, purple prose.

*

Quick, before I forget it . . . the dazzle of the lights on the white tiles, the dismal moans and clatters from the darkness, less like trains than the calls of departing ships; the voice of the announcer over the tannoy. I took out of my pocket a map, folded to the right square, and looked at it as I had done many times on the journey; my heart lurched a little, and small fires of apprehension ran behind my ribs, little flames leaping along the bones. I was a child, and I had been nowhere until now.

I picked up my suitcase, which was dragging my arm out of its socket, and began to lurch forward with it through the early evening; crisp leaves were falling already in the London squares.

When I arrived at the Hall of Residence, a woman – the warden herself – took me upstairs in a lift. She had a bunch of keys. 'If you had left that' (she meant my suitcase) '*there*' (she said, with a mysterious, impatient gesture) 'then the porter would have brought it up for you.' As things were, she had to keep her finger on the OPEN button while I manoeuvred it out of the lift. I had to trail along behind her, dragging the suitcase like a deformed limb.

My room was to be on the third floor, known as C Floor. The woman led me along a wide corridor, parquet squeaking under her feet. She stopped by a door marked C3, rattled her bunch of keys and admitted us. Inside the door she consulted her list. 'Mac, mac, mac,' she said. 'Miss McBain.' There, pinned to her sheet before she flicked it over, I caught a glimpse of a photograph, the black-and-white photograph that the hall had requested. My mother had taken it in our backyard: I leant against red brick, like a person waiting for a firing squad. Perhaps my mother had never used a camera before. It had been a clear day, but in the photograph my features were wreathed in mist; my expression was shocked.

'So,' the woman said, 'you were at day school in, let me see, Lancashire?' That was true. I was listed somewhere, tabulated, in the heart of this great dark building. At a turn in the corridor I had smelt soup. Lights blossomed out in another building across the street.

The woman flicked over her lists again. 'And there are two of your schoolmates coming along, is that correct, Miss Julianne Lipcott and – ' She squinted at the paper, turning it slightly from the light as if that would remove some of the czs and the djs that rustled and shuffled in proximity, in a surname that I had known since I was four, and which was therefore no stranger to me than Smith or Jones – less, really. I pronounced it for her and said helpfully, 'We call her Karina.'

'Yes, I see. But which of you will share? We don't have rooms for three girls.'

Dormitories, those would be. I tried to imagine us in a row in white beds, Carmel and Karina and Julianne: our hands folded in prayer.

'Since you're here first you'd better decide,' the warden said. 'Whoever is left will be found another partner.' She raised an eyebrow. 'Perhaps you'd rather that be you? Perhaps you don't want to share with either of them?'

I realized that a dubious, timid expression must have been growing on my face. 'Miss Lipcott,' I said quickly. 'Miss Lipcott, please.'

How did I dare? It was not so much that I wanted Julianne's company, or thought that she might want mine. She would be indifferent to it; if you'd asked her who she'd like for a room-mate, she'd have said, 'Have you got any men?' But what she would say if through my neglect or failure of nerve she found herself waking up every day in the same room as Karina?

The warden stepped over my suitcase, crossed the room and drew the curtains. They were grey curtains, with a darker grey stripe, matching the covers of the two single beds that stood foot to foot along one wall. She smiled at me, indicating the room, its wardrobe, wash-basin, two desks, two chairs. 'You'll have first choice then, won't you?' She put into my hand a key; attached to it was a big wooden fob, with 'C3' written on it. 'You'll find it best to lock your door when you leave your room. Hand your key in at the front desk when you leave the building.' She put her lists down on a desk, tapped them together and secured them with a snapping bulldog clip. 'May I take this opportunity, Miss McBain, to wish you every success in your university career? If you have any problems, queries, do come to see me – at some mutually agreed hour, of course.' The warden went out, closing the door quietly and leaving me to my life.

I rubbed my elbow. It felt disjointed, irretrievably strained. Should I be here? A vision came into my head of the home I had left, of the stuffy room, with the glowing electric coals, where I had performed the study, where I had formed the ambition, that had delivered me to this room. A horrible longing leapt up inside me: not the flames of apprehension, but something damper, a crawling flurry in my ribcage, like something leaping in a well. The suitcase lay across the doorway, at an angle and on its side. I stooped, crouching to apply a final effort to it, bracing my knees; as if they had been waiting for the aid of gravity, tears ran out of my eyes and made jagged patches on the sleeves of my new beige raincoat.

I straightened up and opened the wardrobe door. Six metal hangers clashed together on a rail. I took off my coat and hung it up. I felt that it had somehow been spoilt by my crying on it, as if salt water would take off the newness. I could not afford to spoil my clothes.

A clock struck, and as I had no watch – I travelled without such normal equipment – I counted the strokes. I sat down on the bed nearest the window. It would be mine, and so would the bigger of the two desks, the better lit. It was more natural to me, and perhaps easier, to take the worse desk and bed, but I knew that Julianne would despise me for any show of self-sacrifice.

So, I sat on the bed. My fingers stroked the rough striped cover. The sheets beneath were starched and crackling like paper: tucked strap-tight into the bed's frame, as if to harness a lunatic. There seemed to be no traffic in the street below. A lightbulb burned in its plain paper shade. A silence gathered. Time seemed to have stopped. I sat, and looked at my feet. Certain lines of verse began to run through my head. 'Then we let off paper crackers, each of which contained a motto / And she listened while I read them, till her mother told her not to.' I could hear my breath going about its usual business, in and out. I was eighteen years old, plus one month. I wondered, would I ever get any older: or just go on sitting in this room. But after a time, the clock struck again. 'And dark as winter was the flow / Of Iser, rolling rapidly.' I got up, and began to put my clothes into the drawers, and my books on the shelves.

I grew up in a small town, the only child of elderly parents. Our town, a cotton town, had fallen into decay by the time I was born; cheap textiles from the Far East were beginning to flood the markets and those mills that remained struggled on with antiquated machinery, which it was not worth the cost of replacing; the workers too were ageing, and by the time of my middle childhood were like a parody of themselves, a southerner's idea of the north. Under the factory walls of plum-coloured brick, stained black from the smoke and daily rain, plodded thick-set men in bib and brace, with shorn hair and flat caps: and angry-looking women in checked head-scarves, with elastic stockings and shoes like boats. Beyond the mill chimneys, you could see the line of hills.

The streets of our town were lined with brick-built terraces, interrupted by corner shops which gave no credit: by public houses in which people would declare they never set foot: by sooty Nonconformist churches, whose attendance dwindled as the 1960s drew on. There was a time when each of these churches had outside it a wooden board, and pinned to the board a discreet notice in fading type, announcing the times of services and Sunday schools and the names of visiting preachers. But a day came when these notices were replaced by posters, splashed in screaming colours: CHRISTIANITY HASN'T FAILED, IT'S JUST NEVER BEEN TRIED. The town's cinema shut down, and was turned into a supermarket of eccentric design; the Mechanics' Institute closed its doors, had its windows smashed, decayed for eighteen months, and then reopened as a tyre salesroom.

My mother, made redundant from her job in the weaving shed, went out cleaning houses. A change took place in our own form of worship; the priest, now turned around to face the people, spoke a debased lingo that they could all understand. *Opera manuum ejus veritas et judicium.* The works of His hands are truth and judgement.

My father was a clerk; I knew this from quite early in life, because of my mother's habit of saying, 'Your father's not just a clerk, you know.' Each evening he completed a crossword puzzle. Sometimes my mother read her library books or looked at magazines, which she also called 'books', but more often she knitted or sewed, her head bowed under the standard lamp. Her work was exquisite: her tapestry, her drawn-thread work. Our pillowcases were embroidered, white on white, with rambling roses and trailing stems, with posies in plaited baskets, with ribbons in garlands and graceful knots. My father had a different cable-knit cardigan for every day of the week, should he choose to wear it. All my petticoats, cut out and sewn by her, had rows of lace at the hem and – also by the hem on the lefthand side – some motif representing innocence: a buttercup, for example, or a kitten.

I can see that my mother was, in herself, not exquisite. She had a firm jaw, and a loud carrying voice. Her hair was greying and wild and held back with springing kirby grips. When she frowned, a cloud passed over the street. When she raised her eyebrows – as she often did, amazed each hour by what God expected her to endure – a small town's tram system sprang up on her forehead. She was quarrelsome, dogmatic and shrewd; her speech was alarmingly forthright, or else bewilderingly circumlocutory. Her eyes were large and alert, green like green glass, with no yellow or hazel in them; with none of the compromises people have when it comes to green eyes. When she laughed I seldom knew why, and when she cried I was no wiser. Her hands were large and knuckly and calloused, made to hold a rifle not a needle.

My father and myself were fair, lean, quiet people, our features minimal and smooth; our eyes changed colour in different lights. I was a little Englishwoman, my mother said: cool. This struck a chill in me, a deepening chill; I wanted to believe I belonged to another country. My mother and father had both left Ireland in their mothers' wombs, and their workaday north country accents were as flat as mine. My father looked entirely like an Englishman; he could have passed for an earl, or an earl's flunkey. His narrow body bent itself in strange places, as if hinged and jointed differently from other people's. His legs were long and seemed extendable, and his feet were narrow and restless; when he came into a room he seemed to hover and trail about it, like a harmless insect, daddy longlegs.

It was my parents' habit, at intervals, to shut themselves in their bedroom; then my mother would mention, loudly and contentiously, the names of strange towns. Colchester was mentioned, so at another time was

Stroud, and so was a place my mother pronounced lengthily as Kingston – upon – Hull. Later I realized that these were places to which we might have gone to live, if my father had taken up an offer of promotion. But for one reason or another he never did. When I was in my teens they would take me into rooms separately, and hiss between their teeth – false, in both cases – about who had wanted to go and who hadn't, who had wrecked whose chances. It was beyond me to make any sense of this: to trap them in a room together and get them to have it out, spit out the truth of the situation. Perhaps I already suspected there was no truth to be had; their fictions were interwoven, depending one on the other.

In summer, when I was a small girl, we would take a bus to the outskirts of the town, and walk in the hills, rambling along the bridle paths in clear green air. We were above the line of the mill chimneys; like angels, we skimmed their frail tops.

Once you have begun remembering – isn't this so? – one image springs another; they run through your head in all directions, scampering animals flushed from coverts. Memory's not a reel, not a film you can run backwards and forwards at will: it's that flash of startled fur, the slither of silk between the fingers, the duplicated texture of hair or bone. It's an image blurring, caught on the move: as if in one of my family snapshots, taken before cameras got so foolproof that any fool could capture the moment.

I remember this.

I am six years old, and I have been ill. After this

illness I am returning to school. It is a spring morning, water gurgling in the gutters, a keen wind. I am still shaky, unused to going out, and I have to hold tight to my mother's hand as she leads me through the school gate. Perhaps I don't want to go; I don't know. There is one tree in our school playground, and the scud and dapple of sun across its leaves is like the feeling in my limbs, now heavy, now light. Everything is new to me. My eyes are clear and cold, as if they have been rinsed in ice water.

Inside the classroom the air is hot and fusty. It smells of damp and wool and of our playtime milk cooking in its bottles beside the radiator pipes, growing glutinous and clotted. Perhaps in summer, when we have our holidays, this smell goes away? In detail: chalk smells of peaches, or I think the word 'chalk' is like the word 'peaches', because of the texture both sounds share, the plushness and the grain. Rulers smell of their wood, of their varnish, and of the salt and flesh of the hand which has warmed them: as you draw them beneath your nose you feel each dividing notch, so that each fraction of an inch has its measured segment of scent. My teacher will snarl – her eyes popping at me – that in all the time I've been off sick she thinks I *might* have learnt to draw a straight line. But that's later; for this morning there's an element of sweetness, and this shivering light. It is as if my teacher has forgotten who I am, and that when she last saw me she threatened to hit me for singing. My renaissance has called out of her a vague good-will. 'Let me see,' she says, looking around the classroom. 'Where would you like to sit?'

The luxury of choice. My fingers curl into my palms like snails. I know what I would like: to sit next to someone who has a certificate to show that there are no insects in their hair. Eggs, my mother says, eggs are what you find, but I cannot imagine eggs unless they are hens' eggs. While she scrapes my scalp with the steel comb she always emphasizes that lice are democratic, that they visit the rich as well as the poor – though we don't, I think, know anyone who is rich – and that they like, they positively *prefer*, clean heads over dirty ones. I come into the category of clean heads, and she tells me this so that I will not look down on the insects' victims, or taunt them in the playground, or chant at them.

I look around the room. Under their pullovers – which might be maroon, or a mottled grey – the boys wear grey shirts, their collars springing upwards, twisted and wrung as though they've tucked down their chins and chewed them. They wear striped elastic belts with buckles like two snakes in a headlock. Their hair is either chopped straight across their foreheads or it is shorn off to stubble. When they go home, in bad weather – which is to say, in most weather – they wear knitted balaclava helmets, and one boy has an even more terrible item, a leather helmet, thin black leather like a saurian skin, tight to his skull and fastening under his chin with a tarnished buckle. When I look at the boys I see bristles and snouts, rubber faces always contorting and meemowing. They are always lolling their tongues and wriggling their ears, or polishing their noses with the flats of their palms, working the cartilage violently round and round. Their not-yet-hairy limbs are pliable as ruddy clay, as a doll I have called a Bendy Toy; I can almost smell the rubber and feel the boneless twist I give its legs. I think I will not sit next to a boy.

I look at the girls and the girls look back at me, various expressions of dullness or spite on their faces. Their hair is braided tightly into stubby plaits, or chopped short below their ears; if the latter, it is parted at one side, and pinned off their faces with a great black grip. They have an assortment of navy cardigans, some of them washed out and shrunken, with the buttons through the wrong holes. Some have pleated skirts, or gym-slips like blue-black cardboard, like solid ink; some have cotton frocks under their cardigans, frocks that are limp and soft and pastel. I think, as the lesser evil, I will sit next to a girl.

But there are two difficulties here. One is that I have been away so long that I do not have a friend. The other is that my mother has embroidered a gambolling lamb and a frieze of spring flowers right over the skirt of my blue cotton dress. It is a sky-blue dress, and otherwise plain; I see them looking into my sky. They both want and don't want it. I can expect no mercy.

I sway on the spot. The hem of the dress brushes the tender skin at the back of my knees.

'Well . . . make up your mind,' my teacher says.

Miss Whittaker, who teaches the next class, is said to make a speciality of hitting pupils on the backs of their knees. Knuckle-rapping has gone quite out of style.

I look around, and see Karina. There is a chair empty next to her. She lifts her broad face to the light, and gives me a benevolent smile. She is wearing a yellow cardigan, yellow and fluffy, the colour of a new chicken in a picture book. Her plaits are fat and bound with white ribbons looped into flamboyant bows. From the braids and all around her head tiny threads or wires of hair stand out, white-blonde, quivering. Her face is like the sun.

'There, please,' I say.

Complacently, Karina begins to rearrange her possessions on the table: square up her ruler, her pencil, the cardboard box in which (at this tender age) we keep our lined paper for writing, and our squared paper for sums.

Next day when Julianne arrived, I was lying on my bed smoking a cigarette. 'My God!' she said, shrieking inside the doorway. 'Your hair! My God!'

I sat up, smiling solemnly. My hair, which had been down to my waist at the end of the school term, was now clipped close to my head, scarcely an inch long all over. Glimpsing myself in shop windows this last week, I had whirled around to confront the stranger who seemed always at my shoulder; it was myself. My head felt light and full of possibilities, like a dandelion clock.

Julianne crossed the room, picked up my packet of cigarettes, and fitted one into her full red mouth. 'Why did you do it? Did you have nits, or is it a symbol?' She caught sight of herself in the mirror. Put up a large hand to touch her own hair, silky hanks the colour of butterscotch. 'This mirror is useless,' she grumbled.

'Duck.'

She bent her knees. 'Useless. It's not the top of my head I need to see, it's the rest of me.'

'Perhaps we might rehang it.'

'And knock a lump out of the bloody wall.'

There was an oblong coffee-table in the middle of the room, centred on the striped cotton rug that was centred on the polished floor. Julianne tested the table with her hand and then stepped up on it. A piece of her came into view through the mirror: her knees, coloured tights, the swish of her short skirt. The table groaned. 'Careful!' I said. She stretched out a hand, palm forth, like an orator. We were stuffed with education, replete with it: 'Make a speech,' I suggested.

'Gaul is divided into three parts,' she proffered, in Latin.

'That isn't a speech.'

'Carthage must be destroyed.' She studied her reflection. 'Not bad.' She stepped down, glowing.

'Your case,' I asked. 'Where is it?'

'I left it for the porter.'

'Lawdy me!' I thought of my dislocated limb. 'Now he will carry it up for you, and you'll have to give him a tip. That will be embarrassing for you.'

'You don't have to tip this kind –' She broke off. She smirked. She saw how it was going to be. We were free now, to enjoy each other's company; free and equal, to be as silly and as sharp as we liked. 'I smelt soup,' she said.

'I'm afraid you did.'

'Christ.' She said it with a volume of disgust.

'Do you remember at school, when Laura took that message over to the kitchens, and they were putting the cabbage on at half-past nine?'

A further blank distaste fell into Julianne's eyes. 'We'll

not discuss our academy,' she said. 'But I must say for it, that at least at the end of the day they let us go to our own homes to eat and have baths.'

'There are communal arrangements,' I said.

'Are there mirrors?'

'What?'

'Are there full-length mirrors? In the bathrooms?'

'No. Only pipes. Steam. The water is hot. There are white tiles, not much cracked, and scouring powder on a ledge, for when you've done.'

'I don't see how you're expected to manage it. To take a bath without a mirror.'

I kept quiet. It had never seemed to me essential. Even important at all. 'They're only along the corridor,' I said. 'Three bathrooms in a row. There's no reason why I should describe them to you.'

'I like to have you describe things,' she said moodily. 'Descriptions are your strong point. God knows why you want to be reading law. Vanity, I suppose. You want to show your frightful grinding omnicompetence.' She looked about her. 'I see you've taken the best desk. The best bed.'

She sat down on her own bed, and began to simper. 'At the hair,' she explained. 'Come now, Carmel, how can you bear to leave the old country behind? A girl like you, brought up with every advantage . . . the rag rugs, the flying ducks on the wall . . .'

'We don't, actually, have any flying ducks. Though my aunt has them.'

'Maybe not, but I expect you have one of those fireside sets, do you, with little gilt tongs and a gilt shovel?'

I smiled, in spite of myself.

'Shingled,' she said. 'Would that be the word? Cropped. Shaved.' She pointed. 'Do you know how that head of yours affects me? Sitting behind your straggly pigtails year in, year out, with your ribbons with the ends cut in Vs like they do them on wreaths – '

'I didn't know that.'

' – and then to walk in here, Miss, to a room in London in this Hall of Residence, where we are confined at Her Majesty's Pleasure . . . What do you think, would they let us move out and get a flat?'

'Together?'

'Why not?'

'What about my lower-class ways?'

She blew smoke at me. 'I have an urge to say to you, Bejasus!'

'Is that so?'

'It would be nice if we went about and talked like an Edna O'Brien novel. It would suit us.'

'Yes, it would become us,' I said. 'We haven't the class for Girls of Slender Means.'

'Speak for yourself. You charwoman's daughter.' Julianne wiped her eyes, but then she began to laugh again almost at once.

I told her about the poems that ran around in my head. She said, 'You need to be taken out of yourself. We should go out and do some living. We could go to some students' union or other, we must belong to them now. We will have a bottle or two of Guinness, will we? To build us up?'

There was a sound of revelry by night, I said to

myself. I could have bitten the secret tongue in my brain that said it. Why did I think I was preparing for the Battle of Waterloo? Julianne made everything seem normal, but it was not normal for me. Her home was recoverable; she could travel to it next weekend, if she wished, and tumble into her frilly bed in her familiar room. I could not return until Christmas – at which point I could reclaim a fare from my local authority. Her parents, she had said, had offered to drive her down, see her installed, inspect her room and add a luxury or two; but she thought it better to make the break, get clean away on the Euston train, and besides, they must realize her accommodation was shared, and I might have brought my own luxuries with me.

I fought off self-pity: which Julianne's words, on the whole, seemed designed to stimulate. I felt homesick already, and poor, more with the apprehension of poverty than with an actual lack in my purse; my right arm, that racked limb, did not feel as if it would support the weight of a bag of textbooks. If only the work would begin: the ink, the files, the grit behind sleepless eyes, the muffled tread of the invigilators. That was what I had come here for: to make my way, to make my living.

There was a knock on the door. Julianne bounced across the room. It was the porter, bringing her suitcase. 'Put it there!' she sang. She stretched her arms wide – Lady Bountiful. There was a plum cake inside her travelling bags, baked at home and sealed in a tin. She knew how to manage her life, how to go away from home. I thought of her father, the doctor; of her three brothers, who at their school played lacrosse. Brothers are an advantage, in the great world; they give a girl the faculty of easy contempt for men. Julianne's skin seemed polished; she was altogether more apt for adventure, more translatable.

'Julianne,' I said, 'you haven't mentioned the obvious fact.'

She stretched her eyes. 'Where is it obvious, where, the obvious fact?'

'You know I mean Karina.'

'Spare me,' Julianne said.

'She hasn't got here yet, at least so far as I . . .'

'Even so. Spare me.'

'They asked if you wanted to share with her.'

Julianne stared at me. 'Where in God's name did they get that idea?'

I smiled inside. 'They only asked. I think it was a formality.'

'I hope you requested them to put her very far away, in the lowest, highest – '

'In fact she's next door.'

'You're not telling me you let them – '

'No, OK. I'm lying. She's on this corridor. C21.' For I had seen the warden's pencil moving swiftly over the lists, allocating numbers and floors. 'Quite far away.'

'Who with?'

'A stranger.'

'It would have to be. A stranger, it would have to be. If you had pulled some trick,' she said, 'and left me with Karina, I would never have spoken to you again.' She thought for a moment. 'I would have run up to you in the street with a specially made snagger and laddered your best tights. I would have got a packet of Durex and written on them "From Carmel to Niall, in anticipation," and I would have taken them out of the packet and stuck pins in them all over and then folded them back in and sealed up the seal and posted them to your boyfriend and written SWALK on the envelope.'

'Finished now?'

'Sealed With A Loving Kiss,' she said.

I wanted to plead, and say, but Karina, we are going to, you know, be friends with her? Aren't we? But I couldn't. It sounded too childish. As if we hadn't moved on. I picked up my packet of Player's and tossed it on to Julianne's bed. 'There you are. I've given up smoking,'

She gaped at me. 'You've only just begun it.'

'Even in my habits I mean to be fickle.'

Julianne laughed. Stiffen the sinews, summon up the blood. Rings on her fingers and bells on her toes.

Two

I never knew what nationality Karina was: or, as I believe, what mixture of nationalities. 'I'm English,' she would say defiantly. Perhaps this hurt her parents. When she was ten or so they wanted to send her off to a Saturday school, so that she could learn to read and write in her native languages, and learn folk-songs and folk-dances, and have national costumes. Stoutly, dumbly, she resisted this. 'Wear a stupid apron!' was all she said. 'Wear a stupid bonnet!'

It torments me now, that I am so vague: were her parents Polish, Ukrainian, Estonian? If they themselves didn't share a native tongue, that would explain why in their household communication was often in rudimentary English. I remember them as shapeless, silent people, in woollen clothes which they wore in many layers. They both worked in the mills, in jobs that required no verbal facility, in rooms where the clatter of the machines was so loud that speech was impossible anyway.

Karina's house was just up the street from mine, just up Curzon Street. The houses on Curzon Street were made of red brick, like the houses in all the streets around. When you went in there was a vestibule and a sitting-room and behind it a kitchen of the same size. There were two bedrooms and no bathroom. The lavatory was outside in the yard. When I was a small child we had a rent man who called every Friday, and who stood filling the vestibule while cash was handed over and an entry was made in our rent book. Every year or so, the landlady would call to look over her property. She owned the whole of Curzon Street, every house, and all of Eliza Street too. She wore a heavy pink dusting of face powder, a dashing trilby with a feather, and a coat and skirt, which people then called a costume. 'Did you see that costume?' my mother would say. Every year she said this. She did not specify what it was about the costume that startled her: just 'Did you see that costume?' Then one year, in a violent outburst, she added, 'I could have made it myself. Run it up for a guinea, on the machine.'

Until I was nine or so, my mother and father and I washed by rota at the kitchen sink, using a pink cake of soap my mother kept in an enamel dish, and sharing a towel that looped on a hook in the cupboard beneath. Mornings were slow work, because of modesty. My mother went first; by the time I was shouted to come downstairs, the mysteries of her bust were preserved beneath hasty pearl-buttoning, only the rough flushed skin of her throat suggesting that she had scrubbed herself half-naked just minutes before. Standing before the mirror, she would swipe the bridge of her nose with her powder-puff; it distributed a different dust from our landlady's, and I would watch her slice down and across and down, practised and ruthless as a man wiping mortar over bricks, obliterating her mottled bits with an overlay of khaki, and slicing off the surplus with the edge of the puff. I would sit at the kitchen table, shivering sometimes, my feet dangling in mid-air below the hem of my nightdress;

I watched while my father shaved. His mouth was stopped by soap, his face tilted as though he were communing with saints; the humiliating female reek of the pink soap leaked from the skin of his freckled shoulders.

But then the landlady yielded to pressure to install baths and hot-water systems for her tenants. Half my bedroom disappeared behind a partition, and became a white, unheated box. On the first day after the installation was finished, I climbed into the tub in my clothes – without the water in, of course – just to see what it would feel like. It felt frozen, glazed, slippery; enamelled cold struck into my bones.

The rent was increased, but shortly afterwards the landlady began to sell off her houses. She must have wanted to be rid of them quickly, because her asking price was only five hundred pounds. My parents went into their bedroom and hissed at each other. A heavy thumping came from the floorboards above. I loitered at the window in our front room, admiring dogs that came and went; I hoped to get a dog, but my mother said the very limit of her tolerance would be a small and perfectly house-trained cat. I strained my ears for the words 'Kingston-upon-Hull'.

My parents came downstairs after two hours. There was a high colour in my mother's cheeks. 'We are to become owner-occupiers,' she said.

Karina's parents did not have five hundred pounds, so they continued to rent their house from the new landlord. 'You think you're so swanky,' Karina said. 'You think you're so well-off.'

Every day Karina and I used to walk to school together. We toddled down Curzon Street towards the town centre, turning left down Eliza Street at the pub called the Ladysmith. Most streets had a pub on the corner, and they were usually named after the younger children of Queen Victoria, or dead generals, or victories in colonial wars; we were too young to know this. We rolled downhill, guided by the mill chimneys and their strange Italianate architecture – yellow brick and pink brick and grimy brick – and everywhere black vistas fell away, railway embankments and waste ground, war damage and smoke; at the end of Bismarck Street we looked down on the puffing chimneys of houses below, ranged in their rows, marching down and down into the murky valley.

We passed the Irish club, and the florist's with its small stiff pink-and-white carnations in a bucket, and the drapers called 'Elvina's', which displayed in its window Bear Brand stockings and knife-pleated skirts like cloth concertinas and pasty-shaped hats on false heads. We passed the confectioner's – or failed to pass it; the window attracted Karina. She balled her hands into her pockets, and leant back, her feet apart; she looked rooted, immovable. The cakes were stacked on decks of sloping shelves, set out on pink doilies whitened by falls of icing sugar. There were vanilla slices, their airy tiers of pastry glued together with confectioners' custard, fat and lolling like a yellow tongue. There were bubbling jam puffs and ballooning Eccles cakes, slashed to show their plump currant insides. There were jam tarts the size of traffic lights; there were whinberry pies oozing juice like black blood.

'Look at them buns,' Karina would say. 'Look.' I

would turn sideways and see her intent face. Sometimes the tip of her tongue would appear, and slide slowly upwards towards her flat nose. There were sponge buns shaped like fat mushrooms, topped with pink icing and half a glacé cherry. There were coconut pyramids, and low square house-shaped chocolate buns, finished with a big roll of chocolate-wrapped marzipan which was solid as the barrel of a cannon.

I waited for Karina to choose one, to go in and buy it, because I knew that her parents gave her money every day, at least 3d. and sometimes as much as 6d. But after examining the cakes for some time, after discussing them, after speculating on their likely taste and texture until my mouth was full of saliva, Karina would fall silent, and turn away, with something obstinate in her face, something puzzled and pained, some expression which was too complicated for me to identify. And so we would go to school.

Two years went by, marked less by scholastic achievement than by crazes. There was a yo-yo craze, and a fashion for paper games. There were whole weeks when we did nothing but beg stiff plain paper to fold and crease and manufacture things we called 'Quackers', disembodied palm-sized beaks that you snapped at people's noses. There were skipping outbreaks and new rhymes, new rhymes and amalgamations and blends of old ones:

'Manchester Guardian, Evening News
Here comes a cat in high-heel shoes.
Clock strikes one,

Clock strikes two,
Clock has a finger and it's pointing at you.
Mother mother I am sick,
Send for the doctor quick quick quick.
Doctor doctor
Will I die?
Course you will and so will I . . . '

Karina was an efficient skipper. Her feet thundered into the pavement. Up, down, her knees drawn up to her chest; her face wore no expression at all.

We passed through the hands of Miss Whittaker, who hit us on the backs of our knees as everyone had said she would; into the hands of Sister Basil, whose malevolence was tempered by absent-mindedness. I picture her always with her arm upraised, her black sleeve falling away, as she chalks on the blackboard in her flowing cursive script the word 'Problems'. And underneath, a complex sum, a sum spelt out in words, like a composition, with no plus signs or minus signs: a discursive sum, with no suggested means of working it. 'If a man buys apples to the value of 1s. 3d., and pears to the value of 2s. 8d., and hands the shopkeeper 10s. in payment . . .' Always these problems were about fruit, coal, the perimeters of fields, railway journeys. If Karina would buy a vanilla slice to the value of 4d., and a chocolate bun to the value of 3d., how many girls could have a nice time?

I was glad when skipping ended. In the middle of the rhyme my mind wandered, and my feet went their own way; the girls who turned the rope set the rhythm, and I couldn't pick it up. I was glad when it was marbles, because I had my marbles in a grubby white draw-string bag given me by my grandad, and anything my grandad gave me was better than a medal blessed by the Pope. I rolled them towards other marbles with great accuracy, as if I were turning a cold eye on their owners. My favourite marble was a cold colour, its iris pebble-grey with the merest hint of blue. In my mind I called this marble 'Connemara'.

Karina still wore white ribbons to seal her short thick plaits, but otherwise her dress had become like that now adopted by the other girls: a skirt and a jersey and a shirt-style blouse that was meant to be white but which looked yellow under the classroom's lights and the cloud-packed skies outside. Her pleated skirt was royal blue – superior to navy, she told me. It settled somewhere under her armpits, for Karina had no waist. She was a big girl, people said – said it approvingly – a big girl, and always very *clean*. We had no washing-machines, and as bathrooms and hot water were so new, cleanliness was a rugged, effortful virtue. A woman with every vice might be granted absolution with one grudging phrase: 'She's very clean, I will say that for her.' To describe someone as 'not clean' was a more dire reproach than to describe them simply as 'dirty'. Dirt might be a transient phenomenon, but being not clean was a spiritual sickness.

Perhaps, in that ghetto beyond language where she lived, Karina's mother had understood this, because there was a scrubbed, scoured quality about her daughter's plump hands and big square white teeth. Karina's skin was like a pink peach, and she seemed to fill it to bursting; if you had touched her cheek, you would have felt it like ripe fruit ready to split. She was a head taller than me and her shoulders were broad, her bones large and raw.

Later, Julianne used to say, 'Karina's a peasant. Well now, isn't she? In England we don't have peasants. Why not? Complex socio-economic factors. But in Europe, to be a peasant is normal. And Karina is normal. For a peasant.'

At the first approach of cold weather, Karina would emerge from her house in the morning in stiff suede boots with a zip up the centre. Over her head she would wear a tartan hood called a pixie hood, or sometimes a kind of nylon fur bonnet with extrusions like nylon fur powder-puffs which nestled over her fleshy ears. If it snowed, she would come to school with tartan trews under her pleated skirt, that part of the trews which is below the knee swirled thickly around her calves and crammed into wellington boots. She had, at the age of eight – and perhaps this was what drew us together – a marked indifference to public opinion.

That I should look nice, that I should look different: this was my mother's aim in life. On my skirts she embroidered whole fantastic landscapes; on my collars she sewed red admiral butterflies, and on my cardigans she set the stars and the crescent moon. I had no truck with navy or even royal-blue pleats, with anything usual, washed-up, faded or thin. I had sashes; I had petticoats with hoops, belling and swaying around my calves. I had bumblebees hovering over clover flowers on a back-ground of grass green, and a jersey specially knitted in the colour of my eyes. My hair, unloosed, was a thin curtain of pale shadow; an indecipherable grey-gold, a colour with no name. 'Can you sit on it?' girls would sometimes say: their grieved fascination edging aside, for a moment, their envy and fright and spite.

You must not think that Karina was kind about my clothes: or that she was any sweeter about my hair than, in our Tonbridge Hall days, Julianne would be. I think again of that sun-shattered, windy morning when I was six years old, and I made my way down the classroom to take my place at the table next to Karina: invited there by her sumptuous smile, and her yellow cardigan.

Small chairs we had, miniaturized; I hitched mine to the table and turned to Karina, smiling in pleasure. Out went my hand, my fingertips, to touch the fluffy egg-yolk wool, which I had convinced myself would be damp to the touch. 'Did you get this for an Easter present?' I asked her.

Karina said, 'Don't talk daft.'

I didn't at once take my fingers away.

'At Easter you get eggs.' She turned her dimpled face towards me, and the fuzzy halo around her hair cast itself into a bobbing disc against the classroom wall. 'Where've you been?' she asked.

'I've been poorly.'

'You're weak,' she said.

'I'm not.'

'It's your hair. Being that long. All down your back. Your strength goes into it.'

'It doesn't.'

'Where else does it go then?'

I was silent. I thought over what she had said. She swung her head away and one jutting ribboned braid was outlined for a moment against the wall. 'This is the cow with the crumpled horn . . .' Once again my fingers stole out to graze the fluff of her sleeve. Karina brought her hand down and chopped it across my fingers so hard that I felt the equivalent of a mild electric shock: a small pain, but dull, bruising and deep.

There were three reasons why every day I walked to school with Karina. The first, and most simple, was that I hoped that, odd as my outfit would be, Karina would be wearing something odder.

The second was that my mother said I must.

The third was that I wanted to make restitution.

I don't know if you understand about restitution. I am always aggrieved − though God knows, I've not set foot in church since my schooldays − by the assumption that Catholics have easy lives: that they sin as and when and where they like, then pop into the confessional and get it wiped off the slate. I'm afraid it's not so simple as that. First, you have to be sorry for your sin. Second, you have to do your best not to repeat it. Third, if there is anything you can do to make up for it, you must do it. If you steal money, you must give it back. If you slander a person, you must spend the rest of your life writing sonnets in praise of their good character. If you injure someone's feelings, you must try to mend the damage.

My tie to Karina had to do with restitution. I had done her a wrong, an injury, and this wrong occurred in the first month after I came to school, when I was four years old.

They say people remember their early years as sunlit. Perhaps this is true for people born in the south, who are richer and have better weather. What I remember largely, is hail and sleet, and the modified excitement when it actually began to snow: neuralgic winds and icicles like stalactites, and poisoned fog in rolling banks of yellow-grey. In one of these climatic exigencies – no doubt in more than one, as they tended to overlap – we were kept in for playtime, and had to work off our baby energies by romping in a cramped and hushed way in our classroom. And there was I, and there Karina was too.

The infants' classroom is not laid out quite like the others: into which we only peep, being deterred by legends of the frightful beatings given out to our seniors. It smells the same – of coke and dust and nuns – but also of the mild creamy flesh of us babies, our skin and hair and wellingtons; and when I think of this, I think of the huge letters in our reading books, which are about a brother and sister called Dick and Dora. I think of the French pleat in the hair of the mother of Dick and Dora, the tweed suit worn by the father of Dick and Dora: and into my mouth seeps the taste, oily and sweet, of welfare-state orange juice. Very well: I am four: I am in the classroom and there is a low cupboard that runs right along one wall. Our paintings are pinned above it: at least, those that are more figurative than abstract.

It is ten-thirty, I suppose. I can't tell the time yet. I know how to chant 'five past, ten past', and the rest, but I haven't realized the relationship between the numbers and the pointing fingers. But let's agree it's ten-thirty; it's raining and dark. I can see the rain hitting the window in discrete splashes then splitting and widening into the Nile delta, though this is a river of whose existence I am not yet informed; I watch the delta become an ocean, a simple roar, a wall of sound. I am sitting on the cupboard swinging my legs. To, fro, to, fro. Fawn socks and lace-up shoes.

Karina comes by. Her pale blue eyes look straight ahead, and her expression is distant but implacable. She has a toy truck, a lorry she is pulling on a string. The lorry is red. In the back of it is crammed a baby doll, a fair, fat, blubbery baby doll, plastic pink and naked. What a game! A baby in a lorry! I think it's stupid.

Before I have time to think anything else, out shoots my foot. Out shoots my foot from the knee. Up sails the lorry, up into the air. Out flies the plastic baby. And smash! Down on the classroom floor, down on its bald pink head. Dead.

Karina drops the string of her lorry. Slowly turns. Sucks in her lips, which are the same pink as her face, between the big square teeth. Then tears – fat tears – begin to roll silently down her cheeks. I sit with my leg still swinging, as if it is a mechanism over which I have no control. Karina menaces me: she raises her arm from the elbow, in a parody of hitting. She is afraid, I can tell she is. She approaches me; the blow lands on my shoulder, soft as pat-a-cake, and a tear falls on to my hand, scorching me. I rub my hand on my dress, and the tear goes away.

Normally if anybody hits me I hit back. I poke their

eyes out. I am four and I am famous as a good fighter. Kick them in the kidneys, Grandad says, they'll not take much of that. I know kidneys: I have seen them on a plate. I know they come from the butcher, and I imagine my enemies toiling up Bismarck Street with a shopping-bag, and their kidneys inside wrapped in bloody paper. In my mind, my leg shoots high and straight, high up to my ear, and I catch them *so*, on the very point of my toe; I send their kidneys spinning.

The butcher writes his prices on the paper; he does adding up, the sum wobbling and warping round the parcel. How much are kidneys? I hardly care. I kick them in the shins too; that's part of their leg. It doesn't matter what you do, Grandad says, as long as you don't hesitate; he who hesitates is lost. Strike, strike hard, strike home.

But I let Karina get away because I know what I did was wrong, to boot her baby like that. I wonder, in fact, why she didn't hit me harder, why she was so plainly afraid; but I think it must have been the mechanical ruthlessness of my foot, swinging and pinging, shooting and booting in its John White's lace-up infant school shoe.

Where was Julianne? Not there: ten miles away in the country, at her private prep school. I imagine her playing with bright plastic shapes on a magnetic board: fitting and manipulating, while a sweet-faced nun smiles above her, and feeds her dolly-mixtures, and says, 'dear little Julianne'.

*

I went home, and said to my mother, 'Karina hit me.'

My mother sat me on the kitchen table. She taught me a song:

> 'Karina's a funny 'un
> She's a face like a pickled onion
> She's a nose like a squashed tomater
> And legs like two sticks.'

'Will I sing it tomorrow?' I cried, beside myself with joy.

'No,' my mother said. 'Sing it to yourself. It's just to help you feel better.'

I understood this perfectly; that if you've learnt something really insulting and gross, a lot of the pleasure is in keeping it to yourself. 'OK,' I said. Kicked my legs a bit. Oh, I was a bright, happy little soul, in those days.

This was the first and last joke my mother made about Karina. At some time in the next two or three years, my mother and Karina's mother held some sort of colloquy in the street, after which my mother came home and cried and mentioned cattle-waggons. What that young woman's life has been, she said, is not to be contemplated, it is not to be contemplated. My father went away and got his model kit out and made a model bomber.

When these grey aeroplanes were done, he would slot them for display on to a Perspex stand, clear thin plastic which was meant to look not there and make you think the planes were flying.

My mother said, 'Now, when you're off to school, you will always call for Karina, won't you?'

Most days, Karina was there already on Curzon Street, waiting and watching for me. Her arm slid through mine, doing what we called linking. I'll link ye, a woman would say to another, slipping an arm through an arm. It was the way for women to get along the street. Nowadays, you would be presumed to be lesbians, I suppose.

Nowadays. Oh, nowadays.

Twenty-four hours after Julianne's arrival in London, I was putting papers into ring-binders and she was lying on her bed, reading the *Evening Standard*. There was a tap at our door.

'*Herein,*' Jule said, thunderously: she mouthed, 'They'll surely think I'm Freud.'

A voice said, 'Oh, may we?'

Two bright faces, one spotty, appeared around the door.

'You may come in entirely,' Jule said. 'The invitation is for more than your heads.'

So in they came: Claire, a large solid-bosomed girl from Bournemouth, and a little sparrow called Sue, who sounded deeply southern but didn't say where she was from. They wore, the both of them, jolly jumpers; beneath, Claire wore a baggy skirt, and Sue wore decent slacks of a polyester type, the kind of thing people's mothers buy.

It was Claire who had the spots. We ran our eyes over them, in that pitiless way girls have at eighteen: to see if there was any battle to be fought. But Jule signalled to me with her big white hand, as if to indicate truce. They were in no case to take our men from us; and there was no man they could possibly attract, that we would care to take from them.

They stood on the cotton rug, their shins brushing the coffee table; they smiled tolerantly at our bookshelves, at our Marx and Leonard Cohen and Hermann Hesse, and tolerantly at Jule's ashtray, and tolerantly at my long thin legs below my tiny skirt. 'I'm at King's,' Claire said. 'And Sue here, she's at Bedford. You're medical, aren't you, Miss Lipcott?'

'Mm,' Julianne said. 'But not dissected anything yet.'

'I say.' Claire laughed. 'Got all that to come, eh?' She shifted her feet; almost her spots seemed to redden, as if she were going to come now to something delicate, possibly embarrassing. 'Look,' she said, 'we've been going around, we're old hands, you see, to welcome the newcomers, and the thing is, we're not an organized group, it's just informal, but if you'd like to join us . . . you see we . . . we get together . . . and we go to church.'

I waited for Julianne to say something very shocking, very deep, and most original. But a curtain dropped behind her extravagantly blue eyes. She said in a dead voice, 'But we're Catholics.'

All next day and the day after that I watched them arriving, girls I had never imagined; girls from Brighton, girls from Luton, girls from bonny Dundee. There must have been times when I stopped and frankly, rudely stared at them; for I only knew about girls from Lancashire. What thoughts had they? What had their lives been? I could not imagine.

I set my accoutrements out on my desk. Pens. Paper.

All squared up. Sweet little Sue put her head around the door. 'What, down to work already? Where's Julianne?'

'Out getting her skeleton.'

'All alone then?' She hovered over me, cheeping. 'Claire and I thought we'd go out for a bite to eat.'

'Thanks. I'm not hungry.'

Sue fluttered off. Her freckled, beady-eyed face stayed for a moment in my mind; annexed to another companion, a girl prettier than herself instead of plainer, she might rise in the world, look less of a gawk. I wondered if she had a boyfriend, and if he was normal or religious. I wondered what she and Claire had in common, besides God. Claire was a year older, felt perhaps some thwarted maternal urge . . . I punched holes in paper, and stacked another file. White sheets, virgins. The punched-out dots skimmed to the floor, precise confetti. I knelt and dabbed them up, one by one.

Julianne brought her skeleton home. We put the skull on the top bookshelf, dead centre. The rest came in a polished wooden box, which Julianne pushed under her bed. 'We need never be bored again,' she said. 'Any night we've nothing to do, we can be like Juliet, and madly play with our forefathers' joints.'

'Aren't they something?' I said. 'These girls?'

'They come from boarding-schools.'

'A lot of them do. You see them at breakfast' (she didn't go down to breakfast) 'getting scrambled eggs.' I thought of how they called to each other down the long dining tables: socialized, fit for the early hour.

'I hear them in the corridor,' she said. 'I hear them, preparing to go down. Calling, "Sophy! Sophy!"'

I thought: Webster was much possessed by death /
And saw the skull beneath the skin.

'By the way, it's female. The skeleton,' Julianne said.
'Women's bones are more interesting, you know.'

Breakfasts at Tonbridge Hall were served on side-plates,
which were grey: as were the breakfasts themselves, small
and grey, and governed by a rota. Most days there was
bacon: a streaky rasher, cut in half to make two. On
Monday a spoonful of scrambled egg, primrose and
liquid; on Tuesday a fried egg, its yolk hard and pale.
On Wednesday with the bacon came a tomato halved,
reduced by a thorough grilling to seed and skin; on
Thursdays a cooling smear of baked beans. On Fridays
with the rasher came a tablespoon of mushrooms, finely
chopped and well-stewed. On Saturdays, boiled eggs
were served to those girls who had not gone away and
who could be bothered to get up for them.

On Sundays there was no cooked breakfast, because
the kitchen was preparing for the fiesta of a roast lunch.

The dining-room at Tonbridge Hall was in the basement of the building, and its tall windows looked out
over one of those inner squares, those inner spaces which
Bloomsbury houses entrap: lightless in any weather, at
any time of day, with etiolated shrubs struggling in
raised beds. We took our places on scarred chairs with
leatherette seats, and the noises of communal dining –
the clatter of stainless steel against cheap plates, the
squeak of trolley wheels as they rolled over the floors, the
voices of slaveys from the kitchen – flew up and echoed
and rebounded in the airy heights, rattled round

39

begrimed light-fittings that no earth-bound cleaner could reach.

I came down to breakfast every day, and tried to get it inside me. I soon understood why the bacon and mushroom day was tops with the Sophies; every scrap was edible. I would eat a bowl of damp cornflakes, then go to the serving hatch to collect my side-plate. After I had picked over the cooked offering I would take two small square pieces of sliced-bread toast, pale yellow in the centre and raw on the outside. I felt the Sophies were watching me; the toast was palatable, but I dared not take more. I longed to eat it with my bacon, as a northerner always would, but I did not dare that either; if I did not come up to scratch, I felt obscurely, I might be sent back home, my education at an end, and have to get some menial job. Butter came in foil portions: a special small size, that they must have manufactured exclusively for girls' halls of residence. It was frozen, always. You opened it and pared it with your knife and laid it on the rubber bread, like wood-shavings.

Dinner at Tonbridge Hall was a very different affair. It was served at seven. At ten minutes to the hour, a mob of inmates would begin to gather outside the locked double doors of the dining-room. Some would lean against the walls, some squat or recline on the lower reaches of the vast dark carved staircase; some would gather in knots, all talking, some laughing, some yelling, so that the volume of noise rose higher and higher and bounced from the walls and echoed in the stairwell: a murmur, then a babble, then a tattered roar, of women in need of their dinner. If the custodians of the doors were a minute late in their unbolting, if they were even a half-minute late, the foremost girls would lean on the glass and peer through and rattle the handles, and a cry would go up, 'It's too bad, really! It's utterly disgraceful! It's an utter, utter shame.'

I hung to the back and watched this performance. I tried to detach myself. I was amused, and a little embarrassed for them. I believed, as strictly as any Victorian mamma, that appetite was unbecoming to women. That girls with the benefit of a university education should hardly need food. My morning battle with myself and the toast – well, at least it was fought in silence, and with dignity.

Once we were admitted, we moved to our habitual tables: four girls to each side, two senior students at each end, taking our places before an array of cutlery suited to a banquet, splashing into tumblers London tap water from tall glass jugs. Soup was always the same, whatever its description on the weekly menu pinned up by the warden's office; it was an uncleaned aquarium, where vegetable matter swam. Or – now I think of it – perhaps there were two kinds of soup. There was the kind I have mentioned – where fragments, deep green, lodged in your teeth. There was also cream soup, beige and very peppery.

Next came the dishes of vegetables, and an oval stainless-steel platter of the evening's meat or fish, placed before one of the seniors to be divided by ten. Justice must be served, and you must picture to yourself the minute forking, the shuffling and the shredding, of a quantity perhaps reasonable for four. How could they do it? I ask myself now. If we'd been boys, they wouldn't have dared do it.

We ate our shred, and our two small potatoes, our vegetables of the root kind; all the time making bright, strained conversation, about our courses, tutors, hopes for the weekend: never high, in my case. It was dark outside now, and we dined in pools of yellow light, and sometimes I would hear the London rain against the windows, and feel bleak and far away from home. Then from the end of the table a plummy voice would be raised: 'There's a tiny bit more, if anyone would care to . . .'

For they were good judges, the shred-monitors, good but not perfect. They always felt they must keep a tiny portion in reserve, in case they had bungled it and the last hungry girl should be short-changed. And there it lay on its platter, and no one could bring herself to speak; for these girls, collectively voracious, were individually all of my opinion, and would rather starve than speak. I used to think, what if, what if a shred-monitor said, Right then, no takers? What if she picked up in her fingers the white sauce or gravy-dripping fragment, and tossed back her head like a sea-lion, and crammed it into her open mouth?

The platters would be returned to the kitchen, each with a slice of flesh remaining. No doubt they noticed this, our rulers, and convinced themselves that we were adequately fed; that we were satisfied, more than satisfied. Why else return to the kitchen food untouched?

A month passed. Our new lives had properly begun. My

file of lecture notes mounted, quarter-inch by quarter-inch, but I took time off to walk. I walked along the Strand and up Fleet Street and on to the City, I walked through the royal parks and up to Camden Town and Hampstead and saw Hampstead Heath. I trekked through Whitehall and Millbank, noting the monuments and learning the views. I tramped through museums and art galleries – anything that was free. Julianne haunted the cinemas with her friends, and the union bar, and the pubs on Tottenham Court Road, and she would speak quite casually of things she had eaten, of by-the-way omelettes and hamburgers, which were a natural part of her evenings out.

I was happy, in those early weeks. There were times when I felt holy, lucky, selected. At Tonbridge Hall there was order and warmth, so I did not care if there were regulations too. My tutors spoke to me with respect, as if I were a sentient and sensitive being; this was a relief after the routine sarcasms of nuns. I felt like a feather-light duchess, skimming down Drury Lane in the mornings; but there was an insistent migraine pain behind my left eye, which pricked at my sensibilities, made me clever and sharp, but which left me shaking sometimes, uncertain in the traffic, unsure of the parameters of my own body. That winter was mild, and so I wore my pale shower-proof until Bonfire Night, and after that a duffel coat which had been donated to me before I left home by a distant cousin. Sometimes, extracting coins from my purse, I travelled on the tube late at night, going God knows where: Arsenal, Angel, Kentish Town. Later I would have to make up for my time off by sitting under the lamp at the desk I had reserved for myself, writing very fast in black ink.

Julianne stayed out all night, every second day. The ponderous front doors of Tonbridge Hall were locked at eleven, and if you wanted to come in after that you had to apply to the warden for what was called a 'late key'. The warden would hear you out, weigh your application, record your destination in a large bound volume which she kept on her desk. But if you were prepared to go out and stay out, who was to know?

On the other day – Julianne's day in – she would go to bed at nine. She fell asleep easily, though my desk lamp burnt far into the night. When she turned she flounced in the bed, making the springs creak and half-waking herself, so that she would mutter a few words and turn again and throw out a bare white arm, to scoop against her breasts a torso of empty air. And I would lean back in my chair, resentful chin on the point of my shoulder, watching her; this easy sleep, I couldn't learn it, I hardly knew if it was becoming. Sleep-starve is best, I said to myself; think of the hours of the night, just the same in quality as the hours of the day, and so many of them, and so much to be done.

In the mornings, Julianne turned over again, as if drugged, delirious, dreaming; it was hard to pull herself to the surface of the day. Sometimes when her travelling clock began its tinny drumming she would pluck it from her bedside table and hurl it towards me; heart fluttering under the single blanket, I would claw for it and clutch it and make the bell stop; smiling a dazed smile, Julianne would tumble back into sleep; myself out at eight, feet on the striped mat, then down the stairs, rubber toast, Sophies, the winter roads. In Houghton Street someone would always say hello, and already there was a seat in the library I could think of as mine. I tore into the work set for me, I rent it and devoured it and I ate it all up every scrap. And still these lines of verse ran through my head, as if I had a brain disease, some epilepsy-variant, some repeating blip in my cells:

I step into my heart and there I meet
A god-almighty devil singing small,
Who would like to shout and whistle in the street,
And squelch the passers flat against the wall;
If the whole world was a cake he had the power to
   take,
He would take it, ask for more, and eat it all.

One morning in the autumn, when I was eight, I went on to Curzon Street and there wasn't Karina: not stumping towards me as usual. Hopefully, I bawled back into the house: 'Hey, Mum, Karina's not here.'

I hoped my mother would say, 'You go on your own, you mustn't be late.'

This damage to routine might free me from Karina, I thought; it would break up the pattern.

My mother shouted back, 'Go and call for her.'

'At her house?'

My mother appeared. 'Yes, just knock on the door.'

'She might be poorly.'

'Well, go and see.'

'They might all be asleep.'

'I shouldn't think so.'

'They might have flitted.'

'What? Moved house? Don't be silly,' my mother said.

I had played my last card. I trudged along Curzon Street and knocked at Karina's door. Her mother called, 'Yes, yes, it is open, it is open.'

I pushed the door and went inside. I had been there many times before and I knew that their house was like our house, with a sideboard and a big black poker for working the fire and a picture of the Pope pinned up on the wall.

'Yes, yes, come on, we are overslept today,' Karina's mother said. Her English came in a rush, the consonants rustling and complex. I thought of when you turn the tap on and put your finger underneath to trap the water; it wobbles like a ball-bearing, and then gushes out in a torrent when you take your finger away.

Karina and her mother were standing in the kitchen. Karina was already belted into her gabardine overcoat, a checked wool scarf tied under her chin. Her mother was not yet dressed to go out but she was wearing thick woollen stockings and a buttoned-up cardigan, with a shawl draped over it. I had never seen a shawl, except in books; you got them in fairy-tales. Karina's mother hadn't a witch face, more the face of a godmother: dough-coloured, unformed, not definitely anything at all. Her eyes were like black grapes, which are not black of course: a dull mobile sheen, purplish, in soft folds of flesh. My mother called Karina's mother 'Mary' when she met her in the street, but I did not think this could possibly be her name.

Karina's mother had both hands full. In her right

hand she had a ham sandwich made with thick white bread; she was holding it out to her daughter. Karina's hands were wrapped around her mother's hand, and she was gnawing at the bread, her head dipping with each bite, and her jaw moving like some greedy animal's: chewing away, while the scarf's bunchy knot bobbed up and down under her chin. In her other hand, Karina's mother held a banana. It was already half-peeled, ready for immediate use. As Karina took the last gulp of ham sandwich she transferred it swiftly to her right hand. Karina closed her own hands again around her mother's, holding the fruit steady; the banana seemed to vanish in three big bites.

Karina straightened up and wiped her hands on her coat. Her mother said something to her in another language. Karina didn't answer. She didn't even look at her mother, acknowledge that she had spoken. Her mother picked up a fat parcel from the kitchen cabinet, wrapped in greaseproof paper. She thrust it into Karina's schoolbag. Carefully, she fastened Karina's coat right up to the neck and twitched her head-scarf forward so that it jutted out, protecting her daughter's flushed cheeks; then she held up Karina's mittens for her to plunge her hands inside. She patted her, on the shoulders, chest, arms, patted her as if she wanted to make sure she was solid all through. Then Karina was ready to seize the day.

I had watched her mother's face while she fed her. She looked hungry, and as if all the food in the world could never be enough.

At eight years old, I wear my hair in ringlets, fat tubes that you can put your finger into. Each night at seven

47

o'clock my mother brushes my hair and then combs it and then rakes it again with the steel comb, in case insects have bred since the night before. If I am free from vermin she gets out the curl rags. These are white ropes of cloth. She unrolls and separates them, then picks up the comb again and divides my hair into strands. At the top of each strand she knots a rope. Then round and round we go, tighter and tighter wrapping, myself delirious with pain and rage and she with set face, mummifying my hair. I cry out that I want my hair cut off, short like other people's and pinned back with a big black kirby grip or a pink plastic slide, and she utters from between her teeth that I don't know what I want. When she has wrapped to the bottom of a rope she ties another big knot, like a fist, like a knuckle bone. When she has finished my whole head, the bound hair springs away from my skull, stiff and white in its casing, as if I had grown legs out of my head: as if I were an alien from the planet Zog, with these swaying white skeleton limbs, knobbled and rickety and shining in the dusk.

When I climb into bed I pray my night prayers. When I put my head on the pillow one set of knots digs into my skull and the other set of knots rolls under my ribs and spine. I toss and turn and come to rest face down, breathing wetly into the sheets. Perhaps Karina is right, perhaps my hair is stealing my strength. I sleep and have dreams.

Next morning the ropes are unknotted and my hair explodes around me. I slide my fingers into the ringlets and pretend I have grown hair on my digits and that I am a werewolf.

*

One day I see Karina standing alone on the corner of Eliza Street, her eyes vacant and her mouth moving around what looks like a cold sausage. I cross over to the other side of the street. I hope she doesn't see me, but she does.

Three

I would like to press on now, to tell you how Karina and I came to meet Julianne Lipcott: to explain how our lives became knotted up beyond hope of severance. But if I hurry I will lose the thread; or the narrative will be like knitting done in a bad temper. The tension goes wrong; you come back later, measure your work, and find that it hasn't grown as you imagined. Then you must unravel it, row by row, resenting each slick twist and pull that undoes, so easily, what you laboured over; and when you work again you must do it with the used wool, every kink in it reminding you of your failure.

Our autobiographies are similar, I think; I mean the unwritten volumes, the stories for an audience of one. This account we give to ourselves of our life – the shape changes moment by moment. We pick up the thread and we use it once, then we use it again, in a more complex form, in a more useful garment, one that conforms more to fashion and our current shape. I wasn't much of a knitter, early in my life. I was perpetually doing a kettle-holder. What is a kettle-holder? you'll ask. It is a kind name for any chewed-looking half-ravelled object of rough oblong shape, knotted up by a day-dreaming nine-year-old on the biggest size of wooden needles: made in an unlikely shade like lavender or bottle-green, in wool left over from some adult's abandoned project: or perhaps from a garment worn and picked apart, so that the secondhand yarn snakes under your fingertips, fighting to get back to the pattern that it's already learnt.

Karina was a good steady knitter. You would see her with her elbows pumping, hunched over a massive clotted greyness; it was as if a crusader had come by and thrown his chain-mail in her lap. I never knew whether she finished her garments or whether her mother and father wore them. All their clothes looked alike; winter and summer they were wadded in their layers, blanketed, swaying heavy and unspeaking along Curzon Street.

When Karina got home her parents were usually at work or asleep, depending which shift they were on. She had her own key, and before she took off her coat she used to put on the kettle and build up the fire and poke it, which I was not allowed to do: but I was allowed to watch her. When the kettle whistled she would swing it up – without benefit of holder – and slosh water into the vast brown teapot. I did not like tea; I did not think children liked it. Karina had a big white cup with blue hoops on it. She drank three cupfuls of tea, each with three heaped teaspoons of sugar.

Once the first cup was inside her she would take out the bread knife, which was something else that, at home, I was not allowed to touch. Karina would saw off four slices of bread and toast them in front of the fire, eating while she worked, slithering on to each slice a raft of margarine. One day she gave me a slice, but the fish smell of the margarine made my first bite come back up into my mouth and stick there. I coughed it back into my handkerchief, and asked permission to put it on the fire. Karina said, 'You'll never gain strength if you don't eat.' She ruminated a while, then said, 'I'm going to have my tonsils out.'

I gaped at her. 'Why?'

'Because our doctor says.' Her tone was virtuous, sage and elderly.

'Why does he say?'

'Because he's our doctor and he knows.'

'How do they get them out?'

'With an operating machine.'

'Do they put you inside it?'

She nodded. 'I reckon.'

I imagined the operating machine. The doctor would help you through a black hatch and you would emerge into a pleasant apartment: a sitting-room with armchairs and a semi-circular rug before the fire, pink carnations in a vase, a standard lamp and a television in the corner. There would be a bedroom and a bathroom; I could not see them, but they would be equally airy and well-appointed. The lights would be on all day, because of course there would be no windows; you would put up with that for the short time of your stay.

Panic fluttered in my throat: a dull bird, a sparrow. I put a hand against it and felt the wings beat. If I had to have my tonsils out I would be put in the operating machine by myself, and I did not know how to live in a house alone. Karina said, 'You get jelly and ice-cream, after it.'

When she had finished her toast she would take her plate into the kitchen, me trailing behind, and roll up her sleeves to peel a sinkful of potatoes. She would tell me what she was going to do later. 'I have to make a potato pie. I have to roast a piece of meat.'

I knew she was exaggerating, if not lying altogether. No child would be allowed to do these things. I wished they were. But when I went into the kitchen at home I said, 'Please, Mum, please, Mum, can I make a cake?' and she'd say, 'Stop messing there. Get from under my feet.' Yet somehow, mysteriously, one had to absorb the domestic arts. There are lessons to be learnt early and learnt well. At the table men are served first, with the best of what's going. It is the woman's part to take the fatty piece of meat and the egg that broke as it slid into the pan.

It was some time around this year – the year I was nine – that I became conscious of a falsity surrounding Karina, a disjunction. My mother – other mothers too – would dote on her and hold her up as an example. Such a clean girl, always looks lovely. She helps her mother. Doesn't have a soft life, both of them at work, had to learn to look after herself and stand on her own two feet. Fetches the potatoes uphill from the market for her mother. Not like you, young lady – everything done for you.

'Don't I help?' I would bellow. 'Don't I dry the pots every night, every single night? Don't I do shopping? Don't I iron – every week, all the straight things?'

'Karina never gives cheek.'

I tried to explain to my mother once, when I was in a reasoning mood and thought she might listen.

'Karina, you see, she's this way and then she's that. She's nice to your face, but horrible. She says horrible things to you. She envies you.'

'I'm not surprised if she envies you. You, with everything provided for you, and nothing to do but get yourself to school and back.'

'No, but the things you've got. Your library book. You think it's nice. Karina says, I wouldn't be reading that muck. Then you used to like it but you don't like it any more.'

My mother looked at me stonily. She did not understand. Soon she would say something about cattle-waggons, as if I were part of the reason for them. I knew it was a waste of time trying to talk to adults; they seemed to miss three-quarters of what was going on in the world. I thought of dogs who smell and hear and never look, cats who just eat and stare at people and creep around till they fall asleep in the sun. Something vital's left out: but with people, something vital seeps out as they age.

The next time Sister Basil asked me a stupid question, I didn't answer her. I just folded my arms and I looked back sadly. She was a small nun, old, who looked as if a cobweb had been draped over her face. 'Come on, come on,' she said. 'Either you know or you don't know, which is it?' I passed my eyes over her. Suddenly she came to life, spitting and dancing like a cat. Two red spots grew on her grey cheeks. She propped up the lid of her desk with one arm while with the other hand she rummaged around for her cane. She stood over me and shouted that I would be caned for dumb insolence. I looked back, sadder. There was really no chance of her caning me because I would not hold out my hand when she asked me; I had made a decision on this. Out of the corner of my eye I saw Karina watching me. Her big pink face had turned white.

I don't really remember what happened next – only that Sister Basil backed off, backed down, found a pretext – and I walked out unmolested at the end of the afternoon, everyone silent around me, and Karina shadowing me with her slapping, rolling, puppy's walk, not offering to link me until she saw which way the wind was blowing. Sister Basil's question was this: Who invented the telephone? I was sure she had the answer at the back of her book. Why didn't she ask questions to which she didn't know the answers? Then she might learn something to her advantage.

I tore a piece of paper out of my rough book. I wrote on it in vast capitals:

ALEXANDER
GRAHAM
BELL

At the end of the day I left it on Sister Basil's desk. So I knew: and she knew I knew.

Karina arrived at Tonbridge Hall two days after Julianne, and was billeted as arranged in Room C21, with a girl called Lynette Segal, who was a third-year student at the School of East European Studies. We met Lynette just after Karina's installation, when she tapped at our door after dinner.

I liked her even before she spoke: she was pale, neat and delicate, with a brunette's glitter and many gold rings. Her eyes were the colour of blackberries. They fell first on the skull on our bookshelf. She said simply, 'I admire.'

Julianne, sprawled on her bed, looked up. 'Oh, we do have taste.'

Lynette stood uncertainly, poised almost on her toes. 'My room-mate says she knows you.'

I nodded.

'So I said I'd ask you round for coffee.'

'And *petits fours*?' Julianne asked.

Lynette rose a little, as if poised for a balletic spring. 'Bendicks Bittermints,' she offered.

Julianne uncoiled her legs. 'I admire,' she murmured.

'Oh, but you must do *something*,' Lynette said. She gave a little sideways hop. 'Or you would die.'

Julianne stood up. Pointed to me. 'May the prole come too? Only half a mint for her, mind!'

Lynette said to me, 'How very short your hair is! But it shows off your beautiful eyes.'

I could see that Julianne had also fallen in love. I think women carry this faculty into later life: the faculty for love, I mean. Men will never understand it till they stop confusing love with sex, which will be never. Even today, there are ten or twenty women I love: for a turn of phrase or wrist, for a bruised-looking ankle where the veins have blossomed out, for a squeeze of the hand or for a voice on the end of the phone. I would no more go to bed with any of them than I would drown myself; and drowning is my most feared form of death. Perhaps I love too easily; I can say Lynette has left a mark on my heart.

So: Julianne reached up and took the skull from the

shelf. 'We call her Mrs Webster,' she said to Lynette. 'Carmel, she will have her little joke.' We skipped and slid along the corridor to C21, passing Mrs Webster between us as if she were a rugby ball.

This is how I came to enter a room that now no longer exists, except in my memory: bursting through the door with a skull poised between my hands. The air of C21 was fragrant with spilt talc and splashed cologne. An electric kettle was steaming into the air. The wardrobe doors stood open and I saw Julianne's eyes pass over crushed silk and cashmere, squeezed over in one half of the wardrobe to leave room for Karina's clothes. On the floor by one of the desks stood three pairs of beautiful boots, like sentinels whose upper part has been assumed to heaven: slim straight-sided high-heeled boots, their aroma of leather and polish blossoming into the room. One pair burgundy: one pair a deep burnished chestnut: one pair black and fluid as melting tar.

And on one of the beds, there basked a fur, a long-haired fox fur, its colours banded and streaked, straw-berry blonde with platinum tips. My eyes were drawn ineluctably towards it, as fingers are drawn to marble or velvet. I stared at it; as I did so, one of its arms slid towards me, as if in languid salute. I watched. The arm flopped itself over and lolled on to the floor. I took a step towards it, genuflected, and lifted it reverently. I tucked it on to the bed, into the body of the coat, feeling as I did so not just the whisper of the fur against my hand but the sleekness of the silk that lined it. 'I would kill for this coat,' I said simply.

57

'Oh, heavens!' its mistress said. 'Don't murder me. Just borrow it. Any time.'

'I couldn't.'

'Go on, try it.' Lynette skipped across the room. The fox fur seemed to leap into her arms and nestle there. Julianne leant against the wall, amused. Lynette whisked my arms into the sleeves. Her supple hands – blue veins and ivory – swept the collar up to my throat. 'Oh, that's lovely!' she said. 'It suits you. Oh, Karina, don't you think? Doesn't it suit her? You're taller, you see, you can carry it off. My father bought it for me, and I do like it, but I wonder if it makes me look like Baby Bear.'

Karina stood by the window. Though it was dark outside the curtains were not yet drawn; we filled the central pane with our shadow selves, like actors on a lit stage, like lively ghosts tossing their arms and twirling in the void. I glanced into the window and saw Karina's broad back, her neck bent like the neck of a toiling ox. Then I looked back into the room and saw her face, its flesh self not the shadow, and I saw – it is easy to persuade myself now, after the event – I saw her patient hatred take root.

Lynette pounced on the kettle. 'Coffee?'

'Black,' said Karina. 'Please.'

'Who got here first?' Jule asked.

'Oh, I did,' Lynette said absently, stooping into the steam.

'She left you the best bed, Karina,' I said. 'The best desk.'

'Mm,' Lynette said. She hummed to herself, spooning out instant coffee. The obvious bit of T. S. Eliot sprang

58

to my mind. 'Not much to do, is it, leave someone a bed? Are you going to have your coffee in your coat, Carmel dear?'

I was staring at myself in the mirror. The fur felt alive around me; there was a faint, disturbing vibration beneath my skin, as if I had acquired another pulse.

'A proper mannequin,' Karina said. 'Isn't she?'

'Yes, well, she has the figure for it,' said Lynette. Her tone, very gently, rebuked Karina's. She caught the coat as it slipped from my shoulders. 'Modom must remember it's here when she wants it,' she said. She curtsied deeply, and cast a glance – abashed – at the wardrobe.

'I told you,' Karina said. 'There's no need to squash your stuff up like that. I've hardly got anything.'

Karina's suitcase was still fastened, standing against the wall by her bed. It was the kind of suitcase people from Curzon Street used to take to Blackpool, once a year during the fifties, with a whole family's clothes inside. It had a check design, like a man's loud suit, though the pattern was faded to fawn, as if summer by summer the rain had washed the colour out; its sharp metal corners were rusty.

'You're entitled to your space,' Lynette insisted. She eased off the lid of the Bittermints. The happy aroma of good chocolate joined the other perfumes in the air.

When autumn came to Curzon Street, the dead leaves blew uphill from the trees in the park, and my father coming home at half-past six brought in on his overcoat the smell of smoke and cold. Our last walk on the hills had been in September. My mother had strode ahead,

59

her coat flapping, leaving my father to make some sort of conversation with me. I knew, though no one mentioned it, that we would not go walking next summer. Their quarrels had changed, and become quieter, more vicious. And I could not keep talking, talking and talking, poulticing the vast bleeding silence. Not without practice; not without a good deal of it.

Karina and I came uphill from school, turned at the pub on the corner; it was half-past four and the street lamps were burning, half-aglow in a wet dusk. 'Let's talk like grown-ups,' I said. 'I'll be Lady Smith.' There was no picture of her on the sign but I thought I knew what she looked like. She would have a tailored costume, like our landlady's. 'You can be my husband,' I told Karina. 'You can be . . .' I searched my inner catalogue of painted heads, '. . . you can be the Prince of Connaught.'

'I don't want to play it,' Karina said.

'Why not?'

'He has got a moustache.'

'We can pretend that.'

'What must I do then?'

'It's easy. You just talk. You say grown-up words.'

Karina had a bag with her, a string bag stretched out with three large loaves. They were stacked one on top of the other, each with its crackling U-shaped top and its fragments splitting through the tissue paper like broken slate. She carried this bag slung over her shoulder, and it made her sway from side to side on the pavement, so that she would move a half-step towards me, a half-step away. 'Pneumonia,' I offered. I didn't mind giving her a word to get her going.

Karina looked sideways at me. 'I am the Prince of Connaught. I have pneumonia.'

I almost thumped her. 'You're not doing it proper.' You have to be that person, I wanted to say to her, put their skin on your back. Grown-up words came bubbling into my mouth: rouge, piano stool, niece. I felt my face blossoming out, round as the full moon, and I smelt the fragrance of pink face powder: I had become Lady Smith. 'I returned home last night,' I enunciated carefully, 'to find my favourite niece seated on the piano stool.'

'Did she have pneumonia?' Karina asked. Her voice was nothing like the Prince of Connaught's: she wasn't even trying. I thought, if I had scissors I could cut her string bag, and her loaves would tumble out and slide down the hill and then she'd catch it from her mother. But this was not the sort of thing I did to Karina, more the sort of thing she did to me. 'Dumb insolence,' she would sometimes say. 'That's bad. Very bad.' It was a whole year since my run-in with Sister Basil; but Karina had appointed herself my spiritual guardian. 'Did you say your morning prayers?' she would ask me, when we met in the street at half-past eight. 'What did you pray for?'

I pictured the loaves picking up speed, losing their tissue paper and collecting dry leaves and bubble-gum wrappers, rolling in at the shop doorway and bouncing back on to the shelves.

'Your father and me have been talking,' my mother said.

That woke me up. I'd never heard them talking. Not in months.

My mother had just come in. She'd been out cleaning. Other cleaning women might come and go in an old coat and a turban, but my mother wore a coat that was no more than medium-old, and a proper scarf, and she put lipstick on, Tan Fantasy. Once when she was in a good mood she let me try it. People take you at your own valuation, she said. Always remember that.

'Can I have a biscuit?' I asked. I thought it might be better not to know what they had been talking about.

'All right, but one, mind, or you'll spoil your tea.' For a moment she was diverted; then, unknotting her scarf, she said, 'We've decided we'll let you sit for the Holy Redeemer.'

I had heard of the Holy Redeemer. It was an academy that Sister Basil often referred to, with a pious, grieving note in her voice, as if it were her land of lost content; though I am sure, now, that she had never set foot inside its portals. I said, 'Sister Basil says the likes of us would never be fit for it in a thousand years.'

My mother snorted. 'Sister Basil? That old nanny goat? What does she know? If you can pass your scholarship you can go. Why shouldn't you? But you have to take their entrance exam as well.'

'Is that harder than my scholarship?'

'Not so hard that you won't manage it, if you apply yourself.'

This was the usual thing. What I asked for was facts: what I got was a sermon.

'Will I have a uniform like Susan Millington?'

'Certainly you will.'

Susan Millington was a big girl who lived near the

park in a detached house. She was the only person I had ever seen who went to the Holy Redeemer. She had passed her scholarship and then she had passed the entrance exam, I said to myself; that was how it was done.

The scholarship was the Eleven Plus. Almost everybody didn't pass it. If boys failed, they sank below my horizon for a few years, then cropped up in a wedding photo, suit sleeves hiding any tattoos; oh, it's a pity, my mother would say, he was a bright little lad, and now look at that trollop he's landed with. If girls failed, they went to St Theresa's up Pennyworth Brow, where they wore navy berets and laddered nylons. Sister Monica, who was in charge of us in the top class, was already priming us for it. 'You will find there is first-rate equipment for domestic science,' she said. 'Electrical sewing-machines. A fully equipped laundry with steam-presses, and a model kitchen fitted out with a range of electrical cooking ranges. In point of fact, everything the heart could desire.'

A thought occurred to me: 'If I go to the Holy Redeemer, I'll have to go on the bus.' A needle of anxiety probed my ribs; a bus, I thought, could get a child lost.

'Two buses, at least,' my mother said. 'Three, if you'd like to save a long walk.' She sounded proud, as if I had already been exalted. 'It'll be worth it, mark my words. Make no mistake about it. An honour and a privilege.'

I wanted to run and put my hand over her mouth. I didn't know why she was saying such things.

*

It was nearly Bonfire Night. The evenings were dry and cold, and smelt of the fires to come. If you're a Catholic you don't burn Guy Fawkes; the Pope says you mustn't.

We went from house to house, cob-coaling.

'We come a cob-coaling for Bonfire Night,
Tally-ho, tally-ho . . .'

Some children hoped that after two lines the person would come out with money in their hand ready, because they didn't know any more words. If the householder was slow they had to stand there just shuffling their feet and droning 'Tally-ho'.

But I liked the words, the complete set. They had no meaning and yet they were crawling with it. I would have sung them for no money at all.

'Down in yon cellar there's an old umberella
And in yonder corner there's an old pepper box.
Pepper box, pepper box, morning till night:
If you give us nowt we'll steal nowt
We wish you good-night.'

By the time it came to the 5th of November, the weather was cloudy, damp and unseasonably warm. The Catherine wheels, nailed to coalhouse doors, twirled brokenly as if they were burning under a towel. Mount Etna and Mount Vesuvius sputtered and coughed, giving a poor impression of their lethal past, and rockets shot into skies ready to receive and extinguish them. My grandad would always give a good firework display, whatever the prevailing conditions: Karina and I stood side by side in his backyard, two among a small crowd, cramming our mouths with parkin. I whispered, through the crumbs, 'I'm going to sit for the Holy Redeemer.'

She turned on me, her eyes narrowed. If she had been less greedy she would have spat out her softening mass of oatmeal and treacle; but as it was she chewed vigorously till most of her cake was gone. 'YOU - ARE - A - LIAR,' she hissed. 'You'll have to tell it in confession.'

'I am not a liar,' I hissed back. 'Susan Millington passed her scholarship and then she passed her entrance exam. I'm going on two buses, if not three. I'll be getting a tennis racquet.'

'If you believe that, you're even dafter than you look.'

The lethargic bonfire put out its tongues: reaching, dull crimson, into heavy air. It was built nice and high – Joan of Arc, I thought – and I could see figures moving against its light; I could see Karina, as she swung her face away. One plait swayed out from under her pixie hood, like a sucker reaching for food. Envy, I thought. One of the Deadly Sins. We were having them in catechism. Cardinal Virtues: Justice, Fortitude, Temperance . . . My memory failed. There was grey smoke going up my nose. Four Sins Crying Out to Heaven for Vengeance. Murder. Sodomy. Oppression of the Poor. Defrauding the Labourer of his Wages.

My grandad gave me a sparkler, from a bunch sparking already in his own hand; he passed one to Karina, saying, 'There you are, my duck.' Turning a little to allow room, we wrote our names on the nearest air. My vast final loop threatened to set Karina's sleeve on fire. As the tip of the sparkler drooped to ash, I wanted to challenge Karina to duel me with what remained, but I knew that duels – swordplay in general – were beyond her poor spirit. 'Blessed are the poor in spirit.' I was happy, even so; frightened, but getting reconciled to being frightened. I sang out: untuneful, smoke-captive: 'Pepper box, pepper box, morning till night . . .'

'STAND BACK,' my grandad yelled.

On our left, a roman candle began to sputter and start, crackling pink and blue hyphens away from itself and by way of an arch into the ground. Another rocket rose, flipped, shot out a trail of subdued white stars and subsided in stifling mid-heaven.

' . . . pepper box, morning till night: / If you give us nowt we'll steal nowt / We wish you good-night.'

The next thing I clearly remember, it was Christmas Eve. We were having visitors from Leeds, and my mother was neatly forking mixed pickles into her cut-glass dish that had been left her in a will. 'If I see you messing with that dish,' she said, 'it'll be a good slap and straight off to bed.'

Earlier, when my mother was milder, we had glued an angel to the window. Frail and phosphorescent, gauzy wings edged thinly with tinsel, she glittered out at Curzon Street. Silent night. Holy Night. From the Ladysmith came the sound of breaking glass. 'Round yon virgin, mother and child . . .' Karina always sang 'Round John Virgin'. One of these years I would tell her: gently, of course. Unless next year I no longer knew Karina; but that seemed hardly possible, as whatever happened about the Holy Redeemer she and I would go on living six doors away from each other. I pictured myself, one year from now, wearing a velour hat like Susan Millington's and gazing out through the angel's wings at Curzon Street: waiting for snow to fall.

Four

Tonbridge Hall: when it came to the night of the roast parsnips, my digestive system rebelled. 'What's the matter?' Lynette said.

'I just can't, that's all. They look like ogres' penises.'

There was a small ripple of shock from the Sophies at the table.

Karina said, 'You were always picky about your food.'

'Not a fault anyone could lay at your door,' Julianne said mildly.

'Just leave it on your plate,' Lynette urged. 'Here, do you want to get rid of it? Give it to me. I'll vanish it from your sight.'

It was too late. A kind of stricture had set in, a tightening in my throat, so that I could not eat the stewed beef that came with the parsnips, and would not be able to manage my square piece of sponge adorned with half an apricot. I do not mean to say that the food at Tonbridge Hall was bad – not bad like school dinners – it was just that some of it, for me personally, was impossible. Since we had got our fridge, our vegetables at home had been Bird's Eye frozen peas; before we got our fridge, our vegetables had been carrots. But these woody things – broccoli – things with great uncooked stems – seemed to me fit only for cattle. The potatoes were hard too, sometimes bullet-hard, doled out sparingly, two per young lady; as if they were bullets indeed, and we were the sheriff's men, who might easily get out of hand.

Now, I would not want you to think that this is a story about anorexia. There have been too many of those, whole novels about moony girls, spoilt girls, girls who dwindle away to wraiths and then blow up like party balloons. No: and yet partly it is a story about flesh, about the bodies that contained our minds. On the whole, during the years when we were educated, we were persuaded into thinking that bodies were an encumbrance, a necessary evil. At least that was the word put out at the Holy Redeemer, where I would first meet Julianne. But we were not so simple, not so tractable, by the time we were sixteen; we knew we lived in the era of the contraceptive pill, and that we had bodies, and that society expected us to get some use out of them. Let us say then it is a story about appetite: appetite in its many aspects and dimensions, its perversions and falling off, its strange reversals and refusals. That will do for now.

When I returned to my desk after dinner, these evenings at Tonbridge Hall, my foot would ruck up the cotton rug on the polished floor, and I would imagine sliding lightly on my back across the room and through the wall, floating out, weightless, over Bloomsbury. Some evenings I took a spoonful or two of soup, made my apologies, pulled on my coat and sped out again into the autumn evening, and I see myself now as if − FLASH − an inner camera has caught me forever, hand flung up before a white face. *Carmel McBain, on her way to a meeting of the student Labour Club.*

In Drury Lane, in the Aldwych, the theatres were

opening their doors; in Houghton Street, a hot little café steamed its fumes over the pavement. I would run up the steps, into my place of work, my palace of wonders; the half-deserted building came with its echo, its ever-burning strip lights, its tar-smell of typewriter ribbons and smoke; in the mazes and catacombs you could sniff out your meeting, guided by your nose towards the dusty scent of composite resolutions, sub-sections and sub-clauses, stacking chairs, tobacco: the reek of Afghan coats and flying jackets, the vaporous traces left in the air they inhabit by weak heads and fainter hearts.

I do not remember that political philosophy was ever discussed, or political issues: only organization, personalities, how the Labour student movement should be run. In Paris, the ashes of the *événements* were hardly cool. Here in London, we discussed whether to go by coach (collectively) or to set out (individually) to some all-day-Saturday students' meeting in some seedy provincial hall; and how much the coach would cost per seat. Whether there should be a joint social evening with the Women's Liberation Group: would that be profitable to both, or end in some ideological and financial disaster?

It was men who spoke; not young and fresh ones, but crease-browed and leather-jacketed elders, men with bad teeth from obscure post-graduate specialities. They would shuffle or lurch to their feet; then would come nose-rubbing, throat-clearing; then their voices would rumble just audibly, like spent thunder in a distant valley. Some would speak slumped in their seats, eyes fixed on the ceiling, ash dripping from a cigarette. Their manner was weary, as if they knew everything and had seen everything, and they paused often, perhaps in the middle of a phrase, to blow their noses or make a snickering sound that must have been laughter. Their remarks reached no conclusion; at a certain point, they would become slower, more sporadic, and finally peter out. Then another would draw attention to himself, with the bare flutter of an agenda in the stale air: and grunting, shrugging, turning down his mouth, begin in the middle of a sentence . . . Dave and Mike and Phil were their names, Phil and Dave and Mike. Young women carried them drinks from the vending-machine, black coffee's frail white shell hardly dented by their light fingertips.

I would put my head in my hands, sometimes, for even I must yawn; I would with delicacy track my fingertips back through my inch of hair, and say to myself, am I, can I be, she who so lately at the Holy Redeemer wore an air of purpose and expectation, and a prefect's deep blue gown? So many years of preparation, for what was called adult life: was it for this? Were these meetings as aimless as they appeared, or was I too un-tutored to see the importance of what was going on, or was I, in some deeper way, missing the point? Yes: that must be it.

As the clock ticked away, a fantasy would creep up and possess me: that if you could stay on and on – if you could stay at the meeting till midnight or the hour beyond – then the masks would slip, the falsity be laid aside, the real business would begin. For it seemed to me that my fellow socialists were talking in code, a code designed perhaps to freeze out strangers and weed out the dilettante. Only the pure of heart were welcome

71

here. They must submit to a new version of the medieval ordeal: instead of poison, water, fire, a Trial by Pointlessness. Once you had passed it – once you had endured the full rigours of a full debate on a revitalized constitution for a revitalized Labour students' movement – then, in the hour after midnight, the chatter would cease – glances be exchanged – the talk begin, hesitant at first, half-smiling, people near-apologetic about their passions and their expertise, quoting Engels, Nye Bevan, Daniel Cohn-Bendit; we would exchange our intuitions and half-perceptions, pass on our visions and dreams, each vision and each dream justified by some reference, recondite or popular. Comrades would say, 'This is what makes me a socialist . . .' and speak from the heart; perhaps someone would mention Lenin, and wages councils, and coal-miners, and the withering away of the state. Dawn would break: gentle humming of the Red Flag.

But in real life, nothing like this occurred at all. By ten-thirty the men would be looking at their watches, drifting and grumbling towards the union bar. I would hover a little, in the corners of rooms, on the edges of groups, hoping that someone would turn to me and begin a real conversation, one I could join in. Stacking chairs squeaked on a dirty floor, the women of the socialists stooped to haul up their fringed and scruffy shoulder bags; in the bar the women stood in a huddle, excluded by the ramparts of turned shoulders, with tepid glasses of pineapple juice clenched in bony white hands. Their eyes avoided mine; they smoked, and muttered to each other in code.

Disillusioned, I would trail back up Drury Lane. The

theatres would have turned out already, and the stage doors would be barred. An empty Malteser box bowling towards the Thames would bear witness to the evening passed. My eyes would be heavy and stinging with cigarette smoke and lack of sleep. Behind my ribs was a weight of disappointment. Still the lines ran through my head, distressing, irrelevent: Is this the hill? Is this the kirk? / Is this mine own countree? The irresponsive silence of the land, / The irresponsive sounding of the sea.

'Why, why,' Julianne said, 'if you were going to have your hair cut, did you have it so stubbled?'

'To last me,' I said. 'Till Christmas.'

'Did you think there were no hairdressers in London?'

'I thought they might be expensive.'

'You really shouldn't be so poor, should you?' Julianne said.

Each morning she flicked her white coat from its hanger, in case they were taken on the wards; her eyes large, soft, alert. She told some Sophies that I had run away from a convent, where my hair had been chopped off; she told others that I was a victim of the IRA, shorn for collaboration after a romance with a squaddie. 'Caught in the Falls Road,' she said, 'her pantyhose around her ankles; her poor mother, if she were dead, would be turning in her grave.'

Pretending to be Irish was a great diversion for Julianne. Lancashire, Ireland, it's all the same to girls called Sophy.

Sophies liked to be engaged to be married by the end of their final year. At breakfast they showed each other their solitaire diamonds. Facets winked as they passed them across the Thursday rasher and the side-plate of baked beans: exchanging them so that they could feel the fatness or looseness of a finger-joint, try on another future.

Claire and Sue, the churchgoers, lived next door to us in C2. 'Come in for a coffee,' Sue would say, fluttering, as we leapt upstairs after dinner: I'd say sorry, got to work, and Julianne would growl, 'They want our souls.'

In C4 was Sophy, the original Sophy: a strapping girl who took fencing lessons, whose big feet lightly danced through Julianne's dream-life as she pranced down the corridor each morning towards her breakfast. Sophy was straight-backed and sound in wind and limb, a girl with large pale eyes and a heavy drift of crimped, dirty-blonde hair; by the side of her mouth there was a mole, flat, definite, a beauty-spot. She looked as if she could stare down a persistent man and bend a useful one to her will. Sometimes she stalked the corridors in her tunic and breeches, with her mesh head tucked beneath her arm; then up in the four-person lift would come Roger, her boyfriend.

I was beginning to puzzle about this sort of thing. I had seen them about the place, various boyfriends: some – like Roger – with purple and throbbing acne, some – like Roger – with hair in their ears, some – like Roger – with vaguely defined middles held in by sagging waist-bands, and in their eyes the pallid cast of mother-worship, and a desperation to put their erections inside some nice girl who would propagate their expectations.

Sometimes, under my desk lamp, when grey morning would filter in through the curtains, and I would rub my eyes, there would pass before me a procession of Sophies and Rogers, brides and grooms. 'What, will the line stretch out to th' crack of doom?' I began to imagine the donors of the breakfast solitaires; their grease-spiked mousy hair, their patronizing attitudes, their welling guts. What was the matter with them, the girls who lived with me on C Floor? Did they think these were the only men they could get? Inferiority was working away inside these girls, guilt at being so clever, wanting so much, taking so much from the world. If they were to have a man as well, it seemed to them right that he should be a very poor specimen.

All this is hindsight of course. FEMINISM HASN'T FAILED, IT'S JUST NEVER BEEN TRIED. If you knew at twenty what you know at thirty-five, what a marvellous life you could have; on the other hand, you might find that you couldn't be bothered to have any life at all.

Every night, or perhaps every second night, Sue's fair head would come bobbing in at the door: 'Carmel, godsake, come on!' I'd become aware that Sue had a struggle with her accent, her lingo, her diction; she was by no means a real Sophy, but Claire had helped her no end, she said, and she had quite a sense of humour when you got to know her, and what with one thing or another she really depended on Claire. 'Honest,' she'd say, 'you really ought to slap those books shut and come on out with us.'

I looked up, my eyes drugged and glazed from the effort of understanding the British legal system. 'Where? Where are you going?'

'Well, dinner was so frightful . . . we thought we might go for a Chinese meal . . .'

'I'm not hungry,' I said. 'Thanks, Sue.'

She looked at me and gave a great sigh. Sweet blue-eyed girl, Sue. I didn't think I could spare the energy to understand her; let Claire do it. I had got a name for studying, a name for dedication. I didn't deserve it, for I daydreamed sometimes, and doodled in the margins of my work. Still, I put in long hours, because I had realized in my second week in London that while I was sitting at my desk in Tonbridge Hall, breathing in the stuffy and recirculated air, bending my gaze beneath the prepaid beam of my lamp, I was not actually spending money.

I had quickly discovered that I would have to count every penny. The fees of Tonbridge Hall were very high, and were deducted from our grants before we received them; they had to cover not just our food but our starched bed linen, the wages of the monosyllabic foreign women who cleaned our rooms, and the ferocious heat chuffed out by the central-heating boiler deep in the bowels of the place. There was no room for negotiation. You could not say, I'll be ten degrees colder please, and get a refund; or say that, being bred to it, you would clean your room yourself. I had sat down with pen and paper, during the first week of the term; though the sums were easy enough to do in your head, pen and paper showed you were putting effort in, and provided against a calamitous mistake. I had deducted my fare for my Christmas ticket home, then divided what was left of my grant into

76

weekly segments, working first on the supposition that I would leave five pounds over for an emergency. The sum per week that was left for me was so impossibly small that I decided I would lump in the reserve with the rest. After all, I said to myself, what kind of emergency costs five pounds?

Each Friday I took the allotted sum out of my bank, which was situated in Lincoln's Inn Fields. It was a pleasant enough place, though later it became home to tramps and derelicts who lived in cardboard houses of their own design. If they'd been in residence then, I might have lost my nerve entirely, brought face-to-face with the consequences of folly or improvidence; but my own imagination yielded such examples that I hardly needed any in the outer world.

My money in my purse, I would sit on a bench, and begin a letter to Niall. I wrote on file paper, letters too fat for normal envelopes to contain, so that I had to buy big tough brown ones; I wrote fast, and I wrote everything, everything that happened and every thought that passed through my head. Each day I sent one of these letters, dropping it into a post-box as I walked down Drury Lane. Each morning, in the pigeonholes of Tonbridge Hall, there was a letter for me, the envelope addressed in the careful writing of a first-year engineer; the numbers as if printed by a machine, the black script upright, precise, as thin as if a pin had traced it. Each morning. Without fail.

Once my letter was fairly begun I would bundle it into my bag and walk down to the student's union, and go into the shop. There were two purchases I had to make, each Friday; a pair of tights, and a pad of file paper for my lecture notes and letters in the week to come.

As an economy measure, I was training my wild hand to be small, so that I could use narrow feint and get in more words per week. This was easy enough, but the tights were more of a problem. The union sold the cheapest in London, so there was no question of obtaining them elsewhere. There was only one size, and, only one colour, a near black.

They were very strange, stretchy garments; it did not matter how carefully you washed them, you could not help the legs getting longer and longer, so that when you drew them from the basin and squeezed them gently they sprang from your palms and lolled about the room like serpents. When you hung them up they dangled obscenely. If the parsnips were ogres' cocks, these were the foreskins of giants: taken as trophies in battle, by an Amazonian band.

At this stage in her life, Julianne had two boyfriends, neither of them ugly. Both of them were somewhere above her in the complex hierarchy of medical students, and both of them had rooms in flats of their own. 'My advice to you,' she said, 'is to get on the Pill.'

I went along to the Student Health Service, where I saw a woman doctor. She didn't sit behind her desk; she had it wedged sideways in the small consulting-room, and gestured to me to sit beside her, as if we were friends. As her chair creaked round towards me, I saw her heavy bursting legs, the lilac veins butting through the stretch of her tights. Dear God, I thought, she must be *forty*, to have legs like that.

'How many boyfriends do you have?' she asked pleasantly.

'Only one.'

She frowned; that is to say, face powder creased in the line above one eye.

'How long have you known him?' She was already reaching for her prescription pad.

'Two years,' I said.

'That's a long time. He must be a boyfriend from home, then. You really should be careful.'

'I am careful. That's why I came to see you.'

She wrote something. 'No. Contraception is one thing.' Dull hair, over-streaked, worn loose, brushed her desk. 'What I mean is, you ought not to get into a pressure-cooker relationship.'

I went out into the street, pondering. Was that what I had? A pressure-cooker relationship? Here I'd been, calling it love. She thought I was too young to love a man, but old enough for screwing. I supposed that she had passed on to me, with her prescription, her malediction: the residue of her disappointment, her let-downs, her sad half-hours under station clocks waiting for men who never came. But how dare she try to sour my life? I imagined myself leaning forward – as in primary-school days – and taking hold of a handful of the woman's denatured hair; then leaning back, firm and leisurely, until a part of her scalp was in my hand and her desk was awash and her notes were bobbing in a sea of blood. The wine-dark sea.

Sometimes my mother had pressure-cooked. Carrots, of course. Quartered potatoes. I remembered the action – packed metal drum, the stacked weights that rolled in your palm before you threaded them on to the dangerous lid; the muttering that rose from inside, as carrot sang to carrot like mutinous slaves below deck. The hiss of steam into cold air, it frightened me . . . I thought the weights might burst up like Annie Oakley's bullets and pierce the ceiling and that our roof might fall in. What did people do for a metaphor, before the pressure-cooker was invented?

Each morning – each morning when she woke up at Tonbridge Hall – Julianne would stand before the mirror looking at her breasts. 'They are, you know.' She'd knead them, look at them narrowly. 'They are. Most definitely. Getting. Bigger. Oh, good old Pill! What did a girl do for tits, before it was invented?'

I collected my prescription from the chemist in Store Street, thinking, Well now, I'm ready for Christmas.

The ludicrous notion stopped me dead in the chemist's doorway. I've got the tinsel, the contraceptives, the roast goose and the holly; I'm ready for Christmas.

The term was almost half-way through. I felt a desolate, excruciating loneliness. Still, I thought, there will come a time . . . and then no more Roman roulette, no more counting the Durex. Already I felt perverse nostalgia for that strange condom texture, slippery and elusive, backed by the firm spike of flesh.

When had we found the opportunity, Niall and I, two

good schoolchildren? At his parents' house when his parents were on holiday. (My parents never went on holiday.) On Sundays, when his parents were visiting their relations, or going to see National Trust properties or gardens open to the public. We had been fucking for years; we were old in fucking. Like me, Niall was an only child; there were no siblings whooping up the stairs to catch us on the job.

No more marking the calendar, I thought. Or that fear. That way of listening to the body, as if you could gauge the peregrinations of each cell; the sick gladness each month as you woke to feel a tension behind the eyes, perhaps a soreness in the breasts, a little tentative cramp. The long breath released; the fingers groping in the drawer for Tampax, of which my mother disapproved.

I could not say that the new dispensation was having much effect on my figure. I was as slim as ever. If anything, more so.

You won't mind, will you, if I call Niall by his real name, and call the other Tonbridge boyfriends by the composite name of Roger? It may seem a confusing technique, but the truth is that all these years on I can't separate them in my mind. One of Julianne's gang – who filled the room, drinking coffee and making a noise, while I worked at my desk with my back to them – inquired of Julianne whether I was, you know, fixed up? She replied that I was practically married, but that the man was in prison. Doing a stretch, she said. It's a shame, but she's very loyal, is Carmel.

Up and down the corrider, the Sophies began to say, 'Have you heard, Miss McBain has a fiancé who's in gaol?'

'Really?' the second Sophy would gasp.

And the first, frowning, careful, 'Oh yes, he's "doing a stretch".'

Claire came tapping at the door. 'Look I – Carmel . . .' Inside her jolly jumper – striped, like a burglar's in a cartoon – she was turning a deep crimson.

'Yes?'

'I heard. Well, you know, I couldn't help . . . I'm so sorry. It must be hell for you. Sue told me not to come, but I thought I must just say a word.'

'Ah now, Claire,' I said. 'Aren't you kind?'

Perhaps I wouldn't have to wait till Christmas. Perhaps one weekend Niall would visit me, when he was in funds. Please God he would visit me, and not let this weary ten weeks stretch out in fretful celibacy and a big hole where my heart used to be. I relished the thought of the dark glitter around him as he trod the corridors. Already I was preparing my little speech . . . Oh, you know, they call it parole . . . The Sophies wanted to ask what his crime was, but they were too polite.

It's a long way to London from the University of Glasgow, and Niall was too proud to hitch-hike.

The day after Claire's visit, I ran into Sue at breakfast. It was fried-egg morning. It blinked up from my plate like a septic eye. Sue gave me a big wink.

Let me go back now to my former life, to 1963. Spring came to the north of England; you wait long enough, and it always does. Timid and experimental buds appeared, high on the black trees in the park. Sister Monica, my class teacher, began to tack sheets of tough blue paper on to a trestle table, and to call it the nature table; in time, we were told, we would have the opportunity to observe the Life of the Frog. The florist that we passed on our way to school began to file daffodils in buckets on the pavement outside the shop. They were brassy trumpets, they were brazen instruments; I touched their leaves, and feared they would slice my finger open.

St Patrick's day was dry but blustery, and the wind bowled us downhill towards school. Twenty minutes to nine, Karina stopped before the florist's. I stopped too; this was something out of the ordinary. She moved from foot to foot, staring into the window, then said to me roughly, 'Are you coming or not?'

I followed her in. The shop bell jangled. I had never been into a flower shop before. It seemed colder than the street outside; wetly, it seemed to breathe. The stone floor was running with water, water swished through recently with a yard brush; the marks were still in it, and the brush stood in the corner, up-ended to give its bristles a chance to dry. There was a smell of torn stems and damp newspaper. A woman came out of the back, pinched and blue and wearing a plastic pinny. On the counter was a box of shamrock, fresh in. Karina pointed to an ostentatious bunch. 'I'll have that,' she said.

'Karina,' I whispered. 'You can't. You're not qualified. You're foreign.'

'I'm English,' she said stonily.

'Yes, but you've got to be Irish.'

'There's no law,' the woman behind the counter said.

She plucked out the bunch Karina had indicated, and shook it gently; silver drops of water scattered into the air. 'I'll pin it on for you, love, shall I?'

'Does it cost extra for the pin?' Karina asked.

'No, the pin's free.'

'That's nice,' Karina said. She stood with her chin raised, stock-still, like a soldier listening to lies before a battle, while the woman fastened the shamrock to her coat. Out of her pocket Karina took a stitched leather purse, a grown-up woman's purse. I gaped at it. The popper, as she opened it, made a muffled explosion. 'How much is that?' Karina inquired.

She peered into the purse. Among the coins she had was a whole shilling piece. She put the money, bit by bit, into the florist's cupped palm, then closed the purse with another thunderous snap.

'Thanks, love,' the florist said. 'Watch the road when you cross.' All grown-up people said that: watch the road. I looked forward to being grown up so I could say it myself. The wind gently rippled the shamrock as we stepped back into the street.

'Karina . . .' I said.

'What?'

'Can I have a bit?'

'Why?'

'I'm Irish.'

'Why don't you buy your own?'

'I've got no money.'

'What, none at all?'

'A penny.'

'A penny!' she repeated.

'Could I buy a pennyworth off you?'

'That'd be about one leaf.'

'Oh, no,' I said. 'It'd be about fifteen stalks with full shamrocks on.'

Just before the school gates, Karina stopped and reached up to her corsage; plucked a single head of shamrock, and placed it in my open and respectful palm.

About a week after that, my mother went down to school to see Sister Monica. As I've said, Karina and I were in the top class now. Every morning we did sums, followed by English, followed by Intelligence. Intelligence was about picking the odd one out: beetroot, asparagus, cabbage, pea. Hen, cow, jaguar, pig; pilot, fireman, engineer, nurse. I hesitated for hours over these questions, sucking the end of my pencil till it was pulp. 'Carmel McBain,' Sister Monica would say, 'if the education committee was disposed to give a bursary for the slowest girl in this class, I'd say you'd get it every time. Don't you realize this will be a timed test, girl, a timed test? You don't pass your scholarship by sucking your pencil, my lady, and if you give me that look once again you'll be out here and have the cane.'

Intelligence was about shapes; about the next number in the sequence. My mother had come to ask Sister Monica to give me extra homework, to increase my chances of passing my scholarship. She returned triumphant. 'And I'm stopping your comics,' she said. 'You'll have no time for all that folderol. Besides, we've to save up now. There'll be your uniform and bus fares. Me and your father will have to scrimp and save.'

My comics were *Judy*, *Bunty*, *Princess* and *Diana*. 'Belle of the Ballet' was my favourite story. Sometimes when I was alone in my bedroom I hung on to the head of the bed and rose on my toes and teetered forward, a hand flailing at the mantelpiece for support; I did this until the bones crumpled, until tears of effort leapt into my eyes and my calves sang with pain. 'Karina,' I said, 'do you get *Princess*?'

'Do I get it?' Karina said. '*Princess*? It's soft.'

Coming back that day from school, my mother had looked thoughtful. 'I've been talking to Sister Monica about Karina. Sister Monica tells me that she's very bright.'

I looked up. I saw that some comment was called for. I remembered Karina's exercise books, besprinkled with red ticks by Sister Monica. Karina was neat, and Sister often said so: not to praise her, but to blame the rest of us. Karina wrote slowly, forming big deliberate letters like house bricks, square at the corners and evenly spaced. She did her numbers the same, and though when she wrote a composition Sister Monica would often scrawl 'More effort required', she usually got nine out of ten for her sums and sometimes nine and a half. Even if she got all the sums right she didn't get ten out of ten, because that was impossible; among human beings, perfection belongs to Our Holy Mother and Our Holy Mother alone.

'Well?' my mother said.

I nodded. 'She's good at sums. Fractions.'

'Better than you?' my mother said. There was an anxious, greedy edge to her voice.

'Yes. But I'm better at compositions.'

'You'll have to work hard at your arithmetic,' my mother said. 'Say your times tables at night before you go to sleep, after you've said your night prayers.' She gnawed her lip and then nodded, as if resolved. 'There's nothing like a good education,' she said, 'of which I personally didn't have the chance.'

Night came. I was a good child and an ambitious one, and I did what I was told, though when I was sleepy the prayers and the times tables got mixed up. Three sevens are twenty-one. Hail, holy queen, mother of mercy. Four sevens are twenty-eight. Hail our life, our sweetness and our hope. Five sevens are thirty-five. To thee do we cry, poor banished children of Eve, mourning and weeping in this vale of tears.

The other story I liked in my comics was 'Sue Day of the Happy Days'. The Days were her family; that was their name. Sue had a snobby elder sister who wore tight skirts and ironed her blouses in the kitchen before she went on dates, but that was really the only disadvantage to Sue's life. Sometimes she got a new classmate who was snobby or unpopular, but it usually turned out there was a good reason for that. Sue Day's mother had a round perm and made gravy and her father was kind in a detached way, like Dr Carr in *What Katy Did*. Her best friend was called . . . Edie Potter? Sue wore a school blazer, and had fair hair that flicked up at the ends. She must have been at least thirteen. Her lips were constantly parted, to show that she was speaking.

Nine sevens are sixty-three. Turn then, O gracious advocate, thine eyes of pity towards us, and after this our exile . . . Ten sevens are seventy.

The next day, when I was coming home from school, I saw my mother and Karina's mother walking together down Eliza Street. They had their heads together. They were deep in conversation; at least, my mother was. And they were linking.

Five

In the first few weeks of term at Tonbridge Hall, we didn't see as much of Karina as I'd imagined we would. Sometimes when I was going in to breakfast she would be leaving, setting off for Euston Square and her college on Mile End Road. 'The mysterious East', Julianne called it. Karina would grunt a good morning, and I'd say, 'Everything all right?' and of course she wouldn't reply, because why should she reply to a question as daft as that?

One night Lynette came to our room, looking defeated and carrying a box of bonbons and candied fruits from Fortnum and Mason. She popped the box on to our coffee table, sat down on Julianne's bed, massaged her tired calves and sighed. 'I've tried to break the ice,' she complained. 'But Karina, it's like – oh, go on, let's have a mixed metaphor – it's like pounding my head on a bleedin' brick wall.'

She finished her sentence with a flourish, a brilliant imitation of Sue's peculiar accent. I said, 'She has a problem with people.'

'A chip on her shoulder,' Julianne said.

'We know her, you see.'

'What language does she speak?' Lynette asked.

'English.'

'Yes, but with her parents – what did she talk at home?'

'English.' I explained the situation, so far as I could.

Lynette frowned. She had been looking forward, she said, to trying out a smattering of this and that, in the cause of making Karina feel more at home. She had done an exchange year, and her Russian was quite fluent. 'I don't think she's Russian,' I said. 'Her father was frightened of Russians, my mother said. He used to take precautions against them.'

Julianne stared at me. 'Like what?'

'Double-locking the door.' At one time I'd been able to come and go freely from Karina's house, but since her mother had taken ill that had changed. Karina's father, never a man to respond to a greeting with more than a grunt, was now as sociable as a corpse. The gas man and the district nurse were let in, if it suited him; they could not rely on it. If old habit drove me to Karina's door in the morning, I had to stand in the street, while mechanisms grated and clanked and chains were lifted from their grooves; when the door opened a crack, Karina had skilfully extruded her body on to Curzon Street without permitting me even a glimpse of the vestibule.

'Well – ' Lynette threw out a hand – 'don't ask me to write you a letter in Romanian, but other than that . . .' She shrugged. She could do the basics in many Eastern-bloc tongues, she said. 'The civilities. The small-talk of the bread queue.' The turn of her sable head was eloquent; it was she who seemed to me a real refugee, one of the glamorous kind who might have diamonds in a silk roll thrust into a lizard-skin vanity-case. When I said this to her she agreed: 'People are always surprised that I grew up in Harrow.'

Julianne offered to go down the corridor to the kitchen to refill our mugs of coffee. We used to drink it black, because the rooms were too hot for us to keep milk. Lynette tore open the bonbons; leaving the room, Jule scooped up a marzipan peach and thrust it into her cheek. Lynette leant forward. 'Please, explain to me while she's out – why does Karina hate her?'

'No special reason.'

'Oh.' Lynette flicked up an eyebrow. 'Fine. But I notice Julianne can be sharp with her.'

'Sharp? That's mild.' I must have grinned. 'You know, Julianne's not what she was. Her character's softening.'

Lynette selected a sugared almond. 'Not a pleasant topic, this. I have to say that Karina doesn't seem to like you either. Not in the least.'

'I'm not sure we can do anything about that.' I bounced a little on my bed. 'Look, Lynette, we're not in a school story. It's not Mallory Towers. We don't have to be . . .' I groped for the word, ' . . . chums.'

'Of course not. It's just that I have to live with her.'

'You do, don't you? Can't you apply for a transfer?'

'No, because who would she find herself sharing with next? You see, I may not be the best person in the world, but I do try to be kind, in so far as one . . .'

'Why?' I said. I was examining the world of motives in those days, trying to find for myself a new place in it.

'Why? I suppose . . . No, I can't think why.'

'We always used to be good in hope of eternal reward. And we were told that every time we said an unkind word, it was another thorn in Jesus' crown. If we committed an unkind action, it drove the nails deeper into his wounds. Well, it won't do, will it? Won't wash.'

Lynette smiled. 'Not really. It's not for grown-ups, is it? I suppose a person . . . a person dislikes confrontation and tries to ease . . . her own way through the world, and that means easing other people's. Inevitably.'

'So being kind is a sort of selfishness?'

'You know the phrase, enlightened self-interest?'

'I thought it meant money-grubbing.'

'Sometimes it's used that way.' The tip of her tongue touched the vanilla-cream centre of a dark chocolate. Julianne was coming back down the corridor, her feet squelching on the parquet. 'Karina's unhappiness is no profit to anyone. And I'm afraid that if she got a new room-mate she might be treated worse than I allow myself to treat her.' She closed her eyes. 'It's just that. That's all.'

Jule handed around the coffee. 'I see we're on the perennial topic.' Her fingers dipped into the Fortnum's box. 'Lynette, you must try to understand that though I know Karina I don't know her. She comes from a social background quite alien to me in every way, and at school if I spoke to her once a year it was as much.'

Lynette laughed, a small gurgle of sarcastic joy. 'What a snob you are, Lipcott, I didn't think – '

'That we had them in Lancashire?' Julianne said coolly. She licked a sugar crystal from her lower lip. 'Anyway, don't ask me about her, ask Carmel. Carmel's known her since they were at infant school.'

Lynette turned to me. A miniature Florentine was poised at her painted lips. 'Well?'

'Yes, I knew her.'

'She was your friend?'

'Not really.'

'So what did you do to her?'

I thought for a moment. 'I kicked her baby,' I said. I glanced up and saw their two faces side by side, gazing at me in uncomprehending shock.

I didn't explain. Or only lamely and partially. Why should I? I had, by this stage of the term, very few words to spare; they were all going into my letters to Niall. And yet the proximity of Karina, the sight of her stumping out into the London traffic and dirt, the presence of her name in our mouths – all these things led me helpless back into the past, memories pulling at me strong and smooth as a steel chain, each link hard and bright and obdurate, so that I was hauled out of my frail, pallid, eighteen-year-old body, and forced to live, as I live today as I write, within my ten-year-old self, rosy-skinned but rigid with fear, on my way by bus to take my entrance exam for the Holy Redeemer.

The surprise – if it was a surprise – had already occurred; I'd known something was up that day I'd seen my mum with Karina's mum, linking each other on Eliza Street. 'I'm sitting for the Holy Redeemer too,' Karina had said boldly, one morning as we went through the school gates.

'You are not!' I said.

'I am so! You can like it or lump it.'

That same night my mother said: I am determined that child should have her chance in life. Why not? She's as good as anybody, isn't she? My father grunted. He was doing a jigsaw puzzle; he did them many evenings now. She has to be a bright girl, my mother reasoned, she must be: running on in her most decisive tone, convincing the empty air. Look at the way she helps Mary in the house. Does all the shopping. Poor Mary doesn't know the price of an egg.

'Why doesn't she?' I said.

My mother frowned. 'Mary has enough to do, working shifts. She has a good capable girl to do her shopping for her.'

I had lost half a crown, once, when I had been sent out on a Sunday for a block of Neapolitan ice-cream. This had never been forgotten, it never would be.

'And she's capable enough to roll up her sleeves when she comes in from school and get her own tea and her father's as well if he's there for it.'

I could get the tea, I thought. My mother didn't need much food – she ran on wrath – and she didn't see that other people might need what she herself didn't. Getting our tea only involved slapping corned beef on a plate, and quartering a tomato. But there was a special way of slapping, a special way of quartering, and any modifications of it I might introduce were subject to my mother's scorn. If I were to fail my Eleven Plus and go to St Theresa's up Pennyworth Brow, with the model kitchen Sister Monica had told us about, I would be doing domestic science. That'll show her, I thought. 'Do they have domestic science at the Holy Redeemer?' I asked.

'Domestic science?' My mother's eyebrows – or the pencil marks which represented them – flew up into her hair. 'Latin and Greek, that's what you'll be doing. Physics and chemistry.'

We had received a booklet, called a prospectus. Among the lines of grey print there were some grey photographs, of two big girls handling test-tubes, supervised by a nun in spectacles; of a hockey team, grinning widely, arranged in a row with their sticks at a regulated angle, and the girl at the centre hoisting a beribboned cup. 'How will I learn to play hockey?' I said. 'I don't know how to do it.'

'Don't worry,' my mother said. 'It'll come to you. When the time is ripe.'

I went to look over my father's shoulder. He was in the early stages of his jigsaw, so you had to look at the lid of the box to see that it represented a thatched cottage on a village green. There was a church spire, and some rambling roses and a bicycle leaning against a gate. 'Be a good girl and you can help me fill in the sky,' he said.

'I'd rather do the duck pond.'

'We're not up to the duck pond yet. We've got to get the edges in first. Can't run before we can walk.'

'Well, will you give me a shout when you're up to the duck pond?'

'Get upstairs, lady,' my mother said, 'and get your homework done, never mind duck ponds. And don't let me come up and catch you gawping out of the window, neither.'

My father looked at his work, just a gap fringed with blue: 'A happy home,' he said, unemphatically.

I went without looking back, up the steep stairs to my room. I closed the door and sat down at the table my mother had lugged up some weeks previously. My homework was already laid out; it was Intelligence tonight. I glanced – just glanced – out of the window, bespattered with spring rain; it was April, still very cold in the house, and as I worked I would sometimes have to put down my pencil and rub my fingers to get some life back into them. My room was papered blue and white, though the white in places was yellow with age; blue Chinamen went to and fro, crossing small bridges over invisible streams. A Chinawoman held up a bird in a cage, her eyes mere slits: strange combs, like knitting needles, stuck out of her hair. Was the caged bird singing? If you got very close you could see that its tiny mouth was open to emit sound, like the mouth of Sue Day of the Happy Days. I imagined its warble, repeated again and again as the pattern repeated, as the Chinamen crossed their bridges, as the pavilion door creaked open, as the string of lanterns swayed.

I sat down, took up my pencil, began to work away at Intelligence: fill in the next letter in this sequence. To help me I had written out the alphabet on a piece of scrap paper. It made it easier to count backwards and forwards, though I would not, as Sister Monica pointed out, be able to have such an aid when I came to sit my exam. Sister Monica was not a very old nun, but rather young; she had spots, which were a sign of youth, and goggly glasses whose arms slotted away somewhere within the starchy mysteries of her caps and coifs and veils.

Twenty minutes passed. Underline the correct word: As calf to cow, so *leveret* to hare. As flock to deer, so *school* to whales. I had circled a number of triangles and squared some circles, done underlining and filled in the answer on the dotted line. Now I put down my pencil and glanced over my shoulder. I wished there had been a lock on my door, but such a thing would have been unthinkable. Stooping down, I reached into my school-bag, and drew out a copy of *Princess*.

Karina had bought it for me; although she had sneered at me and said it was soft, she had read it herself first, so that the pages were scuffed and grimy and blurred with lard-soaked fingerprints. 'You can owe me the money,' Karina had said; but I was afraid I would never be able to pay her back. I did not get pocket-money; my mother had bought my comics for me, until the day when she turned against them. I did not need money of my own, because I was provided for; everything I needed was provided for my comfort, my mother said. And what did I do in return? She'd like to know that, she said. Very much she'd like to know. She would.

I folded the comic, and held it on my knee, thinking that if she came in I might be able to drag my chair right up to the table and conceal my sin underneath. I wondered what sort of a sin it was: venial, not mortal, I knew that much, but what category of venial? Disobedi-ence to my mother? Stealing from Karina? Or what?

Belle of the Ballet was going through a very exciting stage. The snobby prima ballerina had twisted her ankle, tottering to the floor in a gauzy heap, with a scream of 'Oh – OUCH – help me!' Belle had to step into her role at short notice. What a good thing the special spangled tutu fitted her! Belle was so young, yet for her it was maybe a once-in-a-lifetime chance. In the final frame she would get a bouquet, I expected; but since I had to keep the comic folded I could only have a bit at a time. 'Eet izz a triumph!' some foreign person would enthuse: perhaps a man in a coat with a fur collar, and a cigarette in a holder. But he would probably turn out not to be good for Belle's career in the long run.

I looked up, my vision clouded with glory, the creak of red plush seats and the rustle of silk, the abbreviated moan of the violins as the orchestra tuned up ... My eyes, resting on the wall, encountered the Chinawoman, her deep sleeve and her wicker cage. My mother's foot was on the stair. I doubled up in my chair, panic-stricken, and thrust the comic back into my bag. My face burned and pulsed. I felt contaminated, sick with guilt.

As it was now common knowledge that Karina and I were going to sit for the Holy Redeemer, we were ostracized by our classmates, who considered we were getting above ourselves. This threw us increasingly into each other's company, whether we liked it or not. Privately, Karina was gloomy about our prospects; she did not think we would pass our Eleven Plus, let alone our entrance exam. 'Get away,' she said. 'We'll fail. Everybody fails.' I had not encountered pessimism before – not that deep, ingrained, organic pessimism which was part of Karina, and which of course I have often met in adult life.

It was playtime, and it was only raining a bit. We were leaning against the wall at the back of our schoolyard, looking down over the railway embankment. Karina was finishing her bottle of milk, slurping noisily at the clotted half-inch at the bottom, chasing the last drops around with her straw. 'You still owe me for that comic,' she said.

'I'm saving up to pay you.'

Karina sang, 'When will that be, Say the bells of Stepneee.'

'I've got threepence. My grandad gave it me. You can have it. Here.'

'Put it away,' Karina said. 'I don't want your money.'

'You can have my milk every playtime.' A thought struck me. 'But do you think they'll have milk at the Holy Redeemer?'

'I'm sure I don't know, Said the great bell of Bow. Anyway, I told you. We'll not be going. We'll never pass.'

'But you do want to, don't you?' I said tentatively. Because I did; I had made my mind up on it.

Karina said, 'If wishes were horses then beggars would ride.'

I knew the meaning of that. It had been in English yesterday: explain these proverbs. A stitch in time saves nine. Too many cooks spoil the broth. I thought of St Theresa's and the model kitchen, and the girls with their laddered nylons crowded around, clutching wooden spoons in fingers blighted by flaking nail-varnish. I did not want to be like that; I wanted to be like Susan Millington, solemn and horse-faced beneath a winter velour, a summer boater; I wanted to have big legs like Susan Millington, and stride to the bus-stop in mid-brown thick tights. 'Oranges and lemons ...' droned Karina. Oh, no; she was going to start at the beginning and sing straight through. 'You owe me five farthings ...' She broke off, and said, 'Well, considerably more, actually.' She had begun to use big words, I noticed, on occasion; it was called Vocabulary. 'Considerably more.'

I thought, here comes a chopper to chop off your head. Behind my back I made a covert gesture of violence.

On the day of the entrance exam our mothers escorted us on the two buses, dressed in their best coats, which in the case of Karina's mother was best but not very good. My mother had a handbag with a shiny clasp, and as she sat in the bus with the bag on her knees she kept snapping it open, snapping it shut. The mothers sat on one seat; we sat on the seat in front, whispering and nudging.

'My mother called Sister Basil an old nanny goat,' I said, boasting.

'Your mother will burn in hell,' Karina said.

'Not if she repents.'

'She will burn in hell anyway. She wears lipstick.'

'That's not a sin.'

'It is so. Fornication.'

I kept quiet. I didn't know what fornication was, so she might be right. I felt I needed education, needed it very badly.

'Stop that giggling and messing, Carmel,' my mother said. 'You ought to be thinking about what lies before you.'

'I am,' I said.

I had been thinking about it for weeks, months. Sister Monica, when she broke off her disquisition about the laundry-room at St Theresa's, would address the subject of the Holy Redeemer; like Sister Basil, she seemed to know everything about it.

'The girls' skirts are measured each week with a dress-maker's rule,' she would say, 'to see that they conform to the length prescribed. Woe betide any girl whose skirt does not.'

Woe betide. But I did not see much to fear. They wouldn't go shooting up and down, would they, your hem-lines, unpredictable, beyond your control?

'No jewellery is allowed,' Sister Monica would say, 'but a wristwatch of the plainest type. Hair is to be worn neat at all times and off the face. The speech of the girls is never careless and always refined.'

Then, a little later, while we were labouring over our fractions or decimals, she would begin again, her long, pale, acned face turned up to the spring sunlight, her pointer tapping the blackboard for emphasis. 'Periods of silence are observed, and running in the corridors is utterly forbidden. Footwear is to be of the approved type, and a fringe, if worn, should be above the eyebrows.' Her eyes, shining beneath the limpid pools of her spectacles, fell on myself and Karina, isolated in a front desk. 'There'll be none of your nonsense should you be among the fortunate few who find a place at the Holy Redeemer. Let any girl step out of line and she is put up at the morning assembly to apologize to Mother Superior before the whole school and the staff, both nuns and lay teachers.'

My finger and thumb squeezed my pencil, rolled it back into my palm and clenched it there. What would I say? I was bound to step out of line, if only because I did not know where the line was: if only because I did not know anything. 'I'm sorry, Mother Superior. I apologize.' Would that be enough? Sister Monica approached and stood over us. 'And if that girl does not speak clearly and distinctly, or employs a poor accent, they will mock her and ridicule her until she mends the fault.'

Forty minutes into our journey to the entrance exam, the bus ground into a bus station, and we disembarked. Mary followed my mother, lugging with her the grimy tartan shopping bag she always carried. It was windy in the bus station, oily underfoot, pigeons swooping low under the shelters; my mother shielded her eyes with her hand as if she were looking into the sun, as a way of showing Mary that she was in charge and she would soon hit upon our next bus. 'Over here,' my mother cried, and marched us across the litter-blown tarmac, ducking round the big frames of panting buses, through the diesel fumes and a smell of boiled onions. But it wasn't over there, and she marched us back, and marshalled us into line to wait for the Number 64. 'Oh, if only it were to get a cup of tea,' Mary said, breaking her accustomed silence.

'No time. No time. Tea later,' my mother yelled. I thought I had been to this place before – its name was the Victoria bus station – but I hardly knew what lay beyond it; I was beginning to feel very far from home. When the 64 juddered to a halt before us, I felt a moment of panic. My mother seized me by the arm and I tore my arm away. 'For heaven's sake, just look at you,' she said. She took out her handkerchief, licked it, and worked it round and round on my cheek. It came away filthy; I had been baptized in flying smuts. Two by two, we mounted the 64.

*

'Since you are the only two girls from your area,' the nun said, 'a special arrangement has been made for you. The entrance exam proper was held last month, but Sister — Monica, is she called? — couldn't seem to complete the paperwork on time.' The nun sniffed. Her speech was certainly never careless and always refined.

Outside the studded door of the convent — 'It's medieval, isn't it?' Karina whispered — we had lurked fearfully, until the bell was answered. 'Come in, we are waiting for you,' the nun said. We stepped into a wide corridor that smelt of incense and custard. There were red tiles underfoot, and I stepped on one that was loose or broken; the tile gave under my foot, and made a little sound, tock-tock.

For the entrance exam I was wearing my Scotch kilt, and a white lacy sweater with a frill for a collar, and a narrow scarlet ribbon piercing in and out of the frill's edge. Sometimes my hand would go up to touch it, to feel the confiding smoothness against the bobbly wool; my mother would slap my hand away and snap, Stop that, you'll get it filthy. Karina wore one of her royal-blue pleated skirts and a fluffy jumper made by a factory. It was tighter than it should be, and seemed pasted across her protruding stomach. And — I looked hard — could it be? On her chest there were two pouches, twin flaps where there should be nothing but smoothness, nothing but chest. The nun looked down at us. 'You could have worn school uniform,' she said. 'That is usual.'

'Sister, we don't have a school uniform,' I said.

'Don't you? Oh, dear me. Now that is a sad state of affairs.' She switched her attention to our mothers.

'Please wait here. Tea will be provided.' My mother glanced at Mary, as if to say, I told you so. 'You little ones come with me.'

She led us through that first corridor, and round corners, down three steps and up two, by a drawing-room where we glimpsed a cheerful electric fire twinkling in a grate: under pale arches, by windows and glazed doors that looked out on to lawns, to a fine cedar of Lebanon which acknowledged a light breeze. We had left home in rain and wind; here the sun was fighting through, and the skies were patchily blue. The nun turned to us, and almost smiled: 'Of course,' she said, 'this is not the school. This is the House, where we live.'

Our voyage ended in a long cool room, where two desks, widely spaced, stood waiting for us. Sometimes in dreams I'd been in rooms like this, rooms full of pallid light: the floor of blond wood, the walls as smooth as the icing on a wedding cake. Every movement echoed in its vastness, every breath seemed consequential; I turned my eyes to Karina, to see how she liked it, but as usual her face yielded nothing.

We were standing close together; we continued to stand, stupidly, because we did not know if the desks had been designated to us by name. 'Each sit where you please,' the nun said, recognizing what was the matter: said it not unkindly, not at all how Sister Monica would have said it. We took our places. Above us was infinite air, the ceiling gilded, high high above us; from the great windows, lawns ran away into a misty distance. I could see a flight of stone steps flanked by cold graceful urns;

closer at hand, turned not quite in profile, a statue of Our Blessed Lady, a white statue shining as if in the dusk. Her palms were uplifted, and her robes fell away from them, into a U-shaped valley of compassionate folds.

The nun took two papers out of a big brown envelope and laid them face down, one on Karina's desk and one on mine. My fingers played with the pin of my Scotch kilt; my mouth was dry. 'Sister Gabriel?' the nun said. 'Oh, there you are.' From a door I had not noticed, tucked away in a corner of the room, a young nun appeared, and seemed to glide over the pale polished floor. She wore a white veil, and an expression of uncomprehending serenity. 'I leave you with Sister Gabriel to invigilate,' the first nun said. 'The time allowed is one hour and a half. Turn over your papers and begin.'

Holy Mother of God, I prayed, take pity on me. Make me pass my entrance exam. I directed my prayer to the statue outside the window, its mossy plinth and stone drapery. I undid the pin of my kilt, and stabbed its thick point into the cushion of the little finger of my left hand. A worry doubled is a worry halved, and now I had the pain to think about, as well as the terror: I turned over my paper and began.

I hardly remember the rest of that day. I don't know what I said when I came out of the beautiful room, or how I was escorted by a nun back to our starting point at the studded door; or what Karina said, or whether our mothers wanted to know how it had been, or whether I was slapped for having got blood on my handkerchief.

I do recall that the journey home took many hours, owing to a blunder at the Victoria bus station, and that Mary said once again, 'Oh, if only it were to get a cup of tea.' She seemed small and beaten and baffled as she trailed in my mother's wake, and she nodded sadly when Karina said to her, 'If you're that bothered, you could have brought a flask, couldn't you?'

I turned my head and looked out of the corner of my eye to see if my mother was taking in the way Karina spoke to her mother, but she wasn't taking in anything at all. 'Did you see Carmel's new pen?' she cried, in a high, strung-up, scraping voice. Her handbag's clasp continued to snap, open and shut, open and shut.

'No. What new pen?' Karina said.

'Carmel, didn't you show Karina your new pen?'

'No, I did not,' I said, from the seat in front.

'Well then, take it out and show it to her at once.'

Reluctant, I reached into my bag. I drew forth, slowly, my new fountain-pen. 'Pass it to me so I can show Karina's mother.' A hand swarmed over the seat back. It fastened on my pen and swiped it out of my sight. 'What do you think, Mary?' my mother said. 'I got it for her specially to sit the entrance exam. It cost five shillings.'

Mary made a noise of appreciation. It was not enough.

'Just look at this mechanism – ' my mother began.

'Don't start unscrewing it,' I said in alarm. 'You'll get ink spattering.'

'Indeed ink will not spatter,' my mother said. 'This is a first-rate pen. The very top quality. Here. Show it to Karina.'

This was what I had been trying to avoid. I did like my pen and I was proud of it, but I knew that now my pride would be humbled. I slid the smooth burgundy cylinder into Karina's fingers. 'Here,' I said, toneless. Karina scrutinized it, pulling the cap off and squinting at the nib. 'It's gorgeous, Mrs McBain,' she said, her face hidden. 'I think you must be very wealthy to afford a pen like that.'

Behind us, my mother gave a surprised laugh; I suppose it was a laugh, I can't think what else it could have been. 'Well, I'd not say that exactly. We're just doing our best for Carmel, that's all.'

'Gorgeous,' Karina repeated. 'Simply top quality.' Very low, so that the mothers had no chance of hearing, she murmured to me: 'I could get better pens for one and ninepence.'

When we arrived home my father was waiting by the door. 'Come in, come in,' he said. 'Come and look at this.' His face was aglow. His new jigsaw lay complete on the table. 'The *Cutty Sark*,' he said.

My mother said, 'Put the kettle on and don't be such a fool.'

Next day in school, our classmates looked at us fearfully, as if we were survivors of an ordeal or disaster. 'Let us hope those two girls gave a good account of themselves,' Sister Monica said, tapping the blackboard and staring into space: as if those two girls were only notional, and out there somewhere in the great beyond. 'Let us hope those two girls gave a good account of themselves and did not disgrace the name of this school.'

I put up my hand. 'Sister, I need to know what fornication means.'

Sister Monica swept her eyes around to my face. 'Why do you need to know, Carmel?' Her voice was steady and cool.

'It's General Knowledge,' I said.

'Fornication is any type of bad behaviour with the other sex. Outside of marriage. Those two boys at the back may stop sniggering. Perhaps they would care to stand up and give us their definition of the term, or otherwise they may come out here and have the cane.'

The sniggering stopped.

'Is it to do with wearing lipstick?' I said.

'That could be contributory, in certain circumstances,' Sister Monica said.

It was that night, on our way home, that Karina and I began to talk about the entrance exam. All day we had preserved a silence, a no man's land between us; partly tact, partly squeamishness. 'What did you pick for the home of a badger?' Karina said.

'Set.'

'Oh, right. What did you pick for the female type of sheep?'

'Ewe.'

Karina jumped violently. 'What?'

'You,' I said. 'Ewe.' I realized we didn't speak the same language, after all. Karina didn't read books, and perhaps that was her trouble. She called for me after school on a Thursday, and we would troop off to the library together, me with my own two books on my orange junior tickets and my mother's six Jean Plaidys on buff tickets. I would go swarming in and see what I could get, but we had only one bookcase called 'Junior', and I had read everything in it by now. Karina didn't come into the library at all, but stood outside by the bus-stop, as if she were going somewhere. She had handed me her own orange tickets, and wanted me to be grateful; attempted to turn it into more money I owed her. 'Ewe,' I said. 'You-oo-oo-oo.'

'Oh yes.' Karina trudged on, her jaw set. 'What composition did you pick?'

We were under the pub sign, the Prince of Connaught. He creaked in the breeze, above our heads: a stiff breeze, but the herald of fine weather. It was time for skipping ropes to come out, and for all the summer games to begin.

'I did "My Hobbies",' I said. If all went well, I would be beyond skipping ropes soon. Susan Millington, you may be sure, was never caught skipping.

Karina sneered at me. 'You haven't got any hobbies.'

'I put, reading books.'

'That's not hobbies. Hobbies is stamp-collecting.'

'I put that.'

'You did not.'

'I did because my father collects stamps, so it's the same as me doing it. I put jigsaw puzzles.'

'You lied,' she said. 'They'll know.'

'I did not lie, and I put knitting a jumper.'

'What, that green thing you've been mangling? It looks more like a fishing-net.'

I was angry. How dare she malign my knitting? 'What composition did you do, then?'

'I did "The Person I Would Most Like to Meet".'

'Who did you put?' The possibilities ran though my head. She might have put Cliff Richard. Adam Faith. Marty Wilde.

Karina smiled. 'I put, the Pope.'

'You did what?' I stopped in my tracks. 'The Pope?'

'You should really say, His Holiness the Pope,' Karina pointed out.

I did not have the words for the anger I felt, and the disgust. Disgust and fear: because I knew now that Karina would pass the entrance exam. A small part of me suspected those Holy Redeemer nuns would see through her; a much larger part knew that anyone as smart and smooth as Karina would pass anything she set her mind to. And I had passed too, I felt it in my bones; Karina's piece of hypocrisy spread its great black wings over me, and wafted me towards my future, protected by its stretching shadow. She had vouched for me, in a perverse way, because even though we did not have a uniform, even though we did not know what desk to sit at, she had shown that we were the right stuff: she had not disgraced the name of our school.

So we would go to the Holy Redeemer, shackled together, and I would never have a pen or a book or a piece of knitting or anything else in my whole life that I could like, that Karina would not take away and pass comment on and spoil. It came into my mind that perhaps one day I might want to get married, if I did not become a Sister Superior or lady explorer. If I did obtain a husband, I must be sure Karina did not see him, and spoil my wedding day. I must be sure that if I

110

was ever sent a baby she was not there when it was christened; I pictured her screwing its little fat legs in and out of its hip-joints, and saying she could get a better baby for one and ninepence.

There's a time when childhood ends, and it was then, under the swaying grandee on Eliza Street, under Prince Arthur, the Duke of Connaught. I put down my school-bag so that I had two hands free, and gave Karina a shove into the gutter. She shoved me in turn against the wall, and we went on like that round the corner on to Curzon Street, pushing and grunting and trying to fend each other off, until we reached my front door which was on the latch and I went in and slammed it behind me. I wanted to bawl up the stairs, 'Guess what Karina's done now,' but I knew that my mother was always on her side, and would think the pontiff a smart move, and want to know why I hadn't written something similar.

Nowadays, when the word 'child' comes into my mind, I can never see a particular child, any single flesh-and-blood entity. I can only see one of the plaster cripples that in those days stood outside shops, effigies the height of a two-year-old, their outstretched hands supporting collecting boxes. Some of these effigies were boys and some girls, but their features were the same and their plaster-coloured curls; the only difference was that the boys wore short trousers and the girls a frill of skirt, and beneath this there was a cruel leg-iron, clamped to the lower limb. It was the leg-iron that caused people to drop pennies into the box; that, and the upturned, painted blue eyes.

You're only young once, they say, but doesn't it go on for a long time? More years than you can bear.

Six

I must now tell you about our life at the Holy Redeemer; but first of all I must tell you how we came to be outfitted for it.

We had a list of what we had to get, and these were some of the things on it.

Outdoor shoes
Indoor shoes
Gym shoes
Shoe bag
Aertex blouse
Winter tunic
Girdle − girdle! 'Martin,' my mother said, 'she's required to have a girdle!'

'Girdle!' my father said. This had become his favoured method of communication: repeating what my mother said, as if it were alarming, far-fetched or intrinsically ludicrous.

'A foundation garment,' my mother said.

'She seems very young for corsets.'

'After all, they're nuns, they don't want young women going round . . . sticking out.' She looked thoughtful. 'It says "girdle in house colour".'

Words came into my mouth and stuck there: backed up against my hard palate. I knew these girdles were the kind worn by princesses in distress. They were the kind you used to tether a unicorn, or to throw a lifeline to a gallant knight some ogre had cast from a tower. They were not whalebone, they were not elastic, they were more like ropes or strings, sewn with seed pearls or knitted from your own golden hair.

'You can really only get white,' my mother said. 'Or flesh.' She sucked her lip. Ankle socks white, winter knee socks grey. Underwear as regulation – the approved outfitter will be pleased to advise. 'They don't want to go into detail,' my mother said. 'Not in print. You can understand it.'

Winter hat, grey velour

Summer straw, school colours

Hockey stick

Tennis racquet

TENNIS RACQUET! I said

In summer, white gloves will be worn.

I was precipitated into Constantine & Co. by a push in the small of my back. I was in for a slap when I got home, this had been made clear to me: 'Giggling and fidgeting like that in the bus; you ought to know better at your age!' My mother was wearing a very big daub of Tan Fantastic, which Karina had been mocking. She was wearing a costume with a tight skirt, and pinned to the jacket her best brooch, a gilt wheel of big deep blue stones, deep as the sea. Karina's mother lurched through the swinging glass doors behind us. Her coat came nearly down to her ankles and as usual she was lugging her tartan shopping bag.

This was the first time I had ever been taken to a shop for clothes. Everything I had needed until this point had been manufactured by my mother. I looked at Karina to see if she was any more at ease in this situation. She was standing with her eyes closed, breathing in the deep scent of leather and polish. A saleswoman dressed in black minced towards us over the polished floor, like a panther who has spotted something juicy: like a panther who has spotted something slow.

My mother unclasped her handbag with a big snap and withdrew the uniform list, folded in four.

'The Holy Redeemer,' the saleswoman murmured. She seemed to curtsey as she took it from my mother's hand and opened it. Her fingers brushed her smiling throat as she ushered us towards the curtained cubicles of her choice. The room was built up to its lofty ceiling in glass cabinets and deep wooden drawers, some of which other salesladies slid open enticingly, to reveal stacks of stiff shirts bound in Cellophane; from which they lifted jerseys with their arms strait-jacketed by cardboard, in every size from dwarf to gross.

'In here if you please,' the saleswoman said, as if she were threatening us. The curtain swept behind her. I was shut up with my mother in my own cubicle, at dangerously close quarters. But she was all simpering smiles now: for the duration, I was her darling. She took off her coat and hung it on one of the hooks supplied, and at once her woman smell gushed out and filled the air: chemical tang of primitive deodorant, scent and grease of Tan Fantastic, flowery scent of face powder, emanation of armpit and cervix, milk duct and scalp.

I removed my clothes. I was pale as paper, my body

without scent or flavour of its own. Each of my ribs could be counted; each vertebra was accessible to a casual eye. Around my nipples was a puffiness which looked like a disease. I had been worrying that I would have to undress in front of Karina, who was in advance of me, gently but definitely swollen. I knew I had to get a bosom, but I hoped it wouldn't come on too quickly, because when it did I'd need an 'A' cup, size 32 broderie anglaise bra. And my mother would say, All this costs money, and as we are scrimping and saving for your education . . . The flatter my chest stayed, the cheaper I'd be.

The items required for the Holy Redeemer were brought in one by one, stiff on their glossy wooden hangers, by the saleswoman in black. Only the winter tunic was an exception; she carried it across her arms, palms spread beneath it, as in certain statues and paintings Our Lady bears the weight of the body of her crucified son. The tunic was clay coloured, a stiff deep grey-brown. In the uniform of the Holy Redeemer this colour predominated, but it was offset by a solid purple-red called maroon: and sometimes where you would least expect it, these two colours would collide and form stripes.

I slid my arms inside the chilly sleeves of a cream shirt blouse. My mother twitched the stiff collar into position and began to button it up; she was attending to me as if I were a three-year-old, impressing the saleslady with her maternal skills. When the blouse was fastened it came to mid-thigh. The cuffs hung below my hands as if I'd climbed into the body of an ape. 'I'll move the button,' my mother said. The saleslady made an approving noise, and picked up the tunic. She dropped it over my head and it engulfed me. Daylight vanished. I took a breath inside its clay folds. My arms moved outwards as if I were trying to swim. My mother tugged, and the daylight reappeared. I stood with my arms out from my sides, looking down at my feet, which were visible under the tunic.

'She's bound to grow,' my mother said. 'Bound to.'

'You'll find,' said the saleslady, 'that they have very strict requirements about length at the Holy Redeemer. We may have to adjust a little, upwards.' All three of us stared at my feet. 'Indoor shoes.' the saleslady said. 'I shall be but one moment.'

She came back with a box. On the outside of it was a picture of what looked like a coracle. 'We call this "The Diana",' the saleswoman said. 'Wonderfully durable and absolutely recommended.'

When the shoe was revealed and lifted from its tissue paper, even my mother was taken aback: even she, who for the next seven years would hear not a word spoken against the Holy Redeemer and its dress codes and rules and strange demands. 'Well, it is old-fashioned,' she said, taking it unwillingly from the saleslady's hand. The saleslady smiled, and showed one tooth. The shoe was brown, its toe was round, it had a bar across like an infant's shoe. It had a sort of shelf around it, a running board; its sole looked an inch thick.

'Sit down,' my mother said. She grappled with my ankle. I wanted to curl my toes like a baby, squirm my soles so she couldn't ram them into The Diana. When I stood up again I felt as if the floorboards had been fastened to my feet.

We heard, from outside the cubicle, a rush and clatter as an adjacent curtain was drawn back. 'Show Mary,' my mother said. She manoeuvred me out under the cruel strip lights. Karina and I stood side by side. We were clad, we were uniformed. We did not look at each other. Karina's hands were bunched at her sides.

Karina's mother said, 'She must have vests.'

'There is no mention of an approved vest-style on the Holy Redeemer's list,' the saleswoman said. 'However, we do stock various excellent types which I shall show you without delay.'

'Warm, solid vests,' Karina's mother insisted.

'You'll be needing vests, too,' my mother said reprovingly. I understood that she had to match Karina's mother item for item; never would it be said of a daughter of hers that she went to the Holy Redeemer ill-equipped.

An hour later Karina and I were back in our own clothes, with parcels about our feet, bolsters and boulders which contained the equipment for our new lives. We had yellow woolly vests with three buttons at the neck and big navy knickers of soft furry cloth, and ankle boots for severe weather and tan leather satchels; also grey woollen gloves and lace-up outdoor shoes and presses for our tennis racquets and maroon and clay-colour striped scarves. My mother took out her bulging purse.

I averted my eyes. It seemed to me the cost of this was almost as much as the cost of our house. And I bit my lips, thinking of the humiliation of Karina's mother, who surely would not have planned for this, would not have seen so much money in her whole life. I pictured the knickers and the racquet press confiscated, stacked back on the shelves, the pullover re-imprisoned in its cardboard and Cellophane and consigned again to one of the varnished drawers, and Karina herself sleeving away a tear as she recognized that she would never go to the Holy Redeemer now . . .

Mary hoisted up her tartan shopping bag and unzipped it. The sound of the zip, like God farting, seemed to fill the shop. She plunged in her hands like a woman plunging them into the washing-up bowl, and drew out two fistfuls of one-pound notes. She thrust them at the saleslady and dived back in for more.

Hands full, the saleslady recoiled. I noticed that a smudge of her orange lipstick had come off on her predatory tooth. Karina reached out and pulled the tartan bag from her mother's grasp. I heard from inside it a deep jangle of loose change, half-crowns and two-shilling pieces and big change of that sort. Karina scooped the notes back from the salewoman's hands, and began to count them out, one by one, into her ready palm, counting out loud with deliberation, as though she were at school and this were a test. Then she dipped back into the bag, brought out some more pound notes, and continued the process, until the saleswoman purred and was satisfied, and advanced on the till licking her lips, and left us alone to start stacking our gains into each other's arms.

On the way back to the bus, Karina said to me, 'Are those sapphires, actual gemstones, that your mother is wearing?'

'No,' I said. 'They're glass.'

'I wonder why she bothers,' Karina said thoughtfully. 'Embarrassing, really, isn't it?'

I never thought the day could come, but it did; or at least the eve. On the 11th of September my mother sent me to bed at eight o'clock. It was light outside, and a blackbird trilled in Curzon Street's one bush. I lay between the sheets trying to compel sleep and yet to deny it; I did not want to lie awake the whole long night, and yet I was afraid of the morning. I had heard of knights who, wishing to keep a vigil without nodding, slit the ball of their thumb and rubbed salt into the cut; formerly, my curl-rags had served this function. But the rules of the Holy Redeemer, which my mother and I had both studied, stated that hair was to be worn tied back and off the face, in a neat and restrained style; my mother could see that luxuriant ringlets would not fit this brief. Instead she had set my hair in kirby grips in a series of well-regulated corrugations all over my skull; the rest she was proposing to clamp back in a big plastic-toothed pony-tail comb. As an alternative, she said, I could have plaits. She had bought three yards of approved maroon ribbon from Constantine & Co. Even she could see that I might need a change, from time to time.

I turned over, cheek against the pillow. Kirby grips swivelled and upended themselves and probed my tender scalp. My blouse and tunic were hanging outside the wardrobe, as if to heighten their state of readiness, and mine. Music crept up, from the sitting-room below; we had a TV set now, and I knew my father was seated before it, his jigsaw puzzle unattended on the table, while my mother rampaged about in the kitchen. I would have liked to throw aside the blankets and creep down to them, embrace their knees and say I am one of you: offer my father to fill in the sky, on this puzzle and any to come. But I had seen the pitiless state of my mother's face: pitiless and proud and full of tension, as if it were she herself who were going to the Holy Redeemer in the morning.

I thought of Jane Eyre, the night before her wedding. She thought it was presumptuous to label her effects as Mrs Rochester; she would not anticipate the event. Then the real Mrs Rochester with her blood-congested face and psychotic eyes came down from the attic and ripped her veil in two. Every item purchased from Constantine & Co. was now sewed with a name-tape; for better or worse, it belonged to me. I wished something would come down from the garret and rend my tunic, which glowed like an old corpse in the darkening room.

I must have slept. At six o'clock, when Curzon Street was empty and the air was the colour of a dove, my mother was at my bedroom door, shouting at me to get out of bed *this very minute*. My grey wool socks, striped at the turn-down with two rows of maroon, tugged over my feet and rolled up to my knees; my outdoor shoes clamped on to my feet. My mother plucked out each kirby grip with a flourish. My corrugated hair rolled back from my forehead, reeking of setting-lotion.

My mother looked at me fearfully, as if I were a

prodigy, a monster. She watched me eat, each mouthful. My mouth was dry and my toast rolled up into little pellets in my mouth. 'A pity you could never eat breakfast,' she said. I thought of the likely scene in Karina's house; half a dozen eggs spitting in a pan, Mary gripping a butcher's knife and smiting slices from a side of bacon which dangled on an iron hook from the ceiling.

I pushed my plate aside, with the cold remains of the rubber bread. 'Martin, do up her tie for her,' my mother said.

My father said, 'Doesn't she know how?'

My mother said, 'What do you think she is, Vesta Tilley?'

'Vesta Tilley! That was a bow-tie she wore,' my father said.

My heart had sunk down into my stomach; it felt soft and spongy and as if it were folding up on itself, like a bedroom slipper doubled in two.

The moment came. My mother flung open the door. She clamped my hat on my head and thrust me out into Curzon Street. The morning was mild. Through it a grim shape moved towards me, solid like a tank. It was Karina. Like me, she carried her empty satchel slung over her shoulder; like me, she wore a donkey-coloured coat that came down below her calves. 'Have you ever heard of somebody called Vesta Tilley?' I said.

'Yes,' Karina said surprisingly. 'She is in music-halls. She sings she's Burlington Bertie.'

We turned on to Bismarck Street. The Prince of Connaught swung above our heads. 'Remember when we used to play him?' I said to Karina. I was half-smiling, indulgent, as if this folly were a world away.

'Yes,' Karina said. 'Daft, weren't we?' Her tone was the same as mine; she turned her head, smiled slowly, and put out her hand towards me. We were frightened not to wear our prescribed woollen gloves; our palms brushed and squeaked against each other, then snagged together, then stuck in a clammy fastness. We passed our old school – shuttered, unpopulated at this hour, the playground bare except for blowing litter, the double doors locked fast; this autumn it would go on without us, bursting with screaming children sucking up their milk and spilling their ink and knuckling each other's heads and being searched for lice, chanting their times tables and feeling the cane bruise their frozen fingertips. 'It looks so small, doesn't it?,' Karina said. 'Pathetic.' We turned downhill towards the bus station, cast our satchels on to our outer shoulders, and began to link.

When we arrived at the bus-stop near the market place, Susan Millington was there, standing at the head of the queue. She was in her Holy Redeemer summer uniform, her striped blazer and boater, and this shocked me slightly; obviously, some concession was made to the sun, and I thought that, if my mother were in charge at the Holy Redeemer, no concession of any sort would be made. Susan Millington leant on her hockey stick, which was turned inwards between her feet. Her hands were bare, clothed neither in white cotton gloves nor grey woollen gloves; and they were brown because – as everyone was aware – she had recently returned from a family holiday in Portugal.

'Susan,' I said. 'Hello there.'

Susan Millington turned to me her long horse-face. She looked down at me and moved her lip, as if she were whinnying. Then she turned away, and spoke to her companion, and both of them laughed in a long hectic gust of horse-laughter.

Karina pulled at my coat sleeve. 'You can't speak to her! Her dad's a dentist.'

Both of us licked our teeth, as if we were licking blood from them. Dentistry was done in large houses by the park; Mr Millington's had stained-glass in the windows and a laurel hedge. They'd had a bathroom, my mother said, when such things were undreamt of in this vicinity; they also took shower-baths, because Mr Millington believed it was more hygienic. She could dress well, my mother claimed, on a quarter of what Mrs Millington spent in Manchester, at Kendal Milne and in those madam shops round St Ann's Square.

That morning, as every school day for the next seven years, we crawled away through the grimy terraces, lurching to a halt at traffic lights, snarling and revving past Woolworths and the fire station and the mini-marts with bargain posters in their windows, past net-curtain emporia and pet shops where single goldfish swam hopelessly in their bowls: by Methodist churches and cinemas that before a year was out would be turned into bingo halls. As we reached the outskirts of the town there were shops selling blocks of foam that you cut up for cushions and mattresses; there were coal merchants and scrapyards, and weed-ridden vacant lots with standing pools of black water. Our town did not end but simply, after spreading and diluting itself, washed into the next town, where we ground into the Victoria bus station and changed to the Number 64. Then we would lurch off again, under a viaduct, alongside a river running black; by now the streets would be full of men and women hurrying to work, and among the monochrome of their overcoats and mackintoshes you would see the fuchsia or bluebird-coloured flash of a sari or shalwar-kameez.

In winter the bus's windows would be opaque with filth, but on my first morning, golden by now, I was able to watch this second town run out in a sweep of dual-carriageway; I saw tree tops appear above the roofs of neat semi-detached houses, and watched grime give way to green, to tree-lined roads and striped lawns and mellow walls of rosy brick: to mock-Tudor public houses, bowls clubs, shopping parades, a public park with a floral clock and a bandstand with peeling paint.

This was where we would be educated, Karina and I, among girls whose fathers were solicitors, factory managers, small businessmen and the more prosperous sort of shopkeeper. Their mothers stayed at home to construct Battenburg cakes and cut back hydrangeas. Their first memories were of garden ponds and weeping willows, of the wrought-iron balconies of Scarborough hotels, of the slippery leather of the back seat of the family car. When I think of the early lives of these girls – of Julianne, let us say – I think of starched sun-bonnets, Beatrix Potter, of mossy garden paths, regular bedtime, regular bowels: I see them frozen for ever in that unreclaimable oasis between the war and the 1960s, between the end of rationing and the beginning of the end: fixed in time, their bodies scented with clover honey and Bramley apples: one foot daintily poised, one hand – as their ballet teacher prescribed – gesturing a charming invitation to the years to come. Life, do your worst; we are plump of knee and mild of eye, we are douce, glib and blithe: we inherit the semi, while others inherit the wind.

That night my mother said, 'Did Susan Millington speak to you?'

'No.'

'Didn't she?' My mother was irritated. 'Well, no doubt she'll speak to you tomorrow.'

Our first morning was not much of a disaster. We marched in lines a lot, and answered to our names: in Karina's case, to an approximation of it. We were led up and down the cramped and creaking staircases of the Holy Redeemer, glimpsing the convent's lawns through lustreless Gothic lights, to an echoing cloakroom where we were allocated pegs and where we hung our grey velour hats and changed our shoes. I was reluctant to take my hat off, because of my new hairstyle; when Karina saw it she popped her eyes but reined in her snigger, perhaps as a sign of solidarity. We threaded back to our classroom in the silence prescribed for corridors at all times, our huge feet preceding us, our pullovers reeking of Constantine & Co., our faces stiff with unease. We saw that every other girl except us wore narrow almond-toed sandals, neat and light, in a smart shade of tan. We saw that none of them had a satchel, and all had a briefcase with a gleaming brass lock.

Such support as we offered each other was silent. Karina just whispered, when she got the chance: 'That saleswoman, she saw us coming.' It was the first time I had heard this expression, but I understood what she meant, and I nodded. We never spoke of the matter again. But that night as we were going up Curzon Street, our first homework in our despicable bags, we swung them from side to side and sang 'Herring boxes without soxes, / Sandals were for Clementine.'

In our first week at the Holy Redeemer we learnt several stanzas of 'The Lady of Shalott' and the difference between 'will' and 'shall'. I took all my textbooks home to have protective covers put on them, and my mother covered them in wallpaper, offcuts of the blue-and-white Chinese wallpaper I had in my bedroom; so the caged bird sang like Lesbia's sparrow on the back of *A Course in Latin*, and the Chinawoman winced on her bound feet across the spine of *First Steps in Algebra*.

'Did Susan Millington speak to you?' my mother said.

'No.'

'Well, did you speak to her?'

'One day I did.'

'What did you say?

'Hello, Susan.'

'Does she think she's too good?' my mother burst out. 'You're as good as her now. Yes, and as good as anybody.' I wondered what she would think if she could hear Karina on that topic. Now that we were studying the feudal system I was in a better position to understand Karina's outlook on life. She believed in hierarchy and degree and disbelieved profoundly in the equality of man. She believed in self-preservation by scheming, by squirrelling away, by conserving her efforts and never wasting her breath. She did not believe in justice, or at least she acted as if justice were a luxury; she did not believe in speaking her mind. She was slow and steady and she put her shoulder to the wheel.

She was, as Julianne would say later, a peasant. I saw this, but I never thought she would revolt.

The Holy Redeemer was an academy well-thought-of in the district where it was situated — that is to say, it valued the social manner of its girls above their original- ity or wit. The girls themselves were lively, boastful, vain; a few were shy, a few snobbish, a few rebellious. In the seven years between our arrival as first formers and our departure from the Upper Sixth, characters changed of course — but they didn't change much. It was the girls' appearance that was subject to volcanic, dismaying altera- tions. Little gilt girls grew coarse and dark, gangling girls grew svelte; modest girls grew great bosoms and dragged them about like the sorrows of Young Werther. Others, pale and self-effacing as novices, whispered unnoticed through their days, hardly embodied inside their solid maroon-and-clay uniforms, creeping out of the school at eighteen on the same mouse feet that had brought them in at eleven. A number of such girls secured lovers and husbands at once, without the trouble of looking for them, and began upon tumultuous and dazzling erotic careers. Some needed just a year or two to blossom into women who occupied the normal amount of space and breathed their ration of air. Some of them blossomed at thirty, no doubt, and some will find themselves at forty; some will creep on those mouse feet into old age.

In my first year at school I learnt a great deal of poetry by heart, and recited it in my bedroom at night to improve my diction. My vowels remained long and slow, but – though I continued to wear the shoes with the running boards, and to drag my satchel after me – I became indistinguishable, in a year or two, from my companions who had more privileged home-lives. The nuns and lay teachers, though blinkered and inadequate in some respects, were not so snobbish that they made distinctions between Karina, myself and the others: not to our faces, anyway. Who knows – perhaps they regarded us with interest? We were the first girls from our school – from any school like ours – to go to the Holy Redeemer, and perhaps we were thought of as a worthy social experiment.

In my first-year exams I performed with competence in each subject, and was placed fifteenth in a class of thirty-four girls. I was very satisfied with my modest success; it was unlikely to tempt fate, unlikely to attract envy or spite. But then in my second year – in spite of myself, it seemed – I was placed near the top of the class. A year later, only Julianne and I were serious contenders for the Third-Year Prize. She began to notice me, her blue eyes sliding dubiously over me from beneath the lemony froth of her fringe.

Julianne was a doctor's daughter. She was tall, strong, athletic and fast. She never minded what she said and she never minded what she did. If this were a school story for girls, of the kind that have gone out of fashion now, I would be telling you that she was the most popular girl in the form. In fact, I have to report that she was not particularly popular at all. She never exerted herself on anyone's behalf, never exerted herself on her own. Her academic successes came to her without apparent effort; on the tennis court, she would skid to retrieve a wayward ball and thump it down in an unreachable corner of the far court, without loss of poise or loss of breath. Julianne was perhaps too sardonic to wish to be a leader, too deep: that is what I think now. Nothing about her – her beauty, her confidence, her brilliance – did I admire. To begin admiring Julianne would have been to dig myself a bottomless pit. I did not think there was any hope for me if once I fell into it.

Our convent was not like the convents that are generally described in novels. We were not told that Our Lady would blush every time we crossed our legs. We were not forbidden patent-leather shoes in case boys saw our knickers reflected in them. It was not a hotbed of lesbianism; indeed we were unaware of that tendency or vice, until the books we read – uncensored – informed us of it. No one recruited for the order. I did not know any girl – except myself – who wanted to be a nun.

Still, our lives were neither free nor pleasant. There was an agenda. We were to be useful to society. We would graduate, then marry, then be mothers, also nurses and teachers, brainy, dowdy, overstretched: selfless breeders with aching calves, speaking well of support stockings by the age of thirty-five, finding our comfort in strong tea with one sugar. We would be women who never sat down, women with rough hands and a social conscience, women with a prayer in their heart and a tight smile on their lips; women who, seeing an extra burden offered, would always step forward and suggest 'Try me.' You have heard of schools that train life's officers: this was a school that trained life's foolish volunteers.

We were not physically chastised, at the Holy Redeemer. Frigid courtesy was extended to us, as an example of how to conduct ourselves when we were adults. Our excesses and errors were kept in check by sarcasm. We were never praised. We understood we did well if we were not blamed or held up to ridicule. Discouragement was wielded like an intangible baton; when you had tried your hardest, you would be told with a civil brutality that it was not enough. To court notice – even by excellent work – was to run the risk of a snub. Many of us – I do not say Karina, or Julianne – became anxious, painfully scrupulous and striving beings, always trying to out-best our best, to squeeze out one word or look of approbation, to please those who could never be pleased: who would never be pleased on principle. It was a practical education, an education in a certain old-fashioned virtue. We were not *told* to be humble. We were *made* to be.

We were very curious about the details of the nuns' daily lives, but these details were guarded from us. We did not visit the House unless we were sent on a message, or unless we were suddenly taken ill; we stepped inside it, just, as we processed to chapel for the daily rosary, which was voluntary, or for compulsory Friday afternoon

Benediction. Benediction was incense, plainchant and bump-heads: two or three pupils overcome by religiosity or post-lunch hypoglycaemia, bundled out into the corridor to be offered sips of cold water from a plastic beaker.

When I visited the House I always noticed what I had noticed that first time, when we came for our entrance exams. There was the same smell of incense and custard, blended, I later discerned, with the smell of stewed plums and moth-balls. There was the broken tile, the terracotta tile, that gave under the foot: tock-tock. So acute now is my nostalgia and my desire, that if I had such a room with such a tile I would break it to hear the sound: to remind myself of Karina following behind me – tock-tock – ten years old, innocent then of any sin except the Original one. But in those days, I flashed my eyes into the corners of rooms, to pick up any evidence, crumb, of what a nun's life might be like: where were their baths, lavatories, what would they eat that night? I learnt nothing. It was a blank.

The evidence of their spiritual life was equally guarded from me. In our presence they offered the same prayers as us – the formulations anyone can employ – with a conspicuous lack of fuss or fervour. They spoke in a prosaic way of God's glory, and if their private prayers got results they never told us about them. Why were they nuns then? Did they have a faith that was more faithful, a hope that was more hopeful than ours? They certainly didn't excel in charity. They must have cultivated their virtues in private, after we had gone home; in their dealings with us they were grumpy and exacting, petty and cold.

*

I did not see this at once. When I was eleven years old, I understood that I also was meant to be a nun. Where does one acquire a sense of vocation? In the chapel after a school dinner, a queasy mass of processed peas and tinned apricots rolling slowly through the gut: great girls whooping in the playground with the cold stinging their cheeks, and inside, silence and the scent of winter flowers: the frozen oily touch of holy water: the creak and snap of a knee joint as a sister rises from genuflection. If you stare for a long time at a candle flame you lose all sense of self. I found this: I felt my thin, hungry essence flit upwards towards the gilded roof. I thought that was what holiness was – this loss, this flitting – and I may have been right.

The only jewellery permitted to Holy Redeemer girls was of a Catholic nature – a Lourdes medal, a cross and chain. Karina wore a sharp silver crucifix, over-sized, that was always edging up over the top button of her blouse or summer frock. She used to thrust it back with ostentation – impatient yet reverent – and glance up at the teacher of the moment to see if she was watching. She did novenas, First Fridays, rosaries: obligations over and above weekly Mass and regular confession. When the sacred host was in her mouth she looked as if she were sucking a stone.

One thinks of the loss of faith as a gradual process, a seeping and trickling. In my case it was sudden. I woke up one day, in my Chinese room; I was twelve, and the torpor of adolescence was seeping through me, and I hated mornings. There was a prayer, that Sister Monica had told us to say on waking: Holy Mother Mary, I humbly thank you for preserving your hand-maiden from the perils of the night. Downstairs, my mother was already gushing water into the kettle; soon she would be yelling for me. I sat up and slid to the edge of the bed. Now I beseech you preserve your hand-maiden from the snares and temptations of the day to come. My feet were cold on the linoleum: I looked down at them, narrow and blue. Through Jesus Christ Our Lord – just as I was about to add 'Amen', something made me look up. Perhaps it was God, climbing out through my window, absconding. I looked around the room. What perils? I wondered. My satchel rolled fatly on the floor, stuffed with maths textbooks. My outdoor shoes stood obediently side by side, waiting for my feet. What temptations? I moved to the window and opened it a crack. The sullen morning slid its fingers inside. So I'm doing today on my own, I thought. In that pendant second before my feet touched the lino, God had become *de trop*; I felt vaguely embarrassed that I had ever believed anything.

Soon after this I had a short conversation – my first – with Julianne. It was about God's existence. She took a Voltairean view, that if he did not exist it would be necessary to invent him: 'Anyway,' she said, 'even if it were not necessary, it would be profitable.' She had the placid air of someone who would never let Popes interfere with her pleasures. Not a wrinkle – of doubt, or anything – marred her broad white brow. She might have had perfect faith: might have been one of those unspotted souls we heard about, shining with the purity of a recently cleaned window.

*

In Curzon Street, these were years of home improvements – in some ways if not in others. Some people on the street bought cars, but my father said he didn't see why they'd want to bother. 'If only they realized the worry a car causes. The road tax alone. The traffic jams.' Public transport was good enough for us, he said; always had been, always would be.

But in a car, I thought, you can go precisely where you like. You're the driver. You can even go where there isn't a road.

Our coal fire was abolished, and in the sitting-room an electric fire threw out a vitiating heat, pierced by whistling drafts. The house was showing its age. The back wall was freezing to the touch, icy as the pack of six fish fingers that served the three of us on a Friday evening. My mother never went near a church these days, but she did believe devoutly in fish on Fridays.

It can't just have been the menopause that made her so angry – with life, with me? When I was eleven years old, she seemed to enter on a twenty-year temper tantrum. All her discourse was of disappointment and loss, of let-downs and deceits. If I proposed to go on a school outing, she would say, What do you want to go there for? You won't enjoy it. If I was asked to someone's house, she would say, Why do you want to go bothering with her? Your parents, she would say; that's who you should be bothering with. Nobody else will help you, when it comes down to it. You've only your own family.

I see her saying these things; her face hollow and her eyes without light. At other times she would urge on me the virtues of the outside world: of getting on, getting out, getting out of Curzon Street and getting away for good and all. 'It's not *what* you know, it's *who* you know,' she'd say: if this were true, my homework efforts were useless. She talked as if everything were stacked against me – the money of others, their good looks and breeding and social graces – stacked up into a Matterhorn of prejudice and denial; and yet at the same time it was my job to push at this mountain, to topple it, to bulldoze it with my will. The task in life that she set for me was to build my own mountain, build a step-by-step success: the kind didn't matter as long as it was high and it shone. And as she had told me that it is ruthless people who rise highest in this life, I would slash through the ropes of anyone who tried to climb after me; I would prize out their pitons, and jump about on the summit alone.

But then, twenty years on, when I stood on the heights I had erected for myself, there would be a crumbling, she seemed to say, an inner decay, a collapse: and once again I would realize that she was my only friend.

My father did increasingly complex jigsaws. There was an elaborate still-life with grapes, roses and shellfish. There was an Alma-Tadema picture, of soft-eyed women with marble limbs. There was a jigsaw of the Last Supper; it took him days and days, and then a piece of Judas proved to be missing. My mother turned the chairs up and trounced the cushions; the gap remained, a worm-shaped hiatus in the traitor's ribcage.

When I look back from myself now at myself then, I believe I was a diligent, quiet, undemanding child; hardly more trouble at sixteen than I was at ten. At the time, though – even after I had stopped going to confession and stopped examining my conscience every day – I believed I was a monster of egotism, an incipient tyrant, a source of trouble and agony of mind. My mother said I was, and I didn't query it. I never tried to take out of her hands the direction of my life, or questioned why she and not I should have it. Inoffensive though I was, she treated me as what was known in those years as a juvenile delinquent. Everything I did was suspicious – at least, it aroused her suspicion.

My mother kept a tight hand on my social life, posting me upstairs to the Chinese room with orders not to daydream and not to let her catch me looking out of the window. For three hours each evening I kept company with my five-shilling fountain-pen and a bottle of blue-black ink, with maps and protractors, with tables of verbs and ragged lines of blank verse. In severe winters I worked downstairs; the television was turned off, and I was told that she and my father were prepared to sacrifice their evening's entertainment for the sake of my education. I was seldom let to watch television – not even the news, which my mother did not think of as educational, because after all it was not a subject, and I did not have an exercise book for it. But then, once in the week, I would be told to stop whatever I was doing, and to sit down and watch a quiz show called *University Challenge*. My mother watched me anxiously to see what answers I knew, to see what progress I was making. I pressed my lips shut on the answers; I would not play. The students who formed the teams were elderly and tried to appear lovably eccentric; they had mascots with them, floppy-eared dogs and stuffed trolls, stitched-up penguins and that sort of thing. They were mostly the kind of people you'd cross the street to avoid.

So it was a thin time, you see: the dining table had to do me for a dance-floor, and the electric coals for the electric glow of teenage romance. In my bedroom I carried on improving my diction. 'But at my back I always hear / Time's wingèd chariot hurrying near.' But you don't of course, not when you're fifteen or so. Perhaps I should regret my misspent youth, pity myself for having so little fun. But *carpe diem* is an empty sentiment, now that we all live so long.

The seaside-postcard view of convent schools insists that sex intrudes into every lesson, every hour; that there are saucy little novices yearning for a monk, and pigtailed prefects bursting out of their push-up bras. But I must report that our nuns mentioned sex hardly at all: love, never.

Perhaps they were afraid of our superior knowledge. Sometimes they did mention boys – the wary tension in their voices seeming to capitalize them, so that they became Boys of a special type, not the everyday ones that you saw on the street but another kind that you'd meet when the time was ripe. And the time would be ripe at some social occasion, some occasion under Catholic auspices, in a draughty hall ... I pictured them as awkward poor devils, these Boys, the sleeves of their suits too short and their raw hands hanging down, their round faces shining, their smiles bashful and placatory. They knew their nature – uncontrollable – and were ashamed of it. When my mother stopped my comics –

Bunty and *Judy*, *Princess* and *Diana* – I took to reading her magazines instead: *Woman, Woman's Realm.* Always they had articles about 'unmarried mothers'; they seemed written in a lowered tone, eye-rolling and falsely sympathetic. The tone rankled with me; I saw injustice. I said to my mother, 'People can't help it, can they, if they have a baby before they're married? I mean, if they're sent it? What can they do?'

My mother said, 'You'll find it's usually the nice girls who get into trouble of that sort.'

'Why?' I said. There was a gap here, of information not imparted: slipped between the lines, slipped between the years.

'It's because they're too trusting,' my mother said. She looked severe. 'Those hard madams, you don't find them having babies. Oh no, because they know what's what. It's the nice girls who fall for it every time.'

I took the problem to my enemy. 'Karina,' I said, 'do you know how people get babies?'

'God!' she said. 'Don't you know that yet?' But I could see panic in her face, as if she were a horse being galloped at a fence she would not be able to jump. She hit me, and ran off down the street.

My periods started one Tuesday evening in my first term at the Holy Redeemer. I had just finished writing the character of Cassius – bitter, energetic, ambitious – when I went up to the lavatory and found out what a mess I was in. I did not think I was dying, like girls in novels that pre-date this one; though my ignorance was profound, there must have been some intimation, some hint, some suspicion in the air, that a thing like this might occur. I did not feel afraid, but I felt ashamed. The difficulties seemed practical; I had to lay some plot to get my mother on her own.

My mother was sitting under the standard lamp knitting a Fair Isle pullover. When she was doing Fair Isle she did not like people to speak to her. I went up to her and touched her elbow. She snarled. I looked around, dazed. What if I bled on the carpet? My father was doing a jigsaw of the Tower of London. 'Can you come up to my bedroom?' I whispered. 'Tell you something. I want to. Must, please.'

'What is it you can't tell your mother here?' my father inquired. He slotted into place a fragment of the outer wall of a torture chamber.

'It's a surprise,' I said. I thought it a cool thing to say; I amazed myself.

'Oh, a surprise,' he said genially. After all, it was his birthday in a week. He nodded, and fitted in a Beefeater's knee.

When my mother came up to my bedroom I was already undressing. She gave me a cursory glance. 'Have you got jam on your underskirt?'

I looked at her in astonishment. How on earth did she think I would manage that? Where would I get the jam from, unless she gave it to me? I shook my head. At the thought of eating unsupervised jam.

Twenty minutes later, trussed up in a harness, I was in bed. I wailed that it was not bedtime, but this cut no ice with my mother. I wailed that I had not done my equations, and she said curtly, 'I'll give you a note.' I wailed how long would it go on for, and when would it happen again? 'Every month, or twenty-five days in my case,' my mother snapped. I wailed, how old would I be when it stopped, and my mother said, 'I'll get you a book about it.'

'Will I always have to go to bed early?' I said.

She said, 'Don't be so silly.'

Next day I suffered spasms of pain that left me shaking and winded. I felt as if a big bird – one of the ravens, perhaps, from the Tower of London – had got its claws in my lower back and was rending it apart, prizing flesh from spine. Later the pain moved and I felt as if the dissection were being performed more urgently, surgically; I thought of the skinned corpses of animals hanging in butchers' shops, neatly split down the mid-line. 'Exercise is good for period pain,' my mother said. 'Scrubbing floors, that helps it.'

So here it is. The women's realm.

Mrs Thatcher has told one of her interviewers – not that I study her pronouncements, but this one sticks in my mind – that she had nothing to say to her mother after she reached the age of fifteen. Such a sad, blunt confession it seems, and yet a few of us could make it. The world moves on so fast, and we lose all chance of being the women our mothers were; we lose all understanding of what shaped them.

Unlike Mrs Thatcher, though, I lost my father as well. My mother must have alerted him to what was the matter, when she came downstairs that evening to take up her Fair Isle. He looked at me with wistful disappointment for a month or so. There – I was a woman after all, not his little jigsaw-puzzle companion, not even a mechanism by which he might extract some revenge on life. I was bound to marry – 'bound to', he said one day, in a rare burst of communication. Bound to marry and let some man down; I had passed over to the territory of my mother. He treated me with great politeness after those first few disappointed months, and sometimes discussed with me topics that were in the newspapers, to make sure I was keeping up with current affairs. He let me know, without employing words, that if I were ever in trouble, if there were anything I ever needed, I could not count on him.

Year I, I learnt:
a. The ground plan of a medieval monastery;
b. That it is vulgar to use a ballpoint pen instead of a fountain-pen;
c. That parallel lines meet at infinity.

Year II, I learnt:
a. The products of Ecuador;
b. The mountain sheep are sweeter, / But the valley sheep are fatter;
c. To prefer the active to the passive voice.

Year III, I learnt:
a. The anatomy of a rabbit;
b. That beauty is truth, truth beauty;
c. How to apply liquid eyeliner.

Year IV, I learnt :
a. The ablative absolute;

b. The composition of the blood;

c. Something of the nature of the task before me.

Once, when we were fifteen years old and we were leaving the examination room after our O-level Latin paper, Julianne stepped lightly behind me in the corridor and slid her hand on to my shoulder. She left it there, large and warm and solid, for the briefest possible time. But I remember that her touch was curiously sustaining. It was as if a member of a conspiracy, on her way to interrogation, had met a fellow conspirator by accident, and received a moment's consolation on the stone and winding stair.

Julianne sat behind me, in every successive class; she had her friends, among the bold and the pretty, and I had mine among the mice. Sometimes I sensed within myself – sometimes I felt it strongly – a will, a pull towards frivolity. I wanted to separate myself from the common fate of girls who are called Carmel, and identify myself with girls with casual names, names which their parents didn't think about too hard. I wanted to elect pleasure, not duty, and to be happy, and to have an expectation of happiness.

I think now that this is the great division between people. There are people who find life hard and those who find it easy. There are those who have a natural, in-built, expectation of happiness, and there are those who feel that happiness is not to be expected: that it is not, in fact, one of the rights of man. Nor, God knows, one of the rights of women.

*

During my years at the Holy Redeemer, it was Karina kept me going, as far as food was concerned. She always brought food to school with her, packed up in greaseproof and bursting out of brown paper bags. She'd have a stack of sandwiches, ox tongue or Cheshire cheese, perhaps buttered scones and some of the heavy sponge cakes she made herself. Sometimes on the bus on the way to school, she'd be in the middle of a sentence and her hand would begin absent-mindedly to fumble into her bag, and she'd draw out a piece of bread spread thick with potted beef, and begin to munch away. At morning break she would give herself another ration, and then she would eat up all her school dinner, even when it was the special fish made entirely of bones, even when it was semolina. She would have packed enough to see her right on the journey home; and it was at this point in the day that she would sometimes turn to me and say, 'Are you hungry?' and offer me a sandwich and a cake from one of her bags.

Of course, no girl from the Holy Redeemer was ever permitted to eat in public; there was a prominent paragraph in the school rules, denouncing the practice. So a day came when Mother Benedict hauled me in. 'Who reported me?' I asked.

'Nothing to the point,' she snapped. 'God sees all things.'

But I could not help wondering why only I was in trouble, and not Karina, a constant and habitual public muncher. 'Why did you do this thing, Carmel?' the nun said passionately. 'You have never shown an inclination to such distasteful behaviour until now.'

'I was hungry, Mother,' I said; I could not think of any other reason.

She looked at me, disconcerted. 'You're a healthy girl, aren't you, Carmel? You can surely withstand the odd pang of hunger without having to make an exhibition of yourself? Think of the poor Indians, starving on the streets of Bombay! What about your lunch, didn't you eat it?' She didn't wait for an answer. 'Be sure to eat up every morsel from now on, and if you don't like it you can offer it up for the holy souls in purgatory.'

The truth was though that I didn't think of myself, from day to day, as being hungry. I suppose I knew intellectually that I was, but as far as my body was concerned it was a normal feeling; it was only later, at Tonbridge Hall, that I recognized the hollowness and lightness as being perhaps undesirable.

I found Niall the year before our O-levels, at our town's central library down by the market-place. The boys from the local Catholic grammar school congregated there in the early evening, when they were not at their various games practices, and scuffed up the pages of the encyclopedias while they covertly scrutinized the girls who came and went. I got into the habit of dropping into the library on my way home; there was nothing in the school rules to prohibit hanging around in a reference section. I can't have cut much of a figure, with my velour hat like an inverted dish on my head, but we must suppose that I inspired in Niall a wish to see me otherwise.

It is a mistake, of course, to think that convent girls wait until they're adults to disappoint the expectations of the nuns. In our generation, growing up through the sixties, we quickly developed our double lives. We were women inside child's clothes, atheists at Mass, official virgins and *de facto* rakes. It was not deceit; it was dualism. We had grown up with it. Flesh and spirit, ambition and humility. It was time to make plans for the future; I swung between thinking I could do anything with my life, and that I could do nothing. I still fitted into the blazer bought for my first summer at the Holy Redeemer. My mouse feet had hardly grown, so my indoor shoes were still going strong, and had perhaps acquired a perverse chic. But my satchel was scuffed and battered, and inside it at the bottom corner there was a big ink stain, like the map of a new continent.

Maybe the act of love came too late. As a career move, I should have lost my burdensome virginity at thirteen or fourteen, when there would have been no question of a lasting attachment and no desire for one. As it was, I shook when I removed my clothes and I cried after it was done, not out of pain or disappointment but out of an up-rush of muddling emotion which twenty-four hours later I was ready to call love.

So we formed an attachment, Niall and I, and after three or four months were spoken of by our friends as if we were an old married couple.

Niall said really sensible things to me. He said, Why don't you get a Saturday job? It would give you some freedom. My mother said, no daughter of mine. What, in a shop or a café! What would Mother Benedict say!

Saturdays were for homework: getting into Oxbridge. My mother had heard this term 'Oxbridge' and had begun to use it, and it was making me uneasy. I was afraid she thought it was a real place; when the time came, Oxford or Cambridge would not be good enough, only Oxbridge would be good enough for a daughter of hers.

'Just tell her,' Julianne said. 'Tell her you've no wish to spend three years locked in some musty quadrangle with people who will laugh at your accent.'

We were closer, now we were sixth formers – no longer academic rivals because Julianne was in the science stream and I was doing the girls' stuff. All the advice she gave me was of this twist-in-the-tail kind; but you didn't go to her to feed your self-esteem.

What helped my case was the news that Susan Millington had accepted a place at London University. 'She's going to read law,' my mother said 'She's going to be a barrister, like you see on the television.'

As I became more acceptable to Julianne and her friends, I grew away from Karina. We still travelled together, and sometimes in a burst of irritability she would confide in me: it was always when she was angry or jealous or otherwise caught up with strong emotion that her language would seem to slip sideways and you would remember that she was not English, for all her insistence. Her mother infuriated her these days, she said, by talking about her long-dead, her missing relatives. 'I say the past is over and done with, forget it. Why does she keep harking on about it?'

Karina had changed a lot over the last couple of years – to look at, anyway. At twelve she was one of those matronly little girls, who remind you of the well-upholstered women of sixty who stand at bus-stops with baskets on wheels. Her girdle – in house-colour – would ride up over her non-existent waist, giving her tunic an Empire line; but despite this she was still a handsome child, her blonde hair shining, her cheeks still dimpled and pinkly scrubbed. Adults still smiled on her; 'None of that slimming nonsense with Karina,' they would say.

But by the time she was seventeen, she had become a dark, forceful presence, strong and sulky. Her hair had dimmed to a nondescript brown, her skin thickened and become muddy. Her long disapproval of the world had become overt, and stamped a frown-line between her eyes. Her strength seemed ridiculously disproportionate to the day-to-day demands our schoolgirl life placed on it; she might have been a formidable games player, except that she despised games of any kind. When she followed me on to the bus in the mornings, I felt as if my conscience were coming after me, ready to fell me with one blow. 'Karina runs that house single-handed,' my mother would say. Just as when we were children, she always had money in her purse.

One day in my fifth year, when I was coming home along Curzon Street – late, because I'd stayed behind at school to audition for a part in a play – I saw my mother hammering on the door of Karina's house. 'Mary! Mary! Come down, love, and let me in.'

I turned around, shrugged my satchel on to my shoulder, and went straight back down to the town to meet Niall. It was always easier to meet him without telling my mother where I was going. Of course, there would be a row when I got home; but that was preferable to two rows, one when I got home and one before I went.

It turned out that someone had told my mother that Mary had been taken poorly. An ambulance carried her off, but then returned her a day or two later. Karina's father wouldn't let anybody in the house. I said, 'I'm sure Karina will cope. She's always so capable, isn't she?'

My mother looked at me reproachfully. 'She's got her exams coming up, same as you.'

'Exams? Oh, exams are nothing, to somebody as capable as Karina.'

Rehearsals for the play kept me back at school; in the mornings, Karina yawned her way through our journey, and sometimes sunk her head into a textbook. One day she said grudgingly, 'She's got a wasting disease.'

'A what?' I was looking for something more precise, a scientific label. Karina only repeated what she'd said.

'And what's the prognosis?'

'What do you reckon?'

'Doesn't your father want help?'

'I help him.'

'Don't you want help?'

'Are you offering?'

'Would you take the offer?'

No reply.

Academically, Karina was not the kind of girl who shone; you could not accuse her of that. Sometimes we looked at each other's homework; her answers were like an expanded set of notes covering all the important points, just the kind of answers your teachers urge you to give. She used short words which followed each other in the expected order and in the accepted cadence. Her paragraphs were two sentences long, like those in tabloid newspapers. At sixteen her writing was as clear and legible as that of a neat ten-year-old. She never read a book she didn't have to read. I had the impression that she never forgot anything.

Well ... these schematic virtues must have commended themselves to the examiners. Despite her problems at home, she passed eight O-levels and went into the sixth form on the science side. One gusty day in March, in our final year at school, Julianne came bowling into the common room, seeming propelled by the wind outside. Her face, normally so placid, was aglow with affront. 'You'll never guess what SHE – what SHE has done now.'

'I will never guess,' I said, looking up from my work. In those days Karina was not a topic between us; but from the violence of Julianne's tone I knew exactly who she was talking about.

'She's only gone and got an offer from London.'

Julianne and I had already applied for a place in a hall of residence. She had said, We could share a room: why not, you won't be in my way.

'Has she? Which college?' I said.

Julianne snorted. 'Somewhere in the East End.'

I said, 'Perhaps she won't get the grades.'

'Oh, HER,' Julianne said. 'She'll get 'em.'

'Perhaps she'll go and live somewhere else. There are other halls.'

'Oh no,' Julianne said. 'She will come and live in our hall. She will come and live in our room. In our wardrobe. We'll find her bacon rind in our shoes and her toast crumbs in our beds, and cold chips in our textbooks and Cornish pasties stuck to our mirror, and she'll use our nail scissors to trim pork chops and she'll steal our lipsticks and suck the ends and then they'll taste of suet.'

Later that day I stopped Karina in the corridor. 'I hear you've some good news.'

Karina was wearing a white lab coat. She squeezed the cardboard file under her arm. 'It'll be good news when I've got the grades.'

'Will you be . . . I mean, had you thought you might apply to Tonbridge Hall?'

'Oh yes.' She smiled. Her eyes were cold. 'Unless you think it's too good for me?'

'How's your mum?' I said.

She said, 'What do you care?'

One day, two years before this, I had been travelling home late from school – a choir practice, I think – and it was almost dark when I got off the 64 at the Victoria bus station, the mid-way point of our journey. I began to pick my way through the litter and oil and filth towards the queue for my bus home, and out of the corner of my eye I caught a flash of our colours, of the clay-and-maroon stripe of our scarf. I turned my head and saw Karina.

She was leaning against a wall, and not wearing her hat. She was smoking a cigarette, and three boys, none of whom I knew, were leaning and cavorting and smoking and foot-swivelling and kicking and lounging in her vicinity. They were not boys from St Augustine's Catholic grammar school; they were bus-station boys. They had white peaky faces, full of bones; they had lax lips and bendy legs and zipper jackets. I remembered the boys from our primary school, with their elastic belts and scarred knees and grey flapping shorts: and I realized, with a sense of shock, that these were the youths that they would have grown into.

I drew back into the shadows. In those days I was easily intimidated by men, especially young ones, especially young ones at bus stations, who would jeer at my uniform and laugh in my little pale face. It wasn't so much the men themselves who scared me, but the impulses of rage that leapt inside me at their jeers and leers and off-hand remarks, at the knowledge that they owned the streets. I would have liked to strike them dead with a stare; I wanted to beckon them, let them approach, and then stick them with a hidden knife.

Karina looked perfectly at ease. She barely seemed to notice the boys, yet it was obvious that they were trying hard to attract her attention, that they knew her, that they were tied up with her in some way. Her eyes rested on the shuddering sides of green double-deckers and the tired working people toiling home. She touched her cigarette to her lips.

I was cold, tired and hungry, and this state must have made me invisible, or at least translucent: because though I saw Karina she didn't see me.

One evening my mother hurried down to the corner shop on Eliza Street, to try and get some bread before they shut. She managed to get the last small sliced, and was carrying it back when she looked up at Karina's house and saw a face at the bedroom window. It was a face like a white puffy ball: at first she hardly recognized it, but it was Mary, all the same. She waved, but no one waved back.

Seven

In the fifth week of term at Tonbridge Hall three things occurred. I shall describe them to you in ascending order of complexity.

The first, simplest thing was that the miniskirt fell totally and decisively out of favour. For some months the fashion had been on the wane, but that October a few of the old guard were out on the streets; by November, the maxi-skirts had won, and there was not a knee to be seen between Heathrow airport and the Essex coast.

Women became – suddenly – poised, mysterious and difficult. They wore long belted trenchcoats, like spies, and put on lipstick in public places. Twenty-six became a more fashionable age than sixteen. What could I do? I looked sixteen. And I could not afford a new skirt. Fleetingly, I wondered if I would have used my five pounds emergency money, if I'd still had it. But what would one skirt have accomplished? The cotton shower-proof came only half-way down my thighs; what extended below was to be showered upon freely, like lamp-posts against which any dog can piss. Even the duffle coat passed on by my cousin did not go much below the knee. I began to attract quizzical glances, as winter drew on, and I came down to breakfast in my pelmet skirts and strange stretched brown-black tights. I heard someone say, 'Carmel's so obvious, don't you think?'

Julianne heard the remark too. Afterwards she

bounced across the room, repeating it, extending it, embellishing it. 'Yes, well, you see, where she comes from they do probably still wear such things, and after all, what is she?' A second voice chimed in, just as well-bred. 'A little shop girl, m'dear, a little shop girl.'

What was to compensate me? Admiration in men's eyes? Not really. In previous eras my legs had been admired openly, by Rogers for whom I cared nothing. But now men seemed not to see me. I knew I had lost a few pounds – well, more than a few – but was there really so little left?

The second thing happened on Tuesday at eight-thirty in the evening – at which point you may picture us, the girls of Tonbridge Hall, gross and sated from troughing, lolling like sultanas each upon her divan. In an instant, a vast howling began, a terrible skull-piercing wail. I leapt up from my desk, believing my head would burst. Julianne's textbook slid from her fingers and flapped open on the floor, its leaves fanning over and displaying cut sections of heart, lung, brain.

We were unstrung, terribly agitated; Julianne screamed, 'The devil's tone, what is it, are we at war?' We flung open our door. In the corridor what met our view was a procession of young women, faces screwed up against the din, tramping towards the nearest fire exit. 'Oh, if only they wouldn't,' Sue said, hands clawing her hair. 'If only they bloody wouldn't!' The noise was visceral and sickening, as if someone were scraping your guts with their fingernails.

Sophy passed us, marching, her crimped fair hair drifting: trailing in her wake some respectable perfume, possibly the sugar and orange notes of Je Reviens. We heard Claire's voice, rising, swooping above and below the hideous racket: 'Ladies, do please remember, especially first-year ladies, please do remember, that in the event of fire the lifts will not be working.' Claire, it turned out, was some kind of official fire-minder; they were appointed by the warden, one to each floor, and their job was to boss us down the echoing back stairs that no one ever used, to shoulder open fire-doors that no one had ever seen, to shepherd us into the street, and to count us.

As we skittered down the stairs, Julianne began to cough. 'Why are you doing that?' I demanded.

'Authenticity. We really ought to be down at floor level gasping in the air. We ought to crawl.'

The impact of these absurd words was so powerful that when I look back at this scene I seem to catch a whiff of smoke indeed. I seem to see it curling under the corridor's closed doors, and gradually rising into the air to form a haze at the level of our shoulders; I seem to hear the crackle and spit of threatened timbers deep in the building's heart. But in fact, on that night, there was nothing but the cold air and the siren's wail and our indignant chatter as we poured out into a damp, misty street; the lamplight was fuzzy, like the drowned moon in water. The warden herself – forewarned and sensibly clad in a tweed coat – went from group to group: 'Remember, girls, in the event of fire, don't stop to pick up your handbags or any possessions whatever – property may be replaced, but human life is sacred.'

By my side, Julianne still hacked and spluttered, her

shoulders hunched and knees buckling. 'What is it, Miss Lipcott?' the warden said.

'Consumption, I think.' The warden's face showed a moment's dismay, then with an impatient click of her tongue she moved on to another huddled band.

In the next couple of days two rumours swept the building. One: that there would be another fire-practice next term, and that it would be held in the middle of the night. Two, that the fire-doors – which we had noticed for the first time this week, and which some of us had immediately perceived to be useful – were locked unless there was a drill scheduled. There was no mystery about the motive for this. It was a way of keeping out boyfriends.

Or keeping them in, of course, to be burnt to a crisp. If you had a man stay overnight at Tonbridge Hall, and you were caught, the penalty was expulsion – expulsion into the hard world of the freezing bedsit at the end of a tube line, or the sordid flat-share in an area known for its prostitutes. Strangely, no one went to check, to see if the fire-doors actually were locked; the rumour, the dilemma it presented, was too delicious to refute. We talked about it and we all agreed – if you had a man in your room and the siren went, you would just have to put him in the wardrobe and leave him to take his chance, leave him crouching on top of your shoes and hope it was only a practice. If it wasn't . . . 'Yes, Mrs Smith, I'm afraid this is all that's left of your son Roger: just this molar. Here are his textbooks, brought from his digs, and one or two little mementos we thought you'd like to have. The rest of him? They didn't find much, I'm afraid. His anorak had gone up in the blaze. And his condom. A pity. He was so young!'

The third thing that happened was that I wrote to my parents to say that at Christmas I'd been invited to stay with Niall's family. It was true that I was already becoming very nervous about the invitation, but I saw the advantages of it. Why nervous? Well, how would I go on? What was their bathroom etiquette? I did not possess a dressing-gown. I was accustomed, at Tonbridge Hall, to go into the bathroom fully dressed, and come out fully dressed; slightly damp, but very proper. I imagined that, in a private house, this might be seen as strange. I rehearsed, once again, a little speech, to explain myself to the world: I'd left my bathrobe behind at Tonbridge Hall because it took up so much space in my suitcase, it was really thick, you see, fluffy, you know those towelling ones?

I was beginning to convince myself, as I rehearsed this excuse; my fingers smoothed its pastel pile, which would be (variably) peach, pure white, mint green. So I'll borrow Niall's, I heard myself say, and . . . well, I supposed Niall must have a dressing-gown. I had never seen such an article. We walked about before each other naked, as if we were the fount and origin of the world. If he had a dressing-gown I imagined it to be made of a hairy plaid, brown and white, its collar edged with smooth-twisted cord and its belt tasselled, suggestively swinging, at the centre of each tassel a blunt silken knob. Such a dressing-gown to me seemed far less safe than nakedness; far less acceptable in the family home.

Then again, what about food? I had eaten my Sunday lunch at Niall's house every week for two years. We ate, working by rota, roast lamb, roast beef, roast pork. In my own home, I was still not considered capable in the kitchen. My mother sighed and implied that it was one of the results of thinking too much, that I could not burn a carrot in quite the way she could; 'She's academic,' she would say, 'and I dare say you can't expect anything else . . .'

Niall's mother, though, was eager for any help she could get; her cooking was enthusiastic, and left the kitchen plastered with grease, with vast roasting pans of scalding fat, with snails of pastry sticking to their boards. Every pudding she made required the boosting up of the oven to 500°F: the kitchen would fill with fug and steam, and we would open the windows and lean out, gasping, into the garden where Niall's father was imposing stripes on the handkerchief lawn. Lemon meringue pie: the Everest peaks pale beige and studiedly crisp, the meringue beneath a soft lather of whipped sweetness. Then, even more triumphant, there was Baked Alaska: the oven now so hot that blue wisps seemed to issue from its every orifice, and when the door was opened, the heat knocked us back, laughing, and I would wrap a tea-towel around my hands like a surgeon dons his gloves, and I'd go in, and I'd fetch it out . . . speed was of the essence then, so that we could sink our teeth together, our family teeth, into the hot sweet froth on top and the oily frozen block of vanilla ice beneath.

But . . . stay for three weeks? What would we eat at family meals, routine meals? Bread and cheese? I imagined butter on proper bread, laid like golden pavements. Milk? Yes, Niall's mother would never mind at all if I said to her that I liked to drink milk, could I order some, would she get me an extra pint? But three weeks – would she not glance up one day, see my greedy mouth at work, and notice my relish for the flesh of her only son? After Sunday lunch I always washed up, and Niall would stand behind me, a damp Irish linen towel in his hand, and lick the nape of my neck as I scrubbed and scoured away the gravy and the fat and those burnt-on bits that require you to thrust out an elbow and frown. If I leant forward, to get a better purchase on the grease, he would creep his hands up beneath my skirt and pull down my pants. Three weeks . . . how could we hope to get away with this sort of thing? I knew no other way to do the washing-up.

However: I had made the decision. I could not think how I would survive, otherwise: what, go home to the quartering of a quarter of boiled ham, the meat-paste dole, the three bananas that stood in for a bowl of fruit? I would visit my parents, of course, we would only be five or six miles away.

My mother replied to my letter by return of post. The reply was very long and very bitter, denouncing my ingratitude, my improvidence, the laxity of my morals. As an unmarried girl, she said, I should be under my parents' roof, not under the roof of people they did not know, whose manners and outlook were no doubt frivolous, degenerate, and the talk of the district; and there could be no good reason for my wanting to be away from home unless I was planning to conduct myself in a way which she hoped no daughter of hers would ever think of in a thousand years.

I shook my head over the letter, as I read it; as if there were someone in the room to see me do it. I dimly remembered a time before she had been angry . . . the spring days when we had walked up to the hills, the twilit afternoons when she had told me of her youthful triumphs in dance halls, the day when she had sat me on the table and taught me to sing a rude song about Karina. But after that there was nothing but snarling, and the dull pressure of her finger ends as she pinned and fitted clothes on me; the stutter and hum of her sewing-machine, the swearing and rending of cloth: the reiterated question, 'If this Julianne Lipcott can come top of the class, why can't you?'

The letter was written, I perceived, not on what came to hand – not Basildon Bond, not the back of the milk bill, but on writing-paper that someone must have given her for a Christmas present: white paper bordered with roses, cut roses, pink ones, drooping on their stems, frilled and framed by pale thornless leaves. The envelope, I remember, was embellished in this way: the Queen's head in the right-hand corner, and on the left another rose. The burden of the letter was this, when the verbiage was stripped away: if you're not coming home for Christmas, don't bother to come home ever again.

I was in my room when I read this letter, alone. I felt dazed, and was tempted to sit down on my bed, but I had a ten o'clock lecture and it was already, let me see, it must be . . . I picked up Julianne's travelling clock and stared at it. I had come away from home, you remember, without a lot of ordinary things that people have, and one of those things was a watch. I fed my arms into my duffle coat, picked up my bag of books and somehow arrived in Houghton Street, not having noticed the journey.

Someone asked me was I all right, and I nodded; I had no tutorials, and as far as I remember I didn't speak for the rest of the day. It didn't occur to me that the letter might have been written in haste, that perhaps she was already regretting it. I had grown up believing – indeed, seeing – that my mother was a very powerful woman. She was not someone who changed her mind. Her edicts were handed down and I obeyed them.

I went to the library, took my familiar chair, and read the case of *Donoghue v. Stevenson* (1932) which as every lawyer knows concerns a Mrs May Donoghue, who four years earlier had visited an ice-cream parlour in Paisley, had accepted a bottle of ginger-beer from her friend, and had discovered inside it the remains of a decomposing snail. Was the manufacturer responsible? Had he a duty of care to Mrs Donoghue, with whom he had no contractual relationship? Across the page floated images of roses, of blushing petals and bending stems. I asked myself with a kind of horror, was it possible that I loved my parents? If I did not, why should this matter to me? I felt small, very young, hollow at my centre. And verses, more verses ran through my head: Under the water it rumbled on, / Still louder and more dread: / It reached the ship, it split the bay; / The ship went down like lead.

When it was six o'clock – a wet evening, pavements slick and gleaming – I left the library and returned to

Tonbridge Hall. I didn't go down to dinner. Julianne was not in and there was no sign that she had been in all day and no sign that she would come back. I sat on my bed. The feeling returned, from my first evening at Tonbridge Hall: that I would just go on sitting in this room, that hours would spin into weeks and here I would be, in a bubble of silence, with my verses for company and the feeble ticking of the travelling clock. I got up and put out the light, electing to sit in the dark.

When Julianne came back next day I decided not to tell her about my letter, still less to show it to her. I was deeply ashamed of it, ashamed to belong to a family from which such a communication could issue. Not that I did belong to it, any more. I was cut adrift.

The ship went down like lead.

Now it is time to tell you about our housekeeping arrangements at Tonbridge Hall; this will lead me naturally to the matter of love. You must appreciate that we lived in a townscape, built to an unnatural scale: institutional, impersonal. We had come from our suburbs, villages and market towns, from stockbroker Tudor and inter-war semi with laburnum tree, from cosy terrace or mansion flat, to live in a public landscape of grey brick and Coade stone, the iron railings marching on, the brutal Senate House, the boastful British Museum. We walked to our colleges through streets with famous names, by statues and monuments, and we passed most of our lives in public rooms, seedy or grand, under strip lights or chandeliers. In the evenings we came back, it is true, to our own narrow rooms, but even they recalled the felon's accommodation, maintained at public expense, in some enlightened Scandinavian prison.

So it is not surprising that we tried to set up our own housekeeping routines, to recreate the domesticity of which (I suppose) we must have felt deprived. Our rooms were cleaned for us, and fresh bed linen was placed in our rooms each Thursday. We had very little to do except look after ourselves.

Each corridor had a poky kitchen, hardly more than a broom cupboard, with two gas-rings and a sink. Some girls would use the kitchens to heat milk or soup, but they were good for little else, and not pleasant places to congregate. A better place for pretending to a normal woman's life was the laundry-room on the sixth floor; we would stand about and chat while washing-machines whirred and glugged. You never saw Karina up there. She washed her clothes – hairy jumpers and woollen tights – in the wash-basin in C21. Then she hung them over the radiators.

This did not please Lynette; when you called by she would indicate the dripping garments with a poke of her chin, and roll her dark eyes, but she didn't say anything to Karina. Wet, the clothes looked bigger; the sweaters were elongated, their arms swinging and cuffs groping as if in search of a handhold.

Up in the laundry-room across from the machines there were a half-dozen ironing boards, where a half-dozen girls toiled: not always the same six, I mean, but girls with identical expressions, intent and methodical, martyred yet victorious. What were they ironing? Party dresses? Not at all. Shirts. Men's shirts. Boyfriends' shirts.

Flattening the collar. Pressing the cuffs, easing and turning, finally lifting the garment with a flourish, high into the air like a flag, like a banner of triumph: a banner that told the whole world that I, a Tonbridge Hall girl, have got my man. I have got my man and I know how to look after him. I'm not just a pretty brain, you see; not just a pretty brain.

If I could time-travel I would fly back, back in time to the ironing-room; I would fly back to those girls and slap them. I would like to bring them to their senses; say, how can it be, that after all these years of education, all you want is the wash-tub? Leave this, and go and run the country. And yet I see that what they were up to, these surrogate housewives, was not so spiritless; it was a small rebellion against the lives they had led since puberty.

When men decided women could be educated – this is what I think – they educated them on the male plan; they put them into schools with mottoes and school songs and muddy team games, they made them wear collars and ties. It was a way to concede the right to learning, yet remain safe; the products of the system would always be inferior to the original model. Women were forced to imitate men, and bound not to succeed at it. And this is what we were, when we grew up at the Holy Redeemer; not so much little nuns, but little chappies, little chappies with breasts. At 'bad' schools the girls turned up in the mornings with streaks of mascara under their eyes, they talked dirty and flirted and sipped mixed drinks in violent colours. At 'good' schools the girls had plain faces and thick tights, stout shoes and bulging briefcases. They forfeited today for the promise of tomorrow, but the promise wasn't fulfilled; they were reduced to middle-sexes, neuters, without the powers of men or the duties of women. Our schools kept from us, for as long as they could, the dangerous, disruptive, upsetting knowledge of our own female nature.

But we were released from the collars and ties now. All at once it happened, without preparation or warning, in the course of a day. No wonder we were confused, torn by conflicts no one had hinted at. We were eighteen, nineteen; we wanted high marks, because that was what we were trained to get. We were trained to defer gratification, to pamper and exercise and flaunt our mental powers, but now our bodies were registering their demands. We'd had sex; sex bred the desire for its consequences. The little women inside were looking out through our eyes and waving to the world.

We wanted homes. Houses of our own. Babies, even: the milky drool of saliva to replace the smooth flow of ink. We did not speak of it, but each corridor of Tonbridge Hall seethed with fertility-panic. In the groups who gathered for coffee after dinner, there was always one girl who thought she might be pregnant, one who was celebrating the fact that she wasn't: celebrating outwardly, anyway. When friends met in the morning, or after a weekend away, there was always an undertone, a buzz-note of inquiry, an eyebrow raised – you are? You could be? You're not? Late again! was the distraught mutter; we took the contraceptive pill, most of us, but we acted as if we didn't believe it worked. Our doubts spoke of our desires, of our ambivalence. A blip of the bubble-pack, a sip of water, the tiny taste of sweetness on the tongue; how could these prevail against the huge, mechanic workings of nature? Nature had been driven out with a pitchfork, and was creeping her way back in.

Of course, not everybody shared the fertility panics. I was celibate, though not through choice. Julianne seemed to have her body under control. And Claire, our next door neighbour: 'I do worry about Sue,' she said to me. 'This new boyfriend of hers, you know, she has sexual relations with him.'

I wanted to murmur, that is usual nowadays, but I decided to listen with attention to Claire's fears. 'I don't think Sue knows what she wants,' she complained. 'She – takes risks. She tells me she does.'

'Isn't she on the Pill?'

'Oh, have a word with her, Carmel,' Claire begged. 'You're more a woman of the world than I am.'

Poor Claire, I said to myself. When she spoke of Sue, her head sunk into her pasty hands; the pose showed her to advantage. Her spots were sprinkled over her cheeks as if somebody had worked on her flesh with a red-tipped drill. Her hair had been permed recently, in the round style that had been favoured by the mothers of my friends at the Holy Redeemer; the lustreless curls looked brittle, as if you could snap them away from her skull. The way the world was moving, it was becoming increasingly difficult to find an unattractive woman. I wondered about the girls at school, the ones who'd been big girls when I was a shrimp of eleven. I remembered moustaches, manly chests, sinewy torsos; I thought, they probably look quite acceptable now. Frights like Claire were

a dying breed. Even Karina, with her increasingly thick-
ening figure and baleful expression, was not actively
ugly. Lynette said she could think of lots of ways in
which Karina could be improved. 'Not chew her nails
like that. A decent bra, to stop her flopping. Colours to
suit her – imagine, say, a clear coral pink. Or a strong
blue – not navy. And no, Carmel, not royal.'

Karina came and went, and resisted improvement.
About Lynette, she said, 'I cannot be doing with women
who paint their toenails. I've no time for that sort at all.'

In the seventh week of term Sue's problematical boyfriend paid her a visit. 'She insists I move out of our
room for them,' Claire said. She sat on Julianne's bed.
Her voice was frayed and her hands washed together.

'It's the usual arrangement,' I said. I grinned maliciously.
'She'll do the same for you, when the occasion arises.'

She looked up, amazed. 'You don't think that I – oh,
no, Carmel. That's for marriage. That's what I believe.'

'Yes, love.' My fingers crept into my hair; she made
me anxious, northern, almost kind. 'But before people
marry, you know, these days, they expect to try each
other out. Like cars. You go for a test drive.'

'I don't *think* . . .' she spoke carefully, picking through
the English language as if it were strange to her, 'I don't
think I'll marry . . . One never knows of course.'

Are you a lesbian, then? I wanted to ask. I was
building up in my head a library of the looks I had seen
her give Sue. As if answering me, she said, 'I don't say I
wouldn't like to, if the circumstances were right. But you
can't count on someone asking you, can you?'

I saw a moonlit garden, and Claire in white satin, bias cut; a suitor kneeling in evening dress, proffering a rose. 'I don't think you wait to be asked,' I said. 'I think you sort of tell them.' I considered. 'Perhaps you could marry a missionary,' I said. 'Someone like St John Rivers. And go and aid the poor on the streets of Bombay.'

She looked up. 'You've lost me there.'

'Oh, *Jane Eyre*,' I said. 'Sorry. He wasn't going to marry her because she was pretty or anything, but because she was quick on the uptake and he thought she had a strong constitution. You know, this thing with Sue and her boyfriend, how can you be sure it's wrong, how can you be sure? I know what's in the Bible but has God told you personally?'

It was a serious question. Yet Claire managed a smile. 'Of course not. He doesn't need to. Anyway, however you look at it, it's against all the regulations.' I studied her face; she was soon frowning again. 'If we're thrown out, what will my parents say? Look, Carmel, I don't know what's going through your head, you've probably read several books I haven't come across, the point is I don't mind her having a boyfriend, she used to have a nice boyfriend, she met him at a gospel weekend –'

I didn't ask her what a gospel weekend was; I didn't like to think about it. I just interrupted her: 'Claire, if you were to go away for a day or two, wouldn't it solve your problem? I'm sure your parents would be glad to have you home.'

'Oh no.' She blushed. 'They're divorced, you see.'

'You could go and see a friend.'

'But then I'd just be shirking, wouldn't I? I'd be shirking the responsibility.'

'You're not responsible for Sue.'

'Aren't I?'

'Who then, in law, is my neighbour?' Claire looked closely at me. 'The snail in the ginger-beer bottle,' I explained. 'It's a case I've learnt. 1932. "Who then, in law, is my neighbour? The answer seems to be – persons who are so closely and directly affected by my act that I ought reasonably to have them in contemplation as being so affected when I am directing my mind to the acts or omissions which are called in question." Lacks resonance, doesn't it?'

'Do you have to learn it off by heart, like that?'

'No. I just prefer to.'

Claire shook her head. 'We're all responsible for each other. Don't you think, Carmel? Don't you think we ought to be?'

Sue had given her boyfriend a big build-up. There was an unspoken agreement that in our conclaves we could talk about our boyfriends just so much; everybody, more or less, should get equal time, when the others would listen or pretend to. Some people, like Lynette, never talked about their private lives. Some, like me, had nothing against it on principle, but found it too difficult in practice: because of all the things I loved about Niall, how could I select just one or two for public delectation? But Sue could talk and did, rattled on unchecked by good taste or any notion of self-protection; 'I am sick of the topic of Sue's Roger,' Julianne snapped one evening. He was handsome, he was thoughtful, he was romantic and sensitive; we did not at first associate him with the lanky, frowning figure who appeared on the corridor, loping furtively between C2 and the bathrooms. 'He's so old,' Julianne complained. 'She never told us that, did she? He must be twenty-six at least. Married, do you think? He can't be any good, can he? Or else at that age he'd have money for a hotel.'

Lynette gave a delicate shiver. 'It's so sordid,' she said. 'This signing-in business.'

The signing-in book was kept at the reception desk inside the main door. It was guarded by a sharp-eyed middle-aged woman called Jacqueline, of whom it was said that she never forgot a name and never forgot a face. We were allowed male visitors in our rooms, at any time up to eleven at night, but when they entered the hall they had to sign themselves in and when they left they had to sign themselves out.

So the art of keeping a man overnight was this: he must be signed out by someone else's departing boyfriend. No point even trying it when Jacqueline was in charge and on form; but she could be distracted sometimes, she had to go to the lavatory, and sometimes, even, she took a day off. The system was for the departing boyfriend to stand far below in the street, signalling: thumbs up for 'You're signed out', thumbs down for 'I didn't manage it'. I wonder if passers-by ever saw this ritual, and paused to ask themselves what was going on.

It was a sport for boys, not for grown men. Sue's Roger endured it sullenly. Claire – grim-faced – hauled her mattress to another room, and Sue and her man stayed in bed for most of the weekend. 'Wouldn't you think they'd like to vary their programme of activities just a little?' Julianne said. Each one of us, even though she had a man of her own, was violently jealous of anyone who had a man at that very moment.

'We're getting married as soon as I graduate,' Sue said on Monday morning. 'Roger says so.' She was enrobed in smugness, wrapped in self-satisfaction as if in a cobweb shawl. 'It's a long time to wait, but – well . . .' She tried an optimistic little shrug. I saw the invisible shawl move on her shoulders.

'Will he give you an engagement ring?' Lynette asked.

'Oh, we won't bother with that,' Sue said. 'It's bourgeois.'

There was a strange note in her voice, as if she were lurching off course. Claire stared at her, uncomprehending. 'Is he political?' she said. 'I didn't know that.'

At intervals that week I would take out the letter from my mother and read it. I hoped that it would be different, that the words would somehow unwrite themselves while they lay in the darkness of the drawer, or the flowers at least erase themselves from the edges of the page. When I was little and she went out cleaning, her employers would sometimes try to give her things: surplus food and cast-off clothing. 'I flung it back in her face,' she'd say. At Christmas she did accept gifts of money; otherwise, the only thing she'd ever brought home were roses, ten inches long with flexible stems and plastic thorns. They came free for some months with a certain brand of washing powder, and by the time she lost interest we must have had four dozen of these artefacts in all colours, many of them unknown to nature. My fingers still remember the slimy, pliable plastic; I dipped and twisted the flower-heads, turning them to a pleasant angle. Even the folded petals could be moved, so you could elect the bud or the full-blown rose. You could cram them in the same vase, crimson and stippled apricot, youth and age, the whisper of promise and the rose past its prime; they were scentless, accreting to themselves a sticky grey dust, as if they leaked something that would attract it. Arranging them was my hobby, for quite some time.

There was a hairdressing-room up on the sixth floor, with wash-basins and hand-held showers over them. Some of us used to go up there and experimentally dye our hair with solutions that called themselves 'shampoo in, shampoo out'. They didn't, of course, and one day in this seventh week of term, by some accident of mistiming and absent-mindedness, I coloured my hair a flaming red. What I had been after was a discreet enhancement of my moth-wing tufts: when I looked in the mirror I was appalled, but secretly gratified. A frail wisp crept in, a sad little scholar who missed her straw hat; an incendiary woman swept out.

'Singular!' Julianne said, when we met that evening. 'What will Niall say? When will he be visiting you? I'll make myself scarce, you know.' She came up to me and buffeted my boxer's head with her big soft hands. 'I worry about you. You used to have sex every weekend. You must be frustrated. I worry will you run amok.'

'Likely,' I said. 'Now I've got this red hair.'

'It's so *extreme*,' Julianne said. I glowed. It was the first time ever that – unequivocally – she had praised me. I saw that there was something to be said, for not being Julianne. She could never change; such blondeness, such generosity, such abundant, buttery charm can never become less than itself, can never transform or pretend; it can only slide and accommodate itself to the earth's curve.

'Next week,' I said. 'He's coming next week, Niall.'

Julianne said, 'I'm so glad.' Then she stared hard at me. 'You're losing weight,' she accused. 'I should never have brought that skeleton home. It's giving you ideas.'

The boarding-school girls gave me strange looks in the corridors, but on the whole I liked my new head. For the first time, I commanded respect from strangers; they reacted to me as if I might have a poisoned dagger in my stocking-top.

Next week came, it came at last; and Lynette was going to lend me the fox fur.

I longed to lie naked and quiet in Niall's arms, my head on his chest, tell him about my mother and how she had cut me off, how, at this late stage, she had aborted me; I wanted, also, to feel him sink into my flesh, bite my neck, suck my breasts. But I did not intend to keep him hidden away, as if I were ashamed of him. We would go out and eat a meal, for which Niall would have carefully budgeted; when Sunday came, I would repay him by exercising my right to introduce a guest for Sunday lunch at Tonbridge Hall. The shillings for his lunch were building up in the back corner of my desk drawer.

We went in ceremonial force to C21: Sue, still glowing,

Claire, still grizzling, myself with my new head and Julianne with her amused smile. Karina was at her desk, shoulders hunched. She didn't turn when we came in. 'I hope you're not going to make a racket,' she said. 'I'm doing an essay.'

'Misery-guts,' I said to her. I felt light with glee, because I was going to see Niall. 'Don't you want to witness my transformation?'

Lynette slid the coat from its satin padded hanger and swung it out into the room; it seemed to writhe with its own animal life. Sue seized it by the neck, held it splayed and poised; my stick arms slithered into the silk. The sleeves were long for me; like a Frenchman's kiss, the fur brushed the backs of my hands. I turned to the mirror and smiled at myself. I looked like a whippet which had been kitted out in the skin of a well-fed golden retriever. Lynette took my face in her hands and kissed me on the nose.

'I'm off for the weekend,' Julianne said. 'Leave the field clear for you.'

'What, going home?'

'Yes.' She was packing a case already; but looking at her back I sensed a reluctance in her.

'Don't feel you must. I mean, you could throw your mattress in Lynette's room.'

'Oh no. I'd be afraid Karina would roll out of bed in the middle of the night and fall on me and crush me to death.'

'You could go in with Sue and Claire.'

'Oh, God, no! Either it's a revivalist meeting, or we're

on the topic of bloody Roger and his many wonders.'
She mimicked Sue's whine: '"We've been talking over
where we'd like to live, me and Roger, never too early to
see estate agents . . . Of course, I want a career . . ." Silly
bitch. The only career she'll get is washing his socks in a
council flat.'

'Jule,' I said, 'you're not taking much for the weekend,
are you?'

'I've got what I need. I've clothes at home.'

She usually took something special, when she went
back north; she'd fall in with her old tennis-club set, and
they'd go dancing, drive out to Cheshire restaurants
with log fires and prawn cocktails. I thought, is she sick
of them, the tennis-club set, is she moving on, or is the
devious bitch not going home at all, has she got some
secret new man that she's not telling me about? I could
hardly ask to see her train ticket. Jule snapped shut the
clasp of her white vanity-case, fastened the strap. Her
expression was joyless, remote. 'Here I go then,' she said,
picking up her handbag. 'Have a lovely fuck.' Then at
the door – it was quite unlike her – she hesitated: she
swung back towards me and kissed my cheek. 'Take
care, Carmel,' she said. 'Of course, you always do.'

Niall brought a weekend bag, a solid leather and canvas
bag that belonged to his father, with his father's initials
on it; he gripped it in his square cold hand. When I saw
him walk in at the door of C3 I felt I would faint with
joy; and the room did swim for a moment, the textbooks
and files, the grey striped bedspreads, Mrs Webster grinning on her shelf.

I should have warned him to bring a sports bag, a plastic carrier, something that would not indicate so clearly that he was moving in for two nights. Jacqueline would have marked him with her gimlet eye, I felt sure. But then, there was no provisional, makeshift quality about Niall; his natural age was forty, jangling the keys of a Rover, pulling up before a good hotel which he had heard recommended by friends. The deceit would not suit him, the signing-out, the skulking in the corridors. But how else could we be together?

We kissed. It was a black-out kiss, where eyes close and thoughts no longer flow; his hands swam over me. We came up for air. 'You've lost weight,' he said. He was not displeased; it was the fashion for women to be as thin as they could manage. 'Your hair . . .' He appraised it. 'It was an accident?'

'It was an accident.'

Niall went to the wash-basin and ran the taps. He bent over it and splashed water on to his face, reached for the soap and scrubbed and scrubbed. 'I had no idea,' he said. 'That this town was so filthy.'

I had ceased to notice, I suppose: the grime that ran out of my hair when I washed it, the grime that edged white underwear with grey. I handed him a towel. 'You've changed,' he said. 'London has changed you. I knew it would.'

On Friday night we stayed in my room, in bed. It wasn't easy, a big man and a small girl in a single bed; you had to turn together, you had to fit each other, thigh moving with thigh, arm with arm, foot sliding between feet as tongue slid between teeth. Saturday dawn, Niall complained of backache, and I gave him two soluble aspirin in a mug, melted in hot water from the tap. I joined him, though I would have died rather than complain; our hips jostled as we tried to sit up to an angle proper for medicine. Niall handed me his mug, I put it under the bed; we fell across each other, into an aching sleep.

At nine that morning I tripped lightly to the warden's office, leaving Niall naked and locked in C3. I'd been in too much of a hurry to pull on tights – they'd only have to come off again – but I had jumped into an almost ankle-length skirt I'd borrowed from Lynette, and I thought that nobody would notice I was bare-legged. I caught a glimpse of myself in one of the great shadowy mirrors that peopled the ground floor. My lips flared scarlet, my cheeks blazed and my throat was mottled with an orgasmic flush.

'A late key, Miss McBain?' the warden inquired. 'Another of your political meetings?'

'No.' I expect a stupid smile grew on my face. 'I'm going to a film.'

'Oh, my dear, I'm so pleased,' the warden said. 'There is such a thing, you know, as being too serious.'

'Is there?' I said. 'Too serious for what?'

I was interested; the warden saw I was not being pert.

'For the taste of the opposite sex, I suppose.' She gave a brusque little laugh.

'Yes, but after all,' I said, 'it's not the Dark Ages, I don't see that they have any right to say how serious you should be.'

'I agree . . . oh, I do so agree. But – I've seen it again

and again – they do have a way of making things difficult. Especially for clever girls. Your . . . your young man, are you very fond of him?'

Besotted, I wanted to say. We'll be together for ever and ever. But then she might run upstairs and search my room. I was aware that a teardrop of semen was creeping down the inside of my left thigh. 'Well, it's early days,' I said.

'Yes. That's the attitude,' the warden said. 'I like you, Carmel, you're a very promising gel. You must put yourself first, establish yourself in life before you think of a husband and family. Why, we may see you in parliament one of these days! You'll be interested to meet our guest next month, our guest at High Table. Have a word with me nearer the time and remind me to seat you near her. Now, there's a determined lady who knows what she wants!'

I nodded. Smiled. The taste of the opposite sex was on my tongue; salt-jelly, heat and flesh. The last thing I wanted was a party political scrap with the warden; I wanted to run back upstairs, pull off my clothes and climb back into bed with Niall, who would by now be quite ready for me again. But the image came at once to my mind of the Labour Club concubines, trailing after the comrades; at each midnight meeting almost dropping from their seats with boredom, jerking back to wakefulness to fix soft eyes on the face of Dave or Mike or Phil. It wasn't as if they thought they were Rosa Luxemburg; their role was to fetch packets of cigarettes, to cook stews on one ring in bedsits. Sometimes they were allowed to duplicate an agenda on an inky machine, or crayon a poster to advertise a meeting. They were allowed to stand on street corners, trying to sell Tribune, or rattling a collecting box for whatever worthy body of strikers needed students' coins at the time.

The drop of semen inched downwards and slunk into my shoe. There's a few thousand babies that won't be born, I thought; I wonder if there are any little Beethovens run under my foot, any Tolstoys, any promising England fast bowlers? The warden handed over the key and I signed for it. When I passed the mirror again, my face looked quite pale and severe.

On Saturday evening I put on the fox fur and we went out to eat steak. Niall watched me thoughtfully as I dressed. 'It's a nice coat, isn't it?' I said, when he did not speak.

'I'm not sure it's really you, though.' His tone was matter of fact. 'It's more for somebody glamorous.'

So, if you know anybody glamorous, go out with her, I thought. I was too meek to say it. 'It's because I've borrowed it,' I said. 'That's what you don't like.'

'Yes, that's it. I prefer you in your own clothes. And really, to be honest, I don't think you need so much make-up.'

I paused, my lipstick in my hand, and gazed at him through the mirror. What did he prefer then, the stringy-haired girl in the grey velour hat?

In the restaurant: 'You're just pushing your food around, Carmel,' Niall said. 'Has something upset you? Did I say something wrong?'

'No.' I sighed gustily. I leant back in my leatherette banquette. 'I feel like a fraud,' I said. I put my knife and fork down. 'I've had dreams about this meal. But now it comes down to it, I'm not really hungry.'

In the small hours of Sunday we crept into Tonbridge Hall. On the reception desk a gooseneck lamp cast a fierce white beam on the box where the late key must be replaced. Niall crouched in the shadows while I crept towards it, then we inched towards the staircase, ascended with breath held, jumping at any noise, at a creak underfoot or a winter cough issuing from behind a locked door. Stopping, starting, heart in mouth: I held my nervous palms flat against Lynette's coat as we tippytoed all the way to C Floor. It occurred to me that if I were caught and thrown out, Tonbridge Hall might not refund any of the vast accommodation charge that had vanished from my grant before I saw it. I would be destitute.

'It is humiliating, this,' Niall said, when we reached C3.

'I know.'

I cast off the fox fur, letting it slither to the parquet. We made love again in the single bed, its once-crisp sheets now damp and stained and twisting about our bodies like ropes. 'Carmel,' Niall said, 'I can feel all your ribs.' Later, he said, 'I wish I could afford to buy you some roses.' Later still, he asked, 'Why do we have to be young?'

There was a ripple of interest when Niall appeared in the refectory for Sunday lunch. It was not because of our haggard faces – for two nights we had hardly slept – but because many of the girls had swallowed Julianne's story that Niall was a convict out on licence. To some she had said he was a bank robber, to others that he was a member of the IRA. Conversation died as we passed.

Perhaps he wondered why. I judged it too complex to explain to him. He looked just what he was and nothing else: a prop forward from a northern grammar school, a family man in the making. In later life, I should think, he has learnt to carve.

On that day he took his seat, conscious of his market value though he did not know what had enhanced it. His hair curled damply, his square hand lay loosely on the table; his flecked hazel eyes were open and aware. Sue simpered at him, and Claire turned her head and blushed a deep and unbecoming shade. At eight o'clock that morning, counting on slug-a-bed habits, he'd tried a sprint to the nearest lavatory, semi-erect in Y-fronts. Nothing had warned him of Sue and Claire on their way to church, heading for the staircase, respectably buttoned into their coats. I'd said to him, 'We'll laugh about it, twenty years from now.'

'Hi there,' Sue said brightly. 'We've met, haven't we?'

'Sue!' Claire hissed.

'Hello, Niall,' Karina said. She smiled. 'Long time no see. How's it going?'

Startled, I glanced across at her. Niall looked away. Her face was animated; I saw for a moment the shadow presence of the rosy little girl whom everyone used to praise. Try it, I thought, just try it; any more ogling, and I'll turn you into best minced steak.

I gripped my knife and fork, and stared at her. It had never occurred to me to wonder if Karina had a boyfriend these days. I could hear her, in my mind, saying, 'Love? That's daft. Sex? What do you want that for?' It was Karina's deriding voice; it was also, somehow, my mother's.

As in Niall's house, so at Tonbridge Hall: there was always roast meat on a Sunday. It was the quantities that were different. I have explained how a third-year student at the head of the table would serve out the meat; and it was Niall's misfortune that on this particular Sunday she was either a ferociously principled feminist or a girl with a hard heart and no brothers. However it was, I have the impression that she put even less on Niall's plate than on any other; we're talking about two mouthfuls of meat, as against two and a nibble.

I have seen people at road accidents, I have seen people sacked – God knows, I've sacked them myself. But I have never seen anything to equal the horrified disbelief that grew on Niall's face when he saw what he had been given to eat: the wafer, the comma, the nail-paring of protein that was meant to constitute a Sunday dinner. For a moment I thought he would DO IT – reach out for the stainless steel platter, and salvage the scrap, the quarter-slice, the leave-a-bit-for-Miss-Manners: but (because we were in love then, you see) he would have thrust it not into his own mouth but into mine.

Still, the moment passed. That afternoon Niall sat fully dressed on the edge of my bed. He looked miserable. 'Carmel, you must eat,' he said. 'That kitchen along the corridor, I know it's not much but it's there for your use. You could make eggs. You could buy apples, couldn't you? Apples are good for you. What you should do is to get some packets of powdered soup, and every night you and Julianne should have a mug of it before you go to bed.' He said, 'This is my advice.'

'OK,' I said. 'Powdered soup. We could do, I suppose.'

'I mean, Karina – she's looking well.'

'She's looking like a suet pudding, if you want my opinion.'

'Yes, well – she may not be able to help it.'

At five o'clock Niall had to leave to catch his train. I didn't want to walk him to the door of Tonbridge Hall, because it would only obtain for me another two minutes of his company, and I had to set that against the risk of Jacqueline on the desk seeing us and spotting that we were a couple: still, even two minutes were hard to forfeit. I leant out of the window and watched his every step, until he vanished around the corner, into the London dark.

Then I lay on my bed, agonized, shaking with sobs, tears baptizing the stained bed linen. No matter how you bleed each month, there is always blood left; no matter how much you cry, the salt water still drags down your body, soaks your tissues, drips into your silly woman's veins. Niall's face, when he left, had been set against the deprivation to come. It was three weeks to the Christmas vacation.

Julianne did not return till late the following afternoon. I was sitting at my desk chewing over a knotty problem, and I heard her come in behind me. 'Oh, there you are,' I said. 'Good weekend?' I heard her put her case down. 'Family well?'

She made one of those non-committal noises that indicates that this is not an interesting topic. 'Do anything nice?' I asked. 'Cold at home, is it?'

She didn't answer. Obviously in a mood. Oh well, I'd enough to worry about. I frowned at the column of figures before me. Jule's bed squeaked as she sat down on it. I added up the figures, bottom to top, then added them up top to bottom, as if that would make the answer different. 'Did you bring one of your mum's cakes back?' I asked. She usually brought home-made biscuits, and an iced ginger loaf, or a fruit cake laced with brandy.

She didn't reply. I turned to look at her, over my shoulder. She was slumped on the bed still wearing her coat. She brought her eyes round to focus on my face; it seemed to cost her an effort. 'No, I just brought myself,' she said.

I wanted to say, of course I know you haven't really been home. But she looked tired – worn-out, in fact – and I felt sorry for her: the complexity of her life, all the men she had to keep on a string, the wearing business of waking up in different beds. Life was simple for me – except for this matter of the figures.

'I have to go to the chemist,' Julianne said. 'Do you want anything?'

I shook my head. The door clicked behind her. I turned back to my miscalculation.

In my final year at school my father had obtained his tiny, long-plotted promotion. This blip in my parents' fortunes had raised their income, so that I did not receive a full maintenance grant from the state. All my tuition fees were paid, and most of my living expenses, but my parents were required to contribute twenty pounds a term towards keeping me fed and warm. I had been so careful, so exact, that until this eighth week I had thought I would manage without their money.

But then I learnt for the first time that during vacations we were required to clear everything from our rooms: to empty our wardrobes, our bookshelves, to pack up our lives and disappear till mid-January. I could not possibly carry all my possessions: my files, my books, my Winfield on Tort, my Cheshire and Foote on Contract. I remembered how my arm had ached and my shoulder throbbed, when I had dragged my suitcase from Euston half a lifetime ago. I wondered fleetingly if it would lighten the load if I wore both my coats at once, the duffle over the raincoat: I dismissed it from my mind. There was no choice. I would have to have my effects conveyed by British Rail's carrier service to Niall's house. I had already budgeted for my train ticket, of course; I was getting lighter, but I knew I could not fly.

Phone home? Ask for help? We had a telephone, now. I remembered the blushing roses on the letter, and the waxy feel of stems under my nine-year-old fingers. I could not do it.

I did it. My mother was not unfriendly. She told me our cat had died. When I asked about money, she changed the subject.

I could go without lunch, I reasoned. Anyway, I only had a cup of coffee and a yoghurt, or on very hungry days a roll with grated cheese and a slice of tomato. Who could miss that? I would eat extra toast in the mornings, nerve myself to take a third slice under the startled gaze of the Sophies. I would force the hard butter on it and chew and swallow, and that would last me until dinner at Tonbridge Hall. But what would I do on Labour Club nights, when there was seldom time to get back for dinner? There'd be no question of dashing into the college canteen, gulping down a gristle pie and chips; once or twice I had indulged myself in this way. I'd have to choose: the semi-satisfaction of my appetite, or the semi-satisfaction of my conscience.

When one day I ran out of money for stamps, I knew I would have to borrow. I could negotiate my food intake with myself, but I could not negotiate with the GPO a cheap rate for my letters to Niall.

My guts churning, I made my way along the corridor to C21. After all, I thought, we've known each other almost all our lives. And I knew that Karina would have a full grant, because her mother was disabled now, their income was cut by half. She would have a little more money than me, and if − I must pay her back before the end of term, but perhaps even Niall, his parents . . .

As I was about to knock on the door, my attention was drawn by a sound from the kitchen just across the corridor. I peeped around the door and saw a cheap enamel saucepan jiggling and popping on one of the gas rings. I stepped in and lifted its lid. There was nothing in it but water, water at a rolling boil. I knew somehow that this pan belonged to Karina.

A moment later the door of C21 opened and Karina crossed the corridor, holding a screwed-up Cellophane packet. 'Hello, what are you doing here?' she said incuriously. She lifted the lid of the saucepan, pulling her sleeve down to protect her hand. She frowned at the boiling water. It seemed to be satisfactory. She put down the pan lid and untwisted the Cellophane packet; tubes of cut macaroni plopped into the pan, some catching the rim in their descent and rattling like pebbles. One of them fell by the wayside, on to the scratched and rusting space between the two rings. Steam rising into her face, Karina pinched it in her fingers and dropped it in the pan with the rest. She looked at her watch. 'Excuse me.' She left the kitchen. I leant against the wall, watching the macaroni bob and swirl in the pan, turning from yellow to thick white.

Karina recrossed the corridor, carrying a deep soup bowl and paper cylinders of salt and white pepper. 'Excuse me,' she said again, speaking to me this time as if I were in her way. I stepped aside. She dangled her spoon into the water, slapping at the contents.

'Just for you?' I said.

'You can have some if you're hungry. I only have one bowl, you'll have to fetch your own.'

'Aren't you coming to dinner tonight?'

'I am, but it's not enough, is it?'

I shook my head. Karina fished again with her spoon, trapping a tube against the side of the pan, dredging it from the water, raising it to her lips, which flinched away from the hot metal; then testing it with her teeth. It was ready. Her tongue coiled around the remnant her bite had left; it flicked into her mouth. She took the pan from the heat and moved to the sink, wedging her soup bowl against the side of the pan to drain off the boiling water. 'Careful!' I said. I always said things like this. It came from years of listening to my mother; a concern, reflex or perhaps just assumed, for other people's flesh.

Her shoulders stiffened. 'You're so soft, Carmel,' she said.

So soft. Not a compliment.

The macaroni lolloped into the waiting dish. A plume of steam rose from it. Karina, her face absorbed, sprinkled it with salt and pepper, then picked up her spoon and began to eat. The dish was too hot for her to hold, so she balanced it on the draining board and leant over, her lips darting at the spoon, sucking up the tubes with a little intake of air.

'Don't you have cheese?' I said, aghast.

She looked up, the spoon half-way to her mouth. 'I could have. But I won't be able to afford cheese by the end of term. So I might as well get used to it like this.'

'Jule and me, we have some butter,' I offered.

'I don't want your butter.'

'It might be a bit swimmy.'

Karina picked up her dish, held it against her protectively. Her spoon was poised in mid-air. 'Don't you understand me? I don't want to get used to what I can't afford.'

'Yes. Of course I understand you.'

'Julianne, she can afford all sorts of things.'

'But Karina, how can you possibly . . .' Choke it down, I was going to say. My sentence faltered, faltered to the point where I couldn't be bothered with it any more.

'Look, did you want something?' Karina said. 'Otherwise, will you let me get on with my meal in peace? Before it gets cold?'

I made my way unsteadily along the corridor, back towards C3. My key with its big key fob pressed into my palm, and I was just about to put it in my lock when Lynette came through the swing door at the head of the stairs. She was wearing her soft leather coat; it was a claret colour, almost as deep as blackcurrant. The belt was pulled tight at her waist, not buckled but negligently knotted, and the heels of her black boots made a click-click-click on the parquet.

She saw me. Her eyebrows flew up. 'Carmel, you're ill.'

'I'm fine.'

'You look faint.'

'I went to see Karina. She's in the kitchen, eating this gross bowl of macaroni.'

Lynette looked merry. 'Yuk,' she said. 'Let me in, I'll spend five minutes with you, till she's got through with it. I've seen it, honestly. I offered to get her some Parmesan for next time. She said – ' with a gruesome accuracy, Lynette imitated her accent – ' "What sort of muck's that?" '

'Oh, Lynette, honestly.' I turned the key, smiling. I found it difficult to believe that Karina wouldn't know what Parmesan was, and I wondered, fleetingly, if Lynette's anecdotes of day-to-day life in C21 sometimes made her seem more ludicrous and disagreeable than she was. But no, hadn't I just had the evidence of my own eyes?

Lynette took off her coat. I perched on the edge of the bed, she on my desk chair. From her shoulder bag she took a packet of chocolate biscuits, and began to wind off the Cellophane. 'It's the sweaters, you know?' she said. 'Hairy and grey, like gutted wolves or . . . really, I try all the time to think *what* they are like. You look done for, sweetheart. Haven't you had lunch yourself?'

'No, I never have lunch.'

I ate one biscuit. Any more, and tomorrow would be harder to bear. 'What did you want Karina for anyway?' Lynette said.

A crumb of biscuit seemed to fly back up into my throat. I coughed as it scratched my soft palate. I coughed, and began to speak: long pauses between my words. I was bitterly ashamed of my improvidence. Nowadays, of course, students go into debt; indeed, they're encouraged to. Even in my day, there were overdrafts. But not for people like me; for the daughters of mothers like mine. My mother used to say she had never owed a penny piece, never had and never would. Already I was slipping away from the high standard she had set.

Lynette had never looked more beautiful than at the moment she wrote me a cheque. She slid it to me across the desk, as if willing me to take it without comment and never mention it again. Her thick fringe of black lashes fluttered on a cheekbone frosted by Elizabeth Arden.

'What about Karina?' I said. 'I mean, I know she's got a full grant but that's still not very much. I'd hate it if both of us were trying to borrow from you.'

Lynette closed her eyes tight. 'The grant's very mean. I couldn't manage. It's nothing to be ashamed of. If

Karina were to ask, of course I'd help out. She hasn't, so I can't interfere. Shall we not talk about it? Look, you know that my father gives me an allowance every month. We're not wealthy people, but I happen to be an only child, and – '

'So am I.'

'Really? I imagined you belonging to this big jolly clan – ' I saw us with our songs and japes, our makeshift flutes, our donkey parked outside: our thatched roof and the hole cut for a chimney, and us with big patches on our clothes, the patchwork patches that people have in fairytale books. I smiled and looked aside. She paused; her eyes pursued mine. 'No, Carmel . . . I suppose I knew you were just yourself.'

'And the cat's died,' I said. 'You know, my mother, she just said that. Oh, by the way, the cat's died. But why? It wasn't old.'

'You make me feel a worthless person,' Lynette said. 'Work so hard. Never go out.'

'Lynette,' I said, 'could you please not tell Karina or Julianne that you've given me this cheque?'

'What cheque?' Lynette said. As if irritated, she shook her packet of chocolate biscuits in my direction.

I was tempted; I forgot my resolve, and took another. It was a wafer with orange cream inside. I chatted for a minute or two, about the things that interest law students: Acts of God, contributory negligence. I rose, rather formally, to see her out. As I did so I caught a glimpse of myself in the mirror; a terrible creature with iron teeth, grinding up everything that came in her path.

Eight

I will not say much about the Christmas holidays, except that they didn't go quite as I expected. There were strikes that winter and power cuts, so we had to cook when we could, and sometimes we dined by candlelight. Niall's mother had me in the kitchen peeling potatoes by the sackful; but I could only eat the two small potatoes that were the standard issue at Tonbridge Hall. I fell greedily on steaks that carpeted my plate, but when a quarter of the meat had vanished I would quail and, not liking to put down my knife and fork, spend the rest of the meal transferring vegetables from one side of the plate to the other, raising tiny mounds and making patterns and trying to make the quantity look less.

'Your stomach's shrunk,' Niall's mother said. 'I don't know! How ever will you get to be the first woman prime minister if you don't eat up your steak?'

On Christmas Eve we went to midnight Mass in the unprepossessing red-brick church down by the market-place. Susan Millington was there, wearing a tapestry maxi-coat. Her father the dentist showed his teeth at me, and said, 'Hello, Carmel, how's the wide world treating you?'

As a substitute for a smile, Susan lifted a corner of her mouth. 'Whatever have you done to your hair?'

'It's for when the red revolution comes,' I said politely.

'How's Julianne?'

'She's flourishing. Thriving. She's been awarded a medal.'

'A medal? How odd.'

'It's for A Promising Start in Anatomy.'

It was true; some old dead doctor had endowed it. For the last two weeks of term it had dangled on our shelf beside Mrs Webster. Julianne's parents, when they heard the good news, sent her a cheque, and a letter that said she should buy herself something nice.

'I've arranged my pupillage,' Susan said. 'A set in Lincoln's Inn. Did you hear?'

'No, I don't think it was noised abroad.'

Mr Millington patted his breast pocket, where his wallet snuggled. 'It'll cost me a pretty penny too, while she's learning the ropes. Your parents have all that to come, young lady. Yes, the cost of living in the metropolis . . . and she'll have to have her wig and gown.' He rocked back on his heels. 'Still, I have every confidence in our Susan. Our Susan will make a woman High Court judge.'

'You're intending to be a solicitor, are you?' Susan said.

'No, I'm intending . . .' My voice died in my throat. There was really no limit to my intentions. I turned away, feeling a faint nausea at the thought of the blue-white turkey on the larder shelf, ready for tomorrow's banquet of flesh. 'I think I may become a vegetarian,' I said.

In the New Year Julianne brought a toaster back in her

luggage. 'Why didn't I think of it!' Lynette exclaimed. We plugged it in by Julianne's bedside light.

We were popular now, more popular than ever; Claire and Sue called on a nightly basis, round about ten o'clock, to fill themselves up with white slices tanned a light gold then flipped into the air by this god-like machine; we used to sit watching it, intent, ready to spring forward and catch the hot bread. 'I hope it doesn't encourage Karina,' Julianne growled.

But Karina never came. 'Do you know,' Lynette said, 'she's put on a terrific amount of weight over Christmas. I do feel sorry for her.'

'Yes, I've noticed.' In the holidays I had not visited Curzon Street. I had not seen Karina until she returned to Tonbridge Hall, so I did not know what she had been doing to expand herself so. 'I wish I had a photo of her,' I said. 'When she was little. You'd not believe . . .' And it was true; there was no trace of the silvery fairness she'd possessed in the days when she was an Easter chick. When she rolled down the corridors, her calves seemed to expand before my eyes, ballooning out above her shoes; there was a swag of new flesh under her chin, and her small eyes were sunken into a full-moon face. 'I expect she's been cooking for herself,' I said. 'She always did like cooking.'

'Dumplings,' Julianne suggested. 'Big filthy nasty suet dumplings.'

Lynette sighed. 'More and more of Karina. Less and less of Carmel. How odd it is, I'm sure.'

I had decided that I would have to restrict my food

intake severely in the new term, because it was almost the only head of expenditure I could control. I did not intend to be caught out again without the carrier's fee, and have to borrow; I must re-jig my budget. I will have one luxury, I thought, just one, I will buy myself a garment; as for my diet, the toast will help, toast in the morning and toast at night. I can still go to my Labour Club meetings if I can come home and have toast.

It was the butter that had always been problematical. Our rooms at Tonbridge Hall were maintained at such a ferocious temperature that it dissolved into fatty yellow streams. We had to keep it out on the windowsill, high above the street. I was putting out the butter one night when I realized that, when I was outside Tonbridge Hall, I was usually cold. I will knit myself a jumper, I thought.

At first I thought in terms of some serviceable object in dark green, plain as possible, knit one purl one, easy for me. But then I thought: no, why? Why should I be bored? I'll knit a jumper that my mother would have been proud of, if she'd done it herself: one that would have made her gasp. Since the days of kettle-holders, I'm sure my fingers are nimbler. After all, I now have the expectation of success.

In the new term – as in the old – my essays came back from my tutors scrawled with approbation. If there had been a medal for, let us say, A Flying Start in Tort, I'm sure I would have carried it off. My triumphs should have warmed me; but I could not escape the feeling that my application to texts was a despicable zealotry, and that others – like Julianne – achieved the same results with more grace; I was afraid that my elbows were out, that my hunger showed on my face. Besides, I missed Niall very much, and while ambition gnawed like a pain behind my ribs I felt another gnawing too, of loneliness; I felt I was being eaten away from the inside out. Six weeks, we'd said, six weeks to endure and then he'd visit me; six weeks, then we'd know it was only four to go until Easter.

Midnight again: I came back from the kitchen at the end of the corridor with our clean plates stacked in my hands and our butter knife balanced on top. Julianne was standing at our wash-basin, legs apart, enthusiastically soaping her genitals. I put the plates into her bedside cupboard; she towelled herself, floated damply into her nightdress, and ran a hand through her curls. 'Carmel, about you and Niall. Shouldn't you ever branch out? Explore the options? Is there only one cock in the world?'

'I love Niall,' I said.

'Of course you do. Hardly a reason not to sleep with anyone else, is it?'

'I couldn't do that. Why would I want to?' My flesh would revolt, I thought.

'Experience.' She plumped down on the end of her bed, her large breasts jumping once. Her tongue crept out, its tip cherry red, and smoothed a flake of rough skin on her upper lip; January was proving cold. 'I don't think I knew you, Carmel, when we were at the Holy Redeemer. All this . . . intensity.'

Intensity: it is a word of abuse flung at thin women, at thin women who have any pretence at an inner life. It is a label, less costly than the kind I had put on my suitcase.

'Is experience good for its own sake?' I asked.

I felt Julianne's greedy gaze fasten on me: as if she were going to dissect me. Her eyes stripped me down for a moment, down to the bone. Then she flopped back on the bed and stretched, easing her round ample limbs inside her lawn nightdress: abundant, generous, superbly amoral. It occurred to me that perhaps I was the subject of an experiment, an experiment, let us say, in love; that I lived my life under Julianne's gaze, undergoing certain trials for her so that she would not have to undergo them herself. But how are our certainties forged, except by the sweat and tears of other people? If your parents don't teach you how to live, you learn it from books; and clever people watch you, to learn from your mistakes.

Niall had said he would like to buy me roses; I myself thought how nice it would be to have a pot-plant to enliven C3, with its magnolia walls and grinning skull and cheap teak-veneer desks. It was this fleeting desire that gave me the idea for my sweater.

Perhaps a russet-brown is not the best colour for a newly red-headed girl. But I dreamt one night of the Holy Redeemer, of the hall at the House, of the broken tile that would give under the foot, tock-tock. The next day I went out and bought some wool the colour of a mellow old flowerpot. I made it up in a plain stocking-stitch, narrow at the waist, wide and square at the shoulder, with a turn-over to give a double thickness at the neck: like a flowerpot's top. Every spare moment I knitted, sometimes far into the night. I thought that if I flew at it in this way, maintained the tension and momentum, I wouldn't suffer my old problems of mangled wool and loss of confidence. I dreamt of when it would be finished.

'I'm going to sew things on it,' I told Lynette. 'Drooping stems. Felt leaves. And flowers.'

'It will be strikingly original,' she said. 'It will need to be dry-cleaned.'

'I know that. I won't wear it often. But I shall wear it on Guest Night.'

At Tonbridge Hall, Guest Night came three times in the term. One table – where the warden and staff and Hall President normally dined – was described for the evening as High Table, and two others – also highish – were fitted to its ends, so that one had the familiar wedding reception pattern, an 'E' without its middle. The chief guest was someone distinguished, and the other three or four guests – who would be scattered on the wing-tables – would be cheerful, stoical women dons from various colleges, who were willing – for no payment – to spend the evening among us. Floor by floor, in our turn, we girls were allocated places among the guests; and now it was the turn of C Floor, and the Secretary of State for Education was to visit us. The kitchens made special efforts, of course, and a girl we knew from B Floor who had been at High Table last term said that you got given food in ordinary amounts, approximately twice as much as you would get if you were dining in the body of the hall.

*

I had to work fast on the sweater. Lynette pored over the pattern and advised, but it was Karina whose practical skills came into their own when I had to press it and sew the pieces together. Her hair drooped over the ironing board, and there was a faint oily smell of singed wool. 'Not too hot,' I said nervously.

'Look, relax, I know what I'm doing,' she said. 'Though I still think it's ridiculous. I do, Carmel.'

We hadn't spoken so much in months. We had the ironing-room to ourselves; a window was open, and faint late-January sunlight filtered through the smoggy air. 'Those silver beads you've got to sew on it, they're going to look very peculiar.'

'They're for the centre of the daisies. I've got some gold ones too.'

'Nobody grows daisies in flowerpots.'

'It's not an ordinary flowerpot. It's a surreal one.'

'You can excuse any ridiculous thing by calling it that.'

'It will be unique.' I put my hands on either side of my waist and squeezed. She looked up at me. 'Carmel,' she said, 'why are you such a show-off?'

'Show off? Me?' A sour spurt of anger, like stomach acid, rose up into my throat. I reached across and tore my segments of sweater from under her hands. In doing so I knocked aside the iron, which she was holding loosely in her right hand, and it skimmed the knuckles of her left. I watched the mark appear, blue against the bone. Taking her own time, Karina placed the iron on its heel and raised the back of her hand to her lips and sucked it. 'God, stop it,' I said. 'Rinse it under the cold tap.'

'Saliva's antiseptic,' she said.

I knew. I remembered learning that in biology, Form Four. 'I haven't killed you,' I said. 'It was only on bloody wool setting. Or it ought to have been.'

When I got out into the corridor my knitting was still a hot parcel in my hands, tenuous and floppy, premature. Sabotage! I thought. She might have terminally scorched it, if her big mouth hadn't made me intervene.

When I got back to my room I felt shaky. I had lost my temper, and it was news to me that I had a temper to lose.

That evening, my head bent over my task, I said to Julianne, 'There's something about Karina that makes me damage her.'

Julianne gave me a blue-eyed, glazed look; disengaged herself from my remark. 'Let's see, then. Oh yes, I like the twisty stems.'

I was sewing. My flowerpot sweater was assembled and I was applying its fantastical felt daisies, petal by petal. There were embroidered flowers too, less specific in type, and even the daisies were not the colours they are in life. I had remembered chain stitch, stem stitch and satin stitch, and my fingers moved more cleverly than they'd ever moved under a teacher's eye. I had spilt my little beads out of their paper bags, and corralled them in Jule's ashtray. They looked sinister, as they rolled: like the vital parts of a missile system.

I spread out my work on the end of my bed, so that Julianne could finger it and politely exclaim, with a simple kindness I might have thought foreign to her. 'Vine leaves,' she said, 'couldn't you do vine leaves? It would add a touch of the exotic.'

It struck me that perhaps Tonbridge Hall was drawing us together: who is my neighbour? 'Wake me up tomorrow,' she said. 'I want to come to breakfast.'

I woke at four o'clock and lay in the dark. The bedspread, under my hand, was like gritty sand. Twice I got up to check the travel alarm. For three days I had not heard from Niall. Since Christmas there had been these gaps, of a day here and a day there – but never a gap of three days together.

By seven I was drowsing: too late. I forced myself out of bed and opened the window a crack. The cold entered the room like an intruded knife. Standing over Julianne, I touched her elbow. 'Scrambled,' I said.

'What?' she said.

'Egg.'

Her eyes were closed, her breathing even; her upper lip curled back, as if she might draw blood. Nevertheless, twenty minutes later she stumbled down the stairs with me, pretending to be an invalid and slumping on my arm. 'Wait a minute,' I said, 'I have to check my post.'

'Post? Does it come at this time?'

My hand plunged into the pigeonhole. 'It's my letter. I've been waiting. It's come.'

Julianne seemed dazed. I slid a bank statement and a postcard from her pigeonhole and pressed them into her fist. I carried Niall's letter into breakfast; I wanted to rip it open at once, but I knew I would not get the best out of it if I read it in public. I wanted to be able to dwell on every word, and at intervals press the paper to my cheek, pretending it was his skin. This effort of imagination could only be made in private.

I put the letter on my chair, collected my breakfast from the hatch, picked up the letter again and put it on my lap. Weak tea was poured. There was a patter of rain against the long windows. Lynette had not yet put on her lipstick; her face seemed only half-formed. Karina sat rubbing her eyes. 'Toast, Carmel?' cried Claire. There was a grating cheeriness in her voice.

Sue sat at the end of the table, yawning hugely. 'Don't you think we ought to be allowed to come down in our dressing-gowns?'

'There would be some melancholy sights,' Lynette said.

Claire said crossly, 'Really, if people can't make the effort – '

'What's the matter with you this morning?' Julianne asked her.

'And what's the matter with you?' Claire snapped back. 'We never see you at breakfast. What have we done to deserve this honour?'

'Think of it as a rehearsal for Guest Night,' Lynette murmured.

I looked down the table at Claire: irate, her wood-shaving curls leaping away from her scalp. Sue looked jaundiced, and as if she had not slept. She kept her place when the rest of us trooped up for our scrambled egg. It slid through the tines of our forks, pale and perplexing as ever. Sue began to butter a half-slice of rubber toast, and then lost interest. She dropped her knife rather ostentatiously, let it clatter on to her plate. I glanced at her, sympathizing.

Julianne picked up her teaspoon and tapped it against

the rim of her cup. 'Young ladies, if I may have your attention? You may well ask what I'm doing at breakfast. If this pap is the standard, I've been well out of it, and as for the grace, wit and civility of the conversation – '

'Go and eat worms,' I said.

'They would be a most acceptable substitute: but first I wish to make an announcement.' I noticed a little stir at an adjacent table; they thought it was an engagement, and that soon a diamond would be passed around. 'I thought it was better to do it all at once,' Julianne said. 'I'm going to change my name. I don't want to be called Julianne any more.'

'Why not?' Lynette said. 'It's . . . sweet.'

'So it is,' Julianne said. 'And so I'm not. It's a doll's name. A baby name. I don't want it. From now on you can simply call me Julia.'

There was a short silence. Then, 'Fine,' Claire said. 'If you like.'

Lynette said, 'Perhaps I, myself, should consider . . .'

Karina said, 'It doesn't matter what you're called. It doesn't change what you are.'

This made Julia smile. 'Anyone else want to join in? Carmel?'

'Definitely,' I said. 'Call me Zsa-Zsa.'

'Make me Fifi,' Sue said. Her voice was wobbly. Our heads flicked in her direction. She stood up, gripped the back of her chair; she hung on to it for a second, then blundered towards the door.

I was quickest on my feet, sprinting out after her. She let the heavy half-glazed door swing back in my face, and she was crouching on the floor outside the dining-room when I reached her. I had brought my letter with me of course, but I dropped it so that I had both hands free to scoop her floppy fair hair back from her face. Her hand clawed at my shoulder for support. She was sick on the floor, my right shoe and my letter.

The shoe could be salvaged. Had to be, really. But my letter was illegible and smelt noxious. It was by an act of omission, not commission, that I understood its contents. I heard nothing from Niall for the rest of the week, and on Sunday I took the extreme, panicky step of telephoning him at his lodgings.

There was a delay before he came to the phone, and his voice was reluctant. I burst into tears when I heard it. 'I thought you were dead under a truck,' I said. 'I thought you must be.'

'You didn't get my letter?'

I couldn't seem to make him understand that Sue had been sick on it. 'Why was she?'

'Because she's pregnant,' I said. 'Why else?'

A long breath. It was a bad line, but in time I understood that we were finished, that he wanted – what did he say? I can't remember now. The phrases fade. It seemed to have something to do with the fox fur. That he was afraid of what I'd be like, in ten or twenty years, if that was what I deemed to be the proper solace for a cold night.

The next day I didn't go to lectures. It was the first time I had missed. Sue came to my room mid-morning. Her face was swollen from crying. She had been home for the weekend, and given Roger her news. Her account of events was sketchy, jarring and not entirely coherent, but it was obvious to me that Roger was stringing her along. I worked at embroidering my sweater, because while my face was hidden from her I could evade the task of assuming a suitable expression.

'Want another coffee?' she said. Her voice was blurred, thickened with mucus. All morning she had been walking up and down to the kitchen at the end of the corridor, just for something to do: the grey thin liquid overflowing the beakers, slopping over oblivious hands. She did not drink it, I did not drink it; it sat beside us and went cold, until Sue suggested more.

'I couldn't,' I said. 'You get yourself one.'

'No, I couldn't, I feel bloated.' Sitting on Julia's bed, she leant back against the wall, her hands resting above her navel.

'So what did he say then? What did he really say?'

'Well, he seemed – pleased. Not exactly. Pleased in a way, as if, you know, he hadn't expected it, but – well, he didn't say much, really.'

'So he wants you to have it?'

'We didn't talk – I mean, I think it was pretty much of a shock – '

'Are you going to have it?'

'God, I don't know. My parents will be livid. They'll chuck me out.'

In that year, parents still did. For Catholic girls there were small hospitals run by nuns, in discreet rural areas. Parents paid the train fare, and gave a donation; their daughter returned home when her stomach was flat, and the baby was never seen again. Folklore insisted that the experience was penitential: schoolgirls screaming in a twenty-four-hour agony, while Sister pottered serenely in another room.

Head still bent, I considered Sue's phraseology. 'Livid' – that was a word she'd got from Claire. 'Chuck me out' – could be natural to her, or could be one of those pseudo-robust phrases that boarding-school girls employ. It seemed not surprising to me that, out of all of us, this fate had chosen Sue. She had a partial, permeable quality. Words penetrated her; bits of other people's experience intruded themselves into her, like needles picking up the skin. As she talked I heard all the dislocations in her speech, the strange gaps between word and word, the shift from her lurching southern consonants to Claire's posh rounded vowels. She is a thing of shreds and patches, I thought. A stem grew under my hands. I heard the tiny rasp of wool against wool, as I slid my needle through; the silver beads under my fingertips felt like ball-bearings.

'So . . . it doesn't look as if you're setting up house with Roger, then?'

Sue put up her knuckles and pressed them against her mouth. For a moment I thought that she was going to vomit, then I saw that she was thinking. Her eyes moved, once, in their sockets. 'What would you do?' she mumbled through her fists.

I wouldn't be in your situation, I thought. You must be one of those *nice* girls, that my mother told me about; the nice girls who don't know what's what. 'I'd probably get rid of it,' I said.

She took her hands away. 'Is that your advice?'

'No.'

'Don't you give advice?'

'No.'

'What do I do?'

'You go to the Student Health Service.'

'Would it cost anything?'

'No.'

'Roger hasn't got any money.'

'I see.'

'I've only got my grant.'

'Were you on the Pill?'

'At first.'

'And then?'

'I wanted to know if I could have one.'

I looked up, from the delicate terminal frill of a petal extravagantly curled. 'You wanted what?'

Sue's face had the tint and dullness of well-boiled cauliflower. It couldn't be said that pregnancy suited her. 'Help me, Carmel,' she said. 'Don't blame me. Why should anybody blame me? I just wanted to know, you see, to be sure. It's *natural*. It's natural to want to know. Natural.'

'Natural,' I repeated. I reached for my scissors. I had inserted my final stitch. Nature I loved and, next to Nature, Art.

Lynette had an easy day on Mondays, and was always home by mid-afternoon. 'Zsa-Zsa!' she said. She had bought a toaster, too; out of habit, she leapt to it.

'No, no toast! By Guest Night I want to be perfectly triangular.' I whipped out my sweater from under my arm. 'That belt that you said perhaps – '

Lynette was already reaching for it. It was a wide belt, crushing and severe, made of stiff leather in an interesting shade of glossy deep green. 'Can't think why I bought it,' Lynette had said earlier. 'The colour, it seemed special. I suppose it was foresight.'

We stretched out my flowerpot sweater on the bed and laid the belt against it. 'Yes! Now try on,' Lynette said. I eased my creation over my head. Lynette took the sleeves and helped the cuffs over my hands. She slid the belt around my waist, drawing it in until the silver tongue snagged in the last hole. 'Mirror,' she said.

I had to jump to see myself in it. 'Tell me,' I said.

'Perfect if it were an inch tighter. The belt needs one more hole.' She looked cast down. 'But how to make it? I suppose there must be a way. We've got till Wednesday. Do you know, I expect Karina, she's so practical . . . But no. Not worth it. Jealous little madam, she is.'

'Is she all right?'

Lynette shook her head. 'I hardly see her. She never speaks . . . Well, you've seen how she is at breakfast. I come home in the afternoon and I always seem to have missed her. But I know she's been in because there's a Mussolini.'

'A what?'

'A sweater. Clammy and like a corpse and hanging upside down. And at dinner, of course, she can't speak, for eating. Then she's off across the corridor, making soup.'

I remembered Niall's advice. 'She has always had a pathological appetite,' I said.

*

'We could make a hole with a big nail,' Julia said.

'Yes, but we don't have one about our person.'

Julia put her head into C2. 'Have you got a big nail? Or have you got a pair of scissors, a really huge, powerful pair?'

Claire and Sue were sitting on their beds. They looked up and stared. Both of them were white-faced. Slowly, they shook their heads. Julia drew the door shut.

'What's up with them?' she said.

'Claire says that as a Christian she can't connive at the taking of an unborn baby's life.'

Julia snorted. 'Who's asking her to?'

'Sue might need people to cover for her while she's away for a few days. Tell a story for her.'

'She should have it done on a Saturday,' Julia said. 'She'll be discharged on Sunday, and then she can stay out of sight and say she's got twenty-four hour flu. That will cover it. Has she seen somebody yet?'

'I think she might want to have it.'

Julia gave me one of her looks, what I called her rapacious looks: plundering the thoughts out of people's hearts. 'Tell me everything,' she demanded.

'Not in the corridor,' I said.

We went from door to door, saying to the Sophies, 'Has anyone got a corkscrew we could borrow?'

'What! Celebrating?' the Sophies trilled.

The next morning, on my way down Drury Lane, I called at the shoe-repairers. I drew Lynette's belt out of my bag. It lay on the counter like an intractable serpent. 'I wonder,' I said, 'could you make me another hole in this?'

It was done in a second. I took out my purse. 'We wouldn't charge for that, Miss,' the man said. I thanked him. The smell of the shop – feet, leather, tobacco – made me slightly faint, but I felt pleased at getting something for nothing. It was unprecedented.

That evening, as everyone sat in C3 drinking coffee, I tried out the effect. Neither Sue nor I had been down to dinner. 'A thing called beef cobbler,' Lynette said. 'The last word in grossness. Brown-coloured cartilage in gravy, with some sort of hard pastry islands foundering in viscous mud, a reptilian – oh, sorry, Fifi!'

'It's OK,' Sue said. Her fingers padded the place below her cheekbones, like an anxious woman in an operetta; tenderly, she felt the bones of her face, as if seeking a pressure-point that would postpone nausea and her decision.

Julia sat on her bed with her knees beneath her chin and her arms looped around her shins. I realized that she was trying to be as small as possible so that she could observe Sue without scaring her. The worst had happened, and to one of us; the Tonbridge Hall nightmare had come true, and naturally it was of interest. Julia was still and quiet; myself, I wanted to scream. Mrs Webster sat on her shelf, looking jocular.

'Turn round,' Lynette said to me. 'Good. Yes. The flowers are spectacular, and you are achieving triangulation.'

The belt sat below my ribs, its hard edge seeming to elevate them. I tried to slip my finger between wool and leather: I couldn't. 'And yet . . .' I said. 'A half-inch . . .'

Sue clasped her hands against her diaphragm, and moaned.

'Oh, come on!' Claire said. 'It's stupid, Sue, all this agonizing and attention-seeking. You know the answer, you know the right thing to do. The right thing for you, and for everybody concerned. Just make up your mind – have the courage of your convictions.'

Sue whimpered.

'It's taking a life,' Claire said. 'It is, you know it is.' Her face reddened, her spots glowed. 'Talk to Roger. Sit down and talk to him. Talk to your parents. A family conference, that's what you need.'

'I cannot believe,' Lynette said idly, 'that this advice is sound.'

'Everybody will rally round. You'll see. Listen, Sue, you know the selfish choice is never the right one. Think of the baby. It's part of you. Part of him.'

Julia raised her head. Her cheeks flushed, and her lip curled. I didn't think she would condescend to argue with Claire. Nor did she. 'You get fucked first,' she said. 'Give advice after.'

Next morning – a mild bright day – I went back to the shoe-repairers. 'I'm presuming on your good-will,' I said.

I showed with my finger where the next hole should be punched. 'There you are, my darling,' the man said. 'If it weren't for the wife I'd take you home and fatten you up myself.'

I blushed. I wasn't used to Londoners then. I'm still not. They talk so much. I always want to smash their jaws shut; I realize the reaction may be excessive.

*

Guest Night.

Sue, as if magnetized, as if drawn by some invisible force that did not consult her will, went glassy-eyed along the streets to a gynaecologist's consulting-room. The liberalized abortion law was still in its running-in phase, and nobody ever knew quite how to play it. You had to be prepared, at the least, to swear that if you had the baby you'd go insane; I'd always assumed that you must be ready to loosen your hair, sing, ramble on in verse and scatter some flowers, by way of indication that even after ten weeks you weren't feeling yourself.

Whatever acting was required, Sue didn't manage it. 'I'll be back at three,' she'd said that morning. 'Please, Carmel, you will be here, won't you?'

'OK,' I'd said. I'd have to miss a lecture, but I'd missed a few already, in the shocked dumb days after Niall left me. I worked during the night to catch up; I could do another night. 'OK.'

Three o'clock came. Somehow, as soon as I heard the lift doors crunching open – for Sue had taken to using the lift – I knew there had been a complication. I opened the door of C3. Sue sailed down the corridor. It seemed to me that the way she walked had altered; God, I thought, soon it will start to show. 'Come in. What happened?'

There was a wordless, bovine triumph on Sue's face. 'He says,' she told me, 'that I'm in very good health. He says I'm in fine shape to have a very healthy baby.'

Guest Night.

I said to Julia, as we dressed before the revels, 'She

seems to have talked past the point somehow. She forgot why she went, I suppose.'

Julia snorted. 'Two months from now, then she'll remember.'

'Obviously she wants to have it. So what can you say?'

'You can tell her not to indulge herself.'

'She said she wanted to know if she was fertile.'

Julia was pinning on her medal – the one she'd got for A Promising Start in Anatomy. 'You,' she said, 'have you ever felt that need?'

'No.' I was startled. 'Anyway, my experience is academic, now.'

I couldn't imagine sex. It was something I'd done in a previous life. I felt sealed up again. I was a virgin. My flowerpot sweater slid over my head, stretched over my ribs; its fantastical flowers spilt to my waist, and as I turned to show Julia I am sure that the gold and silver beads caught the light. I cinched it with the broad strong belt; no trouble, as I breathed in, to snag the bar in its new hole. My rib cage was lifted, my diaphragm was constrained, it would be difficult to take a very deep breath . . . but why would I need to? I wasn't going to drown.

'Anyway,' Julia said, 'she's messed it up good and proper. She'll change her mind in a week or two, and then you can bet your life she won't want to turn up to the Student Health Service again. What will she say? "Oh yes, I saw the man you sent me to, yes, I gave him the letter, no, I'm still pregnant, he said I was doing nicely."' Julia snorted. 'She'll have to start again, go private. Where will she get the money?'

An hour before, Claire had caught me in the corridor. 'Please, Carmel,' she hissed at me. 'Just a word.'

I went into C2, closed the door and stood with my back against it. Their decor was not like ours. They had cushions on their beds with buttons in the centre, and a fringed bath mat by the wash-basin. There were soft toys piled on Sue's bed: a pink-and-white mini-elephant, a monkey with pliable limbs and a face of almost satanic ugliness. On the wall above Claire's bed was a poster with a prayer on it in fancy script. It said, *Where there is hatred, let me sow love.* 'Carmel,' she said, 'I wanted to talk to you because I know you have influence with her.'

'Everybody has influence with Sue.'

'Yes, but you have experience.'

I understood. Because I came from the north of England, Claire credited me with an earthy maturity. As if I had experienced many upheavals in life, and an early sexual initiation: incest, possibly, caused by overcrowding in the cellar where I was brought up.

'Listen,' she said, 'you know what she wants, in her heart. And now she's seen this chap, gynaecologist, he's put her mind at rest.'

'Yes. But it wasn't what she went there for.'

'None the less – she's seen sense. So now I want you and Julia and Lynette to rally round and stop her having second thoughts. If she has an abortion it could do her endless damage.' Claire was solemn, her tone ponderous. 'Endless,' she said. 'Psychological. Damage.'

'Yes. I can see that. I can see.' Restless, I deferred to the pieties of the age. My imagination worked; I couldn't think what damage would be greater than that inflicted by an innocent wailing itself into the world, from between my unprepared thighs. 'But I don't think she's really decided, has she? She's only interested in her present situation, just how she feels today. It's a novelty, isn't it? But soon she might regret – either way, she might regret it.'

'But a life would be spared,' Claire pleaded. 'For heaven's sake, Carmel, I thought you were a Catholic.'

'No. Who told you that?'

'Oh, so you're not any more?'

'They'd be different kinds of regrets, wouldn't they, very different? I mean she'd have to feed and clothe it, worry about it all the time –' Her life would be over, I thought. 'You could argue, you know, that having the baby would be just giving into a whim – and it's not a baby yet, is it, it's just cells, and you shouldn't turn cells into a person just for the sake of a whim?'

Claire was not shrewd, but she was shrewd enough to see that I was in mental turmoil. 'But what do you think? What do you really think?'

'Oh, I think she should have the baby.' I studied the prayer on the wall. 'I think maybe you should do what your body wants, while you can.'

I thought of the jelly blob sealed inside Sue's body, quivering with its own life: watery, warm, budding. I thought of the jaundiced cavities of the skull on our shelf: vacant, stony and null. I was at some point in between: in transit. I shuddered.

In the drawing-room, under a bright chandelier, the

warden dispensed sherry – tepid – in specially small sherry glasses. 'Miss McBain!' Her voice was cheery. Her eyes descended, ran down to my waist, then more slowly climbed up again. 'How extraordinary,' she said.

'I made it myself.'

'Yes,' she said. 'You certainly couldn't get it in the shops.'

Julia and Lynette were both wearing boots, as if they might need to whistle up a horse and make an escape; they exchanged glances that suggested this. Julia's were comfortable, scuffed, baggy boots with stacked heels; Lynette's were her guardsman's boots, tall and correct and burnished. Lynette wore a sweeping skirt of indeterminate darkness, and a soft mohair sweater the colour of charcoal; on her left hand, a huge emerald. She twisted it apologetically about her finger. 'Grandma's,' she said. 'I thought I'd flash it. At our guest, because after all, didn't I read she married a millionaire?'

The Secretary of State put forth fingers, and accepted a glass of sherry from the warden. Her eye was bright and sharp and small; she tilted her head, the better to see. Her dress was of the shape that is called ageless, and of a length that is called safe; it was sewn all over with little crystal beads. Her pale hair lay against her head in doughy curves, like unbaked sausage rolls.

When we came into proximity, Lynette began to laugh politely into her hand; some of her sherry came out through her nose. 'Very nice *cocktail* dress,' she spluttered. 'My mother had one of those, but she gave it to a charity shop.'

The warden surged up to us, to give us our designated

places at table. I felt that these had been changed, at the last minute. 'Miss McBain,' she said, staring hard at my chest and waving me away to the last place on a wing. 'Miss Lipcott . . .' She banished Julia – whose medal bounced over her left breast – to an equally remote spot.

We took our places. Soup was served – non-standard soup – and rolls which were hot and definitely not yesterday's. At our highish table, we didn't have to prise out the frozen tiny chippings from their foil; we had butter shaved especially for us, curled into glass dishes.

Just as the guests were putting down their soup spoons, Sue rose from her chair, as if it were time for the speeches. She looked wildly up and down the table; then, holding her napkin to her mouth, she bolted. 'Fifi!' Julia cried.

For a micro-second our guest looked up. Lynette smiled down at me from High Table; I nodded, rose and slid unobtrusively into Sue's place near the Secretary of State. The warden glanced at me and nodded, as if she believed some breach in etiquette had been mended.

And really, it would have looked bad, an empty chair so close; as if we were expecting Banquo. Our guest was not eating, even though she had been served with a voluminous chicken breast; her knife toyed with it. She was leaning over the table, talking urgently to the warden and to the section of High Table on her right. The crystals on her dress seemed to quiver; so did her voice, with the effort of restraint. She spoke slowly; she spoke as if she knew everyone except herself was stupid. She leant forward and smiled, and her hair moved with her, as if it were not just hair but a hat made of hair.

I imagined leaning forward, taking her wrist. Put your cutlery down, please. Turn and study this. I wanted her to see my sweater, examine it, envy it. See these flowers! My mother would be proud.

She turned her head in my direction; she opened her lips to speak, and shards of glass fell out.

That night I dreamt of the food I used to eat when I was three years old, when my grandmother was alive: food with the tint and the perfume of living flesh and skin. I dreamt of the rich dark smell of nutmeg that rose from rice pudding, the straw-coloured sweetness of long-baked milk: of sponge rich as egg-yolk, and the trembling speckled surface of baked custard.

I dreamt that I was dead and that I had become a ghost, and that I sat in my grandmother's kitchen and ate honey from a spoon. I saw my ghost spindle legs dangling down in front of me, and I felt the metal handle of the spoon press against my stripped fingerbones.

'At least she wasn't sick on the Guest,' Julia said. 'I wonder will she ever know how lucky she was.'

Nine

January passed. A man sailed the Atlantic single-handed. A woman didn't.

At breakfast I sat with Karina, after the others had left. We took discarded toast from the racks, and avoided each other's eyes as we chewed it. 'Karina,' I said, 'do you remember when I used to do dumb insolence?'

'Yes,' she said. 'You got away with it.'

I looked at her in surprise. How could she think that? I'd had to live ever since with the knowledge of my own temerity; I'd had to live up to it, and find new situations to test it out. Didn't she know that the winner of one game simply goes on to another, harder game?

'"Do you remember?"' Karina said. 'That's all you ever say to me. You wish you didn't know me.'

I was startled. 'No – I've never wished that.'

'You've always wished it. When we were at school.'

'But I used to sit next to you. Don't you remember?'

'I don't mean then. I mean when we were at the Holy Redeemer. You know when I mean.' Her voice was even. She wiped her fingers on her napkin. Long greasy marks appeared. 'Don't you think it's dirty?' she said. 'Having to roll up these napkins and put them in rings?'

'Yes,' I admitted. 'Paper would be cleaner.'

'I embarrass you,' she said. 'You wanted to get in with Julianne and that set. Oh, pardon me. Julia, I should say.'

'I'm going.' I scraped my chair back. There was enough truth in what she said.

'Sue's not too well, I notice.'

I looked hard at her. I glimpsed a vestige of her old look – downcast eyes, gloating. Did she know, then? We'd tried to keep it quiet.

'Pity you can't eat her breakfast for her, isn't it?' I said.

I'd developed a habit, I suppose, of flouncing out on Karina. I said to myself, when I was a child I was afraid, I was torn between pity and fear, and besides, I was told to be her friend, I was made to be. Now I'm grown up and I don't have to take it; especially since I don't, actually, owe her money. I never thought she was dangerous, except to me: I didn't know that her stubby fingers would tie my past to my future, so that now if I wake in the night, my mind goes right back there, to the narrow beds, the dry heat, the broken heart.

February came in. Decimalization of the currency was about to occur, and shopkeepers all over the city were in a panic; old ladies interviewed in bus queues said there'd never be honest money again. We were still occupied with the matter of Sue and what she carried inside; still the anguished, unproductive evenings over grey coffee. Julia refused to be drawn into it, saying that the solution was perfectly simple. Sue went home for the weekend again, taking the risk that her parents would guess. Her lack of appetite, she explained by saying that she had a tummy bug; 'It's going round at Tonbridge Hall.' Her parents believed her. After all, she didn't look pregnant.

Her shoulders hunched protectively over her midriff, and her face was long and drawn. When she came back on Sunday evening, she must have met up with Roger and had it out with him, because she said she'd never trust any man again, as long as she lived. She was going to be a nun, she said. She locked herself into C2 and wouldn't let anybody in.

'I don't know what to do,' Claire moaned. 'Shall I tell the warden? I could just say she was upset, that we'd had a bit of a tiff, that she needs someone to talk sense into her. I don't want to cause trouble, but I can't sleep in the corridor.'

'No?' I said.

Claire blushed hotly. 'Well, if it came to it, I suppose I could.'

'Have my bed,' Julia said. 'I can take myself elsewhere for the night.'

'But my essay! My essay's locked in there with her, and it's due tomorrow.'

Julia rolled her eyes.

I went downstairs to the pigeonholes where our letters were kept. It was Sunday evening, and of course they were empty. But I had begun to believe all sorts of things. That the postman would come at strange times. That some other girl was taking my letters and hoarding them in her room, but that she would have a change of heart and give them back to me. It was as if I had forgotten the content of my telephone conversation with Niall, or not understood it. A clean break, he had said. As people speak of a sporting injury: 'a clean break, it could have been worse'. The lie seemed written into my body; I felt pieces of my own bones, jagged and splintered and trying to work their way out through my skin. Although I could see there was nothing in the pigeonhole, I used to put my hand in and feel about: as if the essence of a letter might be there, a kind of braille that would blossom into meaning as my fingertips sought it out.

Since the morning I had breakfasted with Karina, I could no longer eat up my toast. It had disgusted me, to see her cram the bread into her mouth. I imagined I had seen a doughy mass churning on her tongue, a mess of crumbs and saliva. There was a quivering inside me, a low-level but constant nausea. Whenever I saw that the pigeonhole was empty, something seemed to turn over in my belly, something that felt alive.

I went back up to C Floor. Lynette and I crouched in the corridor outside Sue's door and negotiated with her. At first she wouldn't speak, but we were conciliatory, kind, gentle; in time, we talked out Claire's essay. We could hear Sue's snuffling sobs as she fed it under the door, a sheet at a time. Claire was delighted: but then she wanted us to talk out her toothbrush. We said, we're not trained negotiators; we're tired, we've had enough.

That night I was conscious of the stranger, Claire, tossing and muttering in the bed that was foot to foot with mine. I lay awake, listening to her, and thinking of her dirty teeth. About three o'clock, the hour at which even London is quiet, I became aware that she was saying her prayers.

It was Lynette who lent Sue the money to have a private termination; 'The easiest way, at this stage,' she said.

She sat for a long time brooding over her chequebook, pen in hand. 'I'd rather not have to do it,' she said. 'Claire always seemed to think we were on opposite sides. Whereas in fact, Carmel, my position is more complicated.'

The operation cost one hundred guineas. There was an elegance about the sum which suited Lynette. It is a depressing fact about the women of my generation: name them a year, ask them the fee for an abortion, and they'll be able to tell you. They know the price of expectation, and how expectation dies. And if they don't know, it's because they repress and refuse the memory; you may be sure that they knew at the time.

Lynette, sitting at her desk, propped her chin on her hand. 'It is overblown, I know,' she said, 'portentous, rather a general observation than anything one might apply to the individual . . . but sometimes I think . . . when one looks back to the war . . . one should just *breed*. Because you never know when . . .'

'Have you ever talked to Karina about the war?'

She smiled sadly. 'She seems to know nothing about her family history. Which is perhaps just as well, really. Either it will be tragic, or discreditable.'

I left it. Left the topic. Said, 'You'll not get the money back, will you?'

'Probably not,' Lynette said. 'But where else will she get it? I can do a favour for a friend.'

'Will she think it's a favour ten years from now?'

Lynette shrugged. 'I'm not an astrologer. Perhaps we can arrange to meet. We'll all meet up, shall we, and then we'll see.' She reached out for her diary, and circled the date. 'Tea at the Ritz? Dinner at the Dorchester? Look, we may as well aspire; I don't see you, ten years from now, digging into chips in a transport caff.' She smiled again, less sadly. 'But I bet Sue won't make it. She'll not be able to get a baby-sitter.'

Later, I was glad I'd heard her say that. It seemed to limit the damage: just to say, just to believe, that life goes on.

When Sue came back from the nursing home, she was tottering and white. With a sober tap on the door and a mutter of 'She's back', Claire summoned us into C2. Sue, still with her coat on, sank on to her bed. Her mini-elephant rolled under her, and with a bleat of irritation she punched it feebly, knocking it to the floor.

'Come on,' Julia said. 'Let's have your coat, my love.' She leant over Sue and began to undo her buttons. I thought, she's changed; it must be part of her training.

Sue did not move: only looked at her dully. 'Let me help you,' Julia said patiently. She took hold of Sue and levered her into a sitting position, then began to ease the coat from her shoulders.

Sue cooperated, slow and baffled, drawing out her arms inch by inch. Julia was thwarted by her clenched fists; Sue nodded blearily towards them, left then right, as if she'd seen them somewhere before. Julia eased open her hands, finger by finger, and drew the cuffs over them. Sue's eyes were closed. Julia lifted her by her elbows and in the half-second she was vertical swept the coat from under her. She tossed it on to Claire's bed. I glanced at Claire. Her face was full of pain. 'Will she be all right?' I said. I was frightened.

'Of course,' Julia said shortly. 'They wouldn't have discharged her if she wasn't going to be all right.'

Professional solidarity, I thought. Sue flopped back on the bed. 'You'll be more comfortable if you lie down the right way up, Sue.' She grasped Sue by the ankles and gently up-ended her, to induce her to follow this advice. Then she began to take off her shoes. They were brown lace-up shoes, like school shoes. The laces were very badly knotted. Julia picked at them. Her occupation made her look humble, like someone in the New Testament.

Sue mouthed something. 'I think she says just pull,' Claire said.

Julia pulled. The stockinged heels jerked out. 'Oh, I see, you never untie them,' Julia said. I thought I heard the voice of Mother Benedict, talking on her frequent topic of shoe-abuse: 'a sluttish habit, and sure ruination to the shape of the leather'.

Julia slotted a hand under Sue's head. She jerked it up and flapped a pillow under it. Sue's head fell back as if half-severed. Her pale hair was dark with sweat. Her skull seemed to have taken on bony contours that I had not seen before. She is quite ugly, I thought: ashamed of myself for thinking it. However did we persuade ourselves that she didn't look pregnant? That was wishful thinking, wasn't it? I could see now, as she lay breathing through her mouth, a scooped hollow beneath her ribs.

'Unpack her case,' Julia said. Claire moved to obey. She brought out a scruffy washbag, blue sprigs of flowers on dusty pink: a packet of aspirin, and a huge rubbery pack of heavy-duty sanitary towels. She stood with them in her hand, turning her head slowly, her expression

225

unreadable. 'Well, what do you expect her to do?' Julia said. 'Stick a Tampax up?' She straightened up from the bed. Her cheeks were pink, with the effort of wrestling with the shoes and in shock at her own crudity. 'Put them where she can find them, Claire.'

I looked down at Sue on the bed. 'She's as white as a sheet,' I said. I was struck that a simile could come true.

'I know it looks dramatic.' Julia was breathing heavily. 'But twenty-four hours from now she'll be fine, honestly. Claire, are you going to be around tonight? See she gets plenty of fluid. She might throw up. Get a bowl or something. Can you do that? Only myself, I'm going out.'

'Of course, Julia,' Claire said. 'Just tell me what to do.' Her mind was relieved; she was ready to be commanded, ready to fuss.

'I just did,' Julia said.

I thought, they do not teach this to first-year medical students. She is not some bedside nurse; she is busy making A Promising Start in Anatomy. She knows bones, not flesh: not flinching feet, jelly legs, dry mouth. As she passed me, speeding to the door, my hand brushed her arm. She gave me a half-glance and a half-smile. Her eyes seemed more deeply blue than ever before, as if someone had punched the blueness into them. Her fringe bounced fatly against her forehead. I remembered that she, too, had sometimes been away for the weekend. And that once she had brought back no news and no cakes: nothing back but herself.

A cold beading of sweat broke out on my forehead: it was another cliché forced into life. We should not be so careless with these images, phrases; they enact themselves. I followed Julia into the corridor, but she had already slammed into C3, and I didn't want to be alone with her, in case I had to ask questions and she had to supply answers.

Claire followed me out. She held the door ajar, speaking in a bedside undertone, as if Sue were unaware of her own situation. And if she bleeds too much? How much is too much? It's her body, I said, she'll know. But if and if? Call a doctor. I couldn't, she said, what about the warden, Jacqueline on the desk . . . Then come for me, I said tiredly, I will do it. I felt past caring, to be honest. I could always employ dumb insolence. I just didn't want anybody to die.

The following day, Sue was up and about: uncertain, looking drained and ill, but no worse than people do look in the course of a London winter. There was an unspoken agreement that we would never again refer to what had taken place. Her child must vanish into the blank badlands of never-was: very different, of course, from the glittering realm of might-have-been.

That evening Lynette came to our room with a bottle of whisky. 'Not one of my more elegant offerings,' she said. 'But now the crisis is over, I think we all need a proper drink.'

Julia slapped her book shut, and so did I. Claire was with us; she had brought her evening's work in, because Sue had been ready for bed and wanted the lights out by eight o'clock. When Claire saw the bottle she excused herself, and said she would go downstairs and sit in the room off the hall that was called the Quiet Room; quiet was what she needed, she said. 'Oh, Claire, come on, loosen up, have a drink . . .' we said; but our pleas tailed off, we weren't convincing. She went, we breathed a sigh, we smiled.

We brought our tooth-glasses; but Lynette had a cut-glass tumbler in her hand, heavy-based and glinting. Julia leant forward and flicked her nail against its rim. A thin melodious note shivered in the air. Julia and I both tried out our tumblers; there was nothing but a dull clink. 'So,' Julia said, 'you are a serious spirits drinker. I knew your vices could not remain hidden for ever.'

Lynette's blackberry eyes sharpened. 'I wouldn't have said they were hidden at all.'

'What do you do for sex?' Julia asked.

'Oh, I get it in Harrow,' Lynette said. 'We go on, you know, pretty much as the rest of the world, but I do have a person back there, and I really don't want to get him mixed up in all this.'

All this: the atmosphere of bath water and parsnips, talc and blood. Some hideous girls used to shave their legs and leave the hairs in the bath. Is it surprising that Tonbridge Hall saw the death of love?

The three of us grew cynical, and perhaps a little drunk. 'The question is, who's next?' Lynette said. 'Would you like to place a bet on my room-mate?'

For a moment the two of us spluttered out our whisky down our noses. Julia said, 'Lynette, I know she's put on weight, but you must understand that she's naturally gross. I mean, imagine, who would look twice – she doesn't bring anyone back, does she?'

'Not that I know. Of course, I've had weekends away.'

'You've never seen her with anybody, have you, Carmel?'

'No.' I fell silent, cherishing my whisky, trying to imagine Karina and her beau – any possible beau – running the gauntlet of the signing-in system. Karina just wouldn't go for it, I felt. If she wanted to bring a boy in, and anybody tried to stop her, she'd square up and curl her lip and then – BIFF!!! – that would be the warden laid out, blood springing from her nose in fountains. I said faintly, 'I suppose she could have met someone outside.'

Julia began to laugh. She fell back on her bed and kicked her legs; this was extravagance, I felt. 'Carmel, you're a riot,' she said. 'Outside? In a park, you mean? You think she did it in a shelter, or under a bush?'

'Not that sort of outside,' I said severely. 'I mean out of here, somebody else, not even a student. Honestly, Jule, this is no laughing matter.'

I felt a thrill of fear.

Julia wiped her eyes. 'I find it so.'

That was a long night. I had to catch up on what I'd missed, but the whisky had flown straight to my head and it was hard to keep awake. I read the case of *Thomas v. Bradbury* (1906) in which an author sued a malicious book reviewer, and won. I rubbed my eyes and adjusted the desk lamp to cast a better light. Julia snored discreetly behind me, the covers flung back and one arm flopping out of bed.

Next I read the case of *Carlill v. Carbolic Smokeball Co.* (1883). This was a case of a quack remedy, backed up by ritzy claims: the smoke ball claimed to prevent influenza and to cure coughs, colds, asthma, croup, neuralgia and a mysterious condition called throat deafness. 'Oh, and snoring,' I said out loud. 'Cures snoring, within a week.' It occurred to me that I hadn't been down to dinner that evening. No particular reason, I'd just been immersed in my work; when Julia said, 'Are you coming?' I'd waved her to go on ahead.

The heating was off; I rubbed my upper arms, and groped for my cardigan. The travelling alarm showed three o'clock. Thoughts of Karina kept sliding into my head. How pathetic if we'd all been so absorbed in Sue – and let's face it, if I'd been so *self*-absorbed – that we had missed, or simply misinterpreted, the fact that Karina was swelling before our eyes . . . But no. Don't be frightened, I said to myself, it's just the macaroni, just the macaroni and the powdered soup and gristle pies and ogres' penises. It's the sheer quantity of food ingested that makes her get bigger and bigger.

I tried to imagine Karina in a man's arms: a romantic encounter, a lace pillow, an orchid. I could imagine only the Victoria bus station. It was engraved on my mind, the day long ago when I'd seen her on the way home from school, smoking with a crowd of boys. I knew – I'd known for years – that Karina had another life, one hidden from me. I just didn't understand the nature of it, and she didn't mean me to.

Now: I ran my fingers through my short hair, I tugged it hard to make myself concentrate. The Smoke Ball Co. offered a reward of one hundred pounds to anyone who contracted influenza after using their product. It claimed that one smoke ball would last a family for months; it produced testimonials. The Bishop of London said the invention had benefited him greatly. The Duke of Portland wrote that he found it most efficacious. Lady Mostyn said she would have pleasure in recommending it to her friends.

I was hungry; it could not be ignored. I had to wait a moment to place the sensation, it was so unfamiliar. When I thought about it, I couldn't remember eating a meal since the day of Niall and the roast-lamb dinner; not positively. I must have done, of course; consumed toast, the odd yoghurt, an egg here and there, a bar of chocolate. But if you asked me what I ate yesterday, or the day before – I had no idea. I thought, I could go downstairs and read the menu by the warden's office; that would give me a clue.

I groped in my bedside cupboard, to see if by chance there was a forgotten half-packet of biscuits. Nothing: there were crumbs, that's all, grit under my fingers. I tiptoed across the room to look in Julia's cupboard. There was an orange, a luminous disc in the darkness. She would not mind my taking this, I thought. After all, she knows I have to sit up and work all night. I dug my fingers into its skin, and the pulp gave beneath them, and the juice ran; I licked it from my fingertips. Mrs Carlill used the smoke ball, but went down with flu just the same. She sued the company for the hundred pounds.

I noticed that my heart was beating very fast: a skipping rhythm. My chest felt tight: perhaps because I was trying to imagine the smoke ball, work out what kind of thing it could be. Some juice dripped on to my file paper. I will talk to Karina tomorrow, I thought. I will go to her room and be friendly, we will sit down and chat, I will have the opportunity to look at her closely and if there's anything she wants to tell me she'll have the chance. After all, I am her oldest friend.

Dawn came. I could sense rather than hear or smell the preparations for breakfast going on below. I shifted in my chair; my legs were stiff, and I had the beginnings of a headache. The whisky, I thought; I'm not used to it. My desk lamp still burnt feebly. I heard Julia stir. I turned, stood up shakily, and saw myself in the mirror that hung beneath Mrs Webster's shelf; I was narrow, a bar of darkness, a shade.

Julia sat up, yawning. 'Is this Wednesday?' she asked. Our faces looked bruised, half in shadow and half in weary light.

I had three tutorials that morning. Getting from floor to floor seemed more difficult than usual, and crossing the narrow street from building to building. At one o'clock I sat in one of the coffee bars over a cup of weak tea and a roll filled with grated cheese. The first oily filament of cheese on my tongue, my heart began to skip again; I put the roll back on my plate. An odd thing had happened that morning. My tutor asked me a question to which I knew the answer – but when I opened my mouth to reply, something completely different came out.

My tutor gave me an impatient smile. 'No, no, no . . . hardly *Hartley v. Ponsonby*. That is the case of 1857, where a sailor obtained remuneration in excess of the terms of his contract because nineteen persons of thirty-six had deserted, leaving only some four or five able seamen. No: I was adverting rather to *Hadley v. Baxendale*. Late delivery of replacement crankshaft for a mill, remember? Your very diligence is defeating you, Miss McBain. You look exhausted. Shall we pass on?'

It must be throat deafness, I thought. What might it be like to inhale a smoke ball . . . perhaps some mixture of disinfectant and steam – my tutor's face altered slightly, slipped out of focus as if its planes had slid and subtly realigned themselves. I blinked. His face returned to normal. Another student was answering the question.

And now – it was another odd thing – I was not convinced that the canteen table was quite solid. When I touched its surface, it felt like last night's orange pulp beneath my fingers: sticky of course, but also yielding. I stood up. I'd better get back to Tonbridge Hall, I thought; I knew that on a Wednesday Karina was home early.

I can dash back to the library later, I said to myself. Perhaps it would be better to miss dinner, as eating didn't seem to suit me. I drank off the dregs of the weak tea; it was a comfort.

My walk home then became a journey; not just a trek, but a voyage full of surprises. As soon as I got out into the street I saw that nothing was solid, not the pavements, not the walls; everything I saw seemed created of waves, water, pure motion. I sailed along the Aldwych, around the bend in the river; paddled the shallows of

Drury Lane until I reached the wide, shining expanse of Holborn. The traffic was hushed and muted, cars become gondolas; Londoners bobbed and floated towards me, buoyant despite their February clothes.

Bloomsbury Street was a rank canal, with green weeds that pulled at my ankles, impeded me, exhausted me. By the time I dripped into Montague Place, my chest was crushed, my limbs quivering: my breathing was harsh and audible. Blood roared in my ears: or maybe it was the sea?

When I swum into Tonbridge Hall, the foyer was deserted and there was no one at the reception desk. Usually I ran up the stairs to C Floor, but today I decided to use the lift. But its door was wedged open, a scrawled 'OUT OF ORDER' notice taped to the wood. I began to walk upstairs. A sound, a certain noise, a rhythmic noise, began to thud in my ears. Surely I must be close to the sea now; I could hear the waves, I could hear the crash and roll of breakers. I have sailed away, for a year and a day, on a boat with a skeleton crew . . .

Somewhere between B Floor and C Floor, I sat down on the stairs. Not at once, but gradually, the sound of the sea diminished; but the world remained liquid, diffuse, unstable. My bag of books floated by my side. I didn't think I would move again; wouldn't ever bother. Just keep my head up, butting for the necessary air.

I grew cold, very cold. After a time, I wondered if I had fallen through ice; if so, the dying was not instantaneous, as I would have expected, but ridiculously prolonged. My head at least was still above the ice-line; while my body froze I engaged my mind in debate, and my still-unfrozen mouth in badinage with would-be rescuers and passers by.

No one came, though. And time passed. Not much, perhaps; but this was early in the year, and soon there was a change, light to dark. I struggled for air, throwing out one arm to get a purchase on the banister. I gripped the wood, but my muscles had no strength any more. My hand slid away. I went under.

I had slipped beneath the sea. I had thought there would be starfish, castles of coral; I saw only wetter, deeper darkness. For a moment I fought. I wanted a spar, a piece of jetsam to save myself. But now I was drowning, and the current was tugging me away: the salt, the oil, the wrecking wave.

The next thing I heard was Karina's voice; and when I breathed, I gulped in not water, but the hot re-used and re-circulated air I had breathed since last October. 'Slumped on the stairs,' she said. 'Lucky I came along, really. She could have rolled right down and broken her neck.' There was an interval of nothingness. I heard a door slam.

I had a dim memory of someone – it must have been Karina, I suppose – diving through the waters that had closed over my head. I remembered hands under my arms, and a terrible, implacable hauling . . . and my feet trailing after me, lifeless and numb. It was something that happened years ago, years ago when I was a child . . . so I told myself. My mouth had gaped, drowned by air; from deep inside came a wailing, panic-stricken, starved, unappeasable.

Now I was on my bed. Julia was leaning over me. She took my hand. It rose up on the end of my arm, floating into the air. She held it in hers for a long time, and felt each separate bone, so that I was hideously conscious of my own mortality.

'Why starve?' Lynette said. 'You wonder.'

'There are many reasons,' Julia said. 'Twisted religiosity. Poverty. Sexual disturbance. Inheritance. Zinc deficiency. Deficiency.'

'I have honey in my room,' Lynette said. 'Unless Karina has eaten it.'

'Yes, honey, that would be good. Do you have milk?'

'No, it was off this morning, I forgot to put it out.' I saw that Lynette was holding her purse. It was a little Italian change-purse, a draw-string bag as soft as skin, soft and puckered and weighted: she bounced it in her hand, waiting for instructions. 'I'll go to the milk machine on Store Street,' she said.

'Get two packets,' Julia said. 'Let's hope she'll keep it down.'

There was an interval of vacancy. The world might have stopped; I don't know. The next thing I remember was that Julia was leaning over me again. She had stacked up three pillows behind me, and now she helped me to sit up, and put a mug of milk into my hand, letting go of it herself only when she was sure I had taken a grip. I began to cry. The tears were painful, as if they were washing gravel from under my eyelids. Iser, rolling rapidly.

The milk warmed in my hand. I slumped back against

236

Julia's enfolding arm; tentatively, as if my skull were glass, she allowed her fingers to brush my temple. They rested on my pulse point; I stopped crying. Julia patted at my eyes with a white handkerchief sewn with her initial. I took it in my fist, gripping it tightly, and blotted my own cheeks. Slowly, my vision cleared.

I looked down at my body. I saw the skeletal line of my ribs. I saw my legs like pallid twigs, ready to snap and bleed. I looked up, questioning. Lynette reached forward, and smoothed my stubbly hair. 'Oh, Carmel,' she said. 'We saw it happening. At first we were pleased for you. But then, we didn't know how to stop it.'

'That's all right,' I said. My voice rasped, as if a rusty blade were in my larynx. 'Everything's repairable,' I said.

And my heart slowed. The lines of poetry faded from my brain. For the first time in months my thoughts were my own; slow thoughts, falling away into nothingness. I breathed; I sipped the milk. I was a machine for breathing: a machine for living.

The milk tasted thick, almost sweet. I drank it, and slept.

Ten

I woke to the sound of a shattering scream. God has turned out hell, I thought, the devils have been evicted; they are loose on the streets, they have climbed up to C Floor, they are bellowing for beds for the night.

The light snapped on, and I threw my arm up to protect my eyes; the brightness intensified the shrieking, so that I thought I would vomit or die or fall apart from the horror of it.

'Come on!' Julia shouted. 'Get up! Fire practice! Bloody hell, what a night to choose.' She was knotting the belt of her dressing-gown. 'Come *on*, Carmel.' She flung a pair of shoes at me. 'If we don't do this right they'll make us do it again next week.'

I moved; too slowly for Julia's taste. She crossed the room, yanked back the covers, gripped me by my upper arms and hauled me out of bed. Vaguely, I was upright. The devils were howling; they went on howling, and a thin stream of bile rose in my throat.

I clung to the edge of my desk. I trembled; I was ineffectual, elderly, one hand across my mouth. 'Put on your SHOES,' Julia yelled. 'Come on, you idiot, put on your SHOES.'

She threw open the door. The corridor was swarming with evacuees. Claire was standing square across it, her arms wide: 'Back,' she said. 'No. Stop. Back. That way. That way.'

'Oh, let us through, Claire . . .' somebody wailed, above the wailing of the siren. Claire shook her head.

I saw her face, her set jaw, and I pulled at Julia's arm. 'It's real?' I said.

We tramped as Claire directed us: our possessions abandoned, empty-handed, some barefooted, a couple of lucky souls in their boots: some shivering already in thin nightdresses, some stout in quilted housecoats. 'Close your doors, close your doors,' Claire bellowed. 'Now move, move, MOVE.' Some girls had their hair done up in elaborate rollers and scarves and pins, and two of the glamorous engaged girls from the third year proved to have identical tartan dressing-gowns and sheepskin slippers. Out into the London night we scattered, like a company of pink and blue bunny rabbits let loose from a nursery tale.

The air was cold and raw, its relief indescribable. I doubled up and retched, felt Julia's hand warm and protect the nape of my neck as milk dribbled painfully into the gutter. Muted now, its job done, the siren sobbed within our walls. The fire brigade was already on hand, and some girls gave little practice screams when they realized, for the first time, that this was an emergency. Someone said, 'I hope Nigel had the sense to bolt.'

Jacqueline, the receptionist, was sharp-nosed in a pink satin wrap; did she possibly, I wondered, have a sex-life of her own? Flapping her hands, she urged a bunch of us across the street. 'Keep back girls, keep back, a minor incident, soon be tucked up in our beds again . . .' But just then another fire-engine bounced down the street.

The roads were being sealed off to stop anyone coming into the area; cones and tapes stopped the traffic from the British Museum direction. 'Where is it, where did it start?' Julia demanded. 'I am sure we are entitled to know.' Half the girls from B Floor had been forced to come down a fire-escape, shocked, half-asleep, a freezing metal spiral tumbling them into the dark. 'It was horrible,' one of them sobbed, 'horrible.' Her friend put an arm around her and looked embarrassed. Girls bleated about their crushed heels, and limped across the road looking for steps to sit on.

The bursar was moving among us with a list. A plume of icy breath issued from her mouth. 'Floor wardens, floor wardens, where are you?' she called.

I became conscious of a presence beside me: white, palely glowing. It was Sophy who moved among the displaced and dismayed, like a column of ectoplasm, like some eighteenth-century ghost. She was wearing her full fencing gear; only her head was exposed, and her face was grey under the street lamps. I turned – and Sue turned – just in time to see Sophy's Roger legging it – bursting from a group of shivering inmates and sprinting away, away towards the safety of Bedford Square: towards the world, green leaves and taxis and safety. Never look back: never look back.

Sue turned to me, her jaw dropping, her eyes alight with a growing glee. 'What – ?' she said. 'Why – ?'

'Some unusual perversion,' Julia said thoughtfully. 'An unusual sexual perversion. On our very corridor. How intriguing.'

The bursar did not see Roger go. She glowered at

Sophy and said, 'Really, Miss Pattison, I hope ye
haven't been clumping about in your room, ruining the
parquet. Really! And in the middle of the night, too!'

It was two o'clock. We were forced down the street by
a cordon of staff and firemen, but like a wave we surged
back. It was clear, by now, that this was no minor
incident; the fire had taken a hold. 'Soon have you
somewhere warm, girls,' the warden called out. Her face
was bleak. A rumour spread that some girls had panicked
and lost their bearings, run down to the basement and
had climbed out through the dining-room windows; they
were caged in the building's inner courtyard, with the
withered shrubs and the smoke and the crackling timbers.
'Oh no, oh please . . .' someone was saying; Claire and
the other wardens buzzed from group to group, saying
not *true*, absolutely *false*, no girls *trapped*, everyone *ac-
counted* for.

I don't know if you've ever been at the site of a
disaster. I seem to have avoided them, except for this
one. What my memory retains is a series of snapshots,
with some sound-effects: the fountains and jets, the steam,
the crump and crash, the mouthing of men and the
gleam of their helmets, the false planets of street lamps
fixed and brooding over all: once, a distant screaming,
and a huge flash of white light. We had forgotten we
were cold; we jostled for a view, craned our necks,
barged against each other in the crowd. The situation –
and what we were told of it was at variance with what
we could see – was changing from second to second. And
naturally we were fascinated to see all our possessions go
up in smoke – our clothes, our textbooks, next week's

ay in note form. Some girls held hands and sniffled; others – how odd people are – were smiling broadly, though perhaps they did not know it. 'That's our room,' others said, pointing. They were picking them out, tracking fingers through the smoke. 'That's ours, C20.'

In front of me, in the quaking, hysterical press, an unknown voice whimpered, whimpered on and on. 'My teddy bears,' she said. 'My Afghan coat.'

'Good riddance,' said her room-mate. 'That coat stinks anyway. And now you'll have to grow up, won't you?' She turned, and slapped the whimperer smartly across the face.

There were gasps of shock; someone said, 'For heaven's sake, Linda, get a grip!'

The firemen said, 'Come on, girls, we'll soon get you taken care of, be good girls and move back now, no use crying over spilt milk.'

I thought, do they go to cliché school? Is it part of their training? Then someone screamed. It was Eva, our near neighbour: the poor sap who shared a room with Sophy. 'Look, oh look! Up there, on our floor!'

I looked. Outlined against a window, I saw a single figure; a silhouette, a blackness against red. It was Lynette. I knew her at once: I would have known her anywhere. I saw her put up her arms, like an angel about to fly. Then flames leapt from her head.

As it happened, no one else died. Tonbridge Hall was gutted, the cause of the blaze never established, not completely; but the lists had worked, the regulations and drills and fire-wardens, the shouted commands and the hurry, hurry, the pitching out into the shivering dark.

At the inquest, it was easily established that Karina was the last person to see Lynette alive. She took the witness-stand, looking monstrous, huge; which was understandable, as we were now coming into March. Her face was grim and set as she told of the moment when the siren went off.

Woken from deep sleep, her first thought had been that the kitchen was opposite, with its fire-extinguisher; she had dived across the corridor to get it. It was not what we had been told to do; but it was natural, and even mildly heroic. But when she was properly awake – 'I'm always a heavy sleeper,' she said – she realized that at this point the fire was not to be seen, not actually there to be fought. Then she did as she had been drilled and directed; she moved as fast as she could to the nearest safe exit. She assumed, of course, that Lynette was ahead of her; yes, the door of their room was closed, there was no reason why she should open it, she knew she must not go back for anything. 'We were told that at the practice,' she said. 'Claire was the fire-warden for our floor, and I remember the rehearsal. Even on that night I heard her shouting, Leave it, save yourself, leave it all, don't go back. And so, of course, I didn't.'

Then once out in the street, in the press and confusion, with the groups of drifting girls, some crying, most distraught; in the cold, under the streetlamps ... there was no reason to miss Lynette. Why look for Lynette, among so many others? There was no chance of looking for her really ... When she thought to search, when she'd thought to call out for her, a fire officer had come along and ordered her down the street . . .

Eva was screaming: she was screaming so hard her body doubled up and she convulsed. Someone in uniform threw a blanket around her. An ambulance rumbled up. We were distracted; so we did not see the very moment when Claire began to run. 'Lynette, don't die,' she yelled: 'I'm coming.'

Our heads and bodies swivelled. We forgot Eva the faintee; we gaped as Claire charged back towards the burning building, her big fleecy slippers slapping the ground at every stride. She meant it; she was going for Lynette. She would die in there, if that was what it took. But what was the point? I would have run in there myself; I valued my life so little. But I knew Lynette was beyond rescue now; I had seen her head on fire, and then a blaze burst out between her ribs.

The firemen caught Claire easily, and turned her back. The warden and an ambulance man supported her as they walked her away, each holding an elbow, hustling her down the street as if she were the last recalcitrant drinker in a closing bar. I saw her eyes, which were empty; her mouth moved.

There was a breath at my shoulder. I felt it. It was familiar. I wanted to hug the breather. 'Karina,' I said. 'Thank God.'

'All right, Carmel?' Karina was wearing a vast flannel nightdress, a marquee: the kind of nightdress grandmother is wearing in her cottage, when the wolf comes calling. She was holding something over her arm; it was

244

a strange draping softness, something limp and slaughtered. My hand crept out to it: Lynette's fox fur. In this light, you could not see its colours; it could have been the corpse of a dog. I glanced down. From its pocket there drooped, there depended, a key fob. C21 was written on it. It was the key to the door of their room.

'Why don't you put it on? Put the coat on, since you've saved it?'

My voice was choked and frail, far away; I hardly recognized it as mine. Karina turned her head, looking where I looked. Her eyes fell on the key fob. She reached to retrieve it. It slithered from its pocket. It clattered to the ground. It lay in the road. I stooped to pick it up. Karina put her foot on it. Crouching, I looked up into her face.

Then a gust of wind came bowling along the street. It rippled the nightdresses of shivering girls, slapped at bare blue legs. It raised the hairs, the short hairs on my neck. It took Karina's vast nightgown and pasted it against her body. I looked up, along her bulk. My head was in the shadow of her great belly. She must be five months, six months gone. She must have been pregnant before ever we saw London.

I squatted at Karina's feet. I saw the classroom, our first classroom; smelt coal and milk and baby-skin. There was the fat smell of wax crayons, the aroma of pencils, the forbidden coldness of a pencil point against the tongue. Tens and units on the blackboard: a blue worm of Plasticine curled on the floor. I saw Karina with her doll, the baby doll in the back of the lorry. Her tongue between her teeth; mother and baby, out for a tow.

I saw my foot swing. I saw it catch the lorry's underside and hurtle it into the air. I saw the rubber trajectory of the pink pseudo-flesh, and the baby face smashed down on to the hard floor.

Now, I stared up at Karina. She was huge, womanly, brooding. The cold of the night had struck into my bones. Karina's expression was hooded, complacent. She knew I would not give her away. After all, I said to myself, I don't know that she is a murderer. Just because she has the key, it doesn't mean she turned it in the lock.

Behind us, someone else fainted. It was a girl from B Floor, one of the fire-escape mob. I moved to take the fox fur from Karina's hands, to throw over the casualty; but I thought better of it. 'Put it on. Hide yourself.'

Something which will not be possible for much longer, I thought. Well, that's your problem. If I speak out, you'll give birth in Holloway. I saw, in my mind's eye, Lynette at the window; her flying arms, the flickering of her melting flesh. It will always be in my mind's eye, of course. I never for a moment doubted that she would die, knew – unlike Claire – that she was ablaze from inside, and that we had caught her in the act of dying, roasted in the wreck of the third floor. I saw Claire's mad fleecy slippers slapping towards the blaze. Claire did not come back, next term; I did not inquire after her. I remembered what Sue had said once: she's really, really a Christian. Always doing good unto you. I'd have liked to keep in contact, but, in my situation, it didn't seem appropriate. Knowing what I did.

Two men jogged up with a stretcher. Stone-faced, they swept up the fallen girl from the ground; swept her up as if they were sweeping the streets. 'Back, girls, back,' called the warden. The street seemed full of swirling smoke. A siren was wailing, getting closer; lights were on in the buildings around, and a forced, yellow day was beginning, a floodlit day, where all motives and deeds would be exposed. There was a tune in my head, at the back of my mind, and then it was in my mouth: before I could stop myself I sang out. I was back in my grandad's yard, the Catherine wheel fizzing damply, the sparklers swirling our names in the air, Carmel and Karina, Karina and Carmel:

'Pepper box, pepper box,
Morning till night . . .'

'Let's run,' Karina said. 'Come on, Carmel! Run! Something might blow up.'

She flung out her hand. I seized it. When the windows blew the noise had knocked us back but when that was over we'd crept forward again; the crowd was eddying, uncertain, confused, unwilling to dramatize, each member of it dreading to appear foolish by a break for safety. But Karina had me by the wrist; she towed me past the barriers, pulling strongly, knowing I was weak. 'Steady, girl!' someone said, but she lashed out at him: with her fist I mean, not her tongue. I gasped and begged as we flew along the street; she didn't hear me.

We halted at last, under trees, under a deep roof of green. I was half-dead. My chest sobbed, my heart was bursting. I folded up and retched again, producing only stained saliva; my knees gave, but Karina caught me, so I fell not on to scarring pavement but on to London turf.

My head dipped towards the pigeon droppings; Karina saved it in her palm. 'Sit up, lovie,' she said. We raised our faces; I thought that dew dripped on to them, and into our hair.

A good many things went up, in the blaze at Tonbridge Hall. My love affair, and my anorexia, and my hopes of being the first woman prime minister: my cousin's duffle coat, and my notes on the Carbolic Smoke Ball. Julia lost her medal, but has no doubt won another since; the Segals lost their daughter. At the inquest Mr Segal wore a stiff, expensive dark suit; he was dark himself, a squat, vehement man who knocked away one tear with a violent back-of-the-hand. Lynette's mother did not disappoint us; tall, frail, veiled, she had sharp shins in pale, expensive stockings, and high-heeled shoes and a bag that might have been made of some rare lizard. Her face was chalky, her lips painted red: she said, 'She was our only, you see. One child only I might have.' They pressed Karina's hands, as if some imprint of their daughter might be left there. To me they just nodded, puzzled and bemused by so many young faces without names.

I would have liked to touch their elbows and say, at least the fox fur got out. Lynette would have liked that; she really would, you know.

I wake up, these days, some time after my husband has left for the train and the city. My house, my street, is eerily quiet; even when the schoolchildren are on holiday, they make a muffled festival of it, and the cries from their bicycles and skateboards are muted by the expensive

248

distance between the houses and the landscaping of the far-sighted architects who have planted us out here among the pines.

And so, sitting by myself with my newspaper, nine o'clock in the morning, I become conscious of all the small noises of the house: the purr of the well-stocked freezer, the expansive tick of the long-case clock. Sometimes it occurs to me that I am hungry. I might boil an egg; I believe in protein now. I make some toast, and butter it thickly with the same type of Danish butter that I ate when I was a child, and which, when I was a student, I was ashamed to be unable to afford.

I put my meal on to a tray – with my small silver teapot, my china cup, my lemon slice – and carry it through to the dining-room, where I sit down with it in great state. The 'dining-room', I am aware, is a bourgeois invention; the upper classes (historically) and the lower classes (now, for all I know) preferred and prefer to do everything in an all-purpose room. Sleep, cry, write letters, make love . . . but that reminds me too much of the era of the Slimmer's Disease.

I pluck out, as I go, a fresh pale linen table napkin, just for me; I am the one who will wash and iron it, but I have reached the stage in life when I am willing to serve myself.

My breakfast table is as far as a table can be from the french-polished object at which I toiled at my homework in my parents' house, on those winter nights when it was too cold for me to be kept upstairs. It is a blond table, a bland table, a table which shows the great beauty of its natural wood, and my touch glides over it with a sensual assurance that I can never feel in the presence of another human being. I trace with my nail the lovely line of the wood's exposed heart, its graceful curves like the fingerprints of those giants on whose shoulders we stand. I place my forefinger on the knots in the wood, those knots that, though they run against the grain, seem more satin-like, more glassy than the wood itself: I think of my life, and the lives of the women I knew, and I say, tapping softly, tapping decisively on the dark and swirling node, that is where we went wrong, just there, that is the very place.

But then in the dappled sunlight, filtered through conifers, the wood seems to dissolve beneath my fingers. The angles of the white room soften and melt around me; and the past runs like water through my hands.